About the Author

R. G. Briggs resides in the United States where he grew up idolizing Ian Fleming and his creation, James Bond. Briggs attended Utah Tech University where he obtained a bachelor's degree in communication (2012). Following that, he worked in journalism for a few years before attending law school at Texas Southern University and obtained his juris doctor degree (2020).

Spy for Hire

R. G. Briggs

Spy for Hire

Vanguard Press

VANGUARD PAPERBACK

© Copyright 2024
R. G. Briggs

The right of R. G. Briggs to be identified as author of
this work has been asserted by him in accordance with the
Copyright, Designs and Patents Act 1988.

All Rights Reserved

No reproduction, copy or transmission of this publication
may be made without written permission.
No paragraph of this publication may be reproduced,
copied or transmitted save with the written permission of the
publisher, or in accordance with the provisions
of the Copyright Act 1956 (as amended).

Any person who commits any unauthorised act in relation to
this publication may be liable to criminal
prosecution and civil claims for damages.

A CIP catalogue record for this title is
available from the British Library.

ISBN 978 1 80016 873 2

This is a work of fiction. Names, characters, businesses, places, events and
incidents are either the product of the author's imagination or used in a
fictitious manner. Any resemblance to actual persons, living or dead, or
actual events is purely coincidental.

Vanguard Press is an imprint of
Pegasus Elliot Mackenzie Publishers Ltd.
www.pegasuspublishers.com

First Published in 2024

Vanguard Press
Sheraton House Castle Park
Cambridge England

Printed & Bound in Great Britain

CHAPTER 1

Jett Fox pondered the mysteries of the world when she exercised. She allowed her mind to wander so that it could accidentally stumble upon a revelation that might work to her favor in any given circumstance. Daydreaming often brought stunning insights, she thought, or at the very least they revealed details about her character. Should she have let the woman with only one item cut in front of her at the grocery store? Did she call her grandfather enough? How many vodka martinis were too many? Who was the man skulking near the pool and doing a horrendous job of pretending to not watch her swim?

Yes, that last one! Jett Fox was used to strange men pretending to not watch her do *anything*. However, this particular gentleman caught her eye as she lifted her head on the upstroke of her front crawl. Her face splashed back into the water with each powerful heave through the Olympic-sized pool. Why was this man doing such a terrible job of watching her from a distance?

At last, Jett Fox casually glided across the pool opposite where the man sat. She pulled herself up the steel railing and gazed out on the exquisite view of the Hassan II Mosque overlooking the Atlantic Ocean from the Casablanca shoreline. Fox enjoyed staying at this particular hotel because of this exact view. She made time wherever she went to escape the doldrums of her profession long enough to enjoy the world's grandeur, and Casablanca's beauty seized the very depths of her romantic heart. A smile crept upon her face as she watched the late afternoon sun begin its descent toward the west, teasing the orange hue that would magnify Casablanca's beauty that much more.

Of course, Jett Fox was in Morocco on business, and she guessed that the man watching her with the subtlety of a Labrador had important details regarding said business. She grabbed the towel from her chair and dried herself, staring directly at the man seated near the pool entrance. Fox took stock of his features. Even seated, she could tell the man was tall, well over six feet. He dressed casually so as to not raise suspicion, Fox thought, and it gave her an impressive view of his muscles that stretched the T-shirt. His face was handsome. He had a strong jawline, high cheekbones, and thick brown curls that covered his head. He wore sunglasses, so Fox was unable to see his eye color. She raced through the files in her mind, trying to pinpoint his name. He was a British agent, but Fox didn't remember his name.

She watched the man long enough for him to know that his cover was blown. He hadn't left, which meant that the man wanted her to see him, an invitation of sorts. A smirk appeared on her face as she swept the towel over her black hair one more time. She flung the towel around her neck and slipped her feet through her sandals. She made her way across the pool area toward the hotel entrance. But instead of continuing on to the entrance and back to her room, she veered to the veranda where the strange man sat. She said nothing when she reached him. She simply sat in the chair across the table and smiled.

The man was the first to speak. "Don't flatter yourself. I gave myself away immediately."

The English accent poured out of the man's mouth like frosting. Fox felt a sense of pride that she knew he was British. This was surely the man she was sent to Casablanca to visit. Was he a spy, as well? Her instructions were unclear, as they always were on initial visits, but she did not expect her client to be a British spy.

"Starting out on the defensive," Fox said. "I take it you didn't expect me to see you as quickly as I did."

The man sat forward and removed his sunglasses. Fox got her first look at the man's blue-gray eyes. They were a striking feature to add to an already impressive looking man.

"I wanted to make sure you were competent before I spoke with you," he said. "I'm putting my career on the line by coming to your agency, and I had to know you weren't an amateur."

Fox was appalled at the man's audacity. "Surely my boss provided a suitable demonstration for you that we are legitimate."

"Yes, she was quite persuasive, but it's one thing to hear the sales pitch and another to see the agent in action. You should know that I'm moderately impressed."

Fox bit her lower lip and calmed herself before responding. She wanted to slap the arrogance right out of the man. Instead, she called him out on it.

"You're quite confident for a professional that's coming to a lowly operative in the private sector," Fox said. "Are you sure you really need our help? It would save you a lot of money to handle the problem on your own."

The man sighed. He nodded in defeat. "I apologize. I'm not used to being on this side of a case. I wanted to get to know you a little better, and unfortunately these conversations aren't the best way to learn about someone. Seeing you work is the best way for me to get to know you. Besides, I assume you already know who I am, just as I know you."

Fox allowed herself to relax. "You work for MI6, but your name escapes me."

The man smiled. "Well then it's good to know I can still hide myself." He paused and then extended his hand. "Harry Pyne."

Fox reached out and accepted the gesture. "Jett Fox."

They released their grips and Fox spoke. "Now, if you'll excuse me, Mr. Pyne, I prefer to not talk shop in my swimsuit. Should we meet at La Terraza in two hours?"

"Of course, Miss Fox, I'll see you then."

Fox sauntered toward the hotel and pondered Harry Pyne's demeanor. She assessed that Pyne was used to being in control of every situation, and this was the first time that he didn't have complete control. That could become problematic later on. She also noticed that Pyne's instincts were to tease and charm, but something underneath kept him from embracing his usual persona during their meeting by the pool. Pyne felt something personal for the case they were about to discuss, and Fox knew that her services required a deft touch.

CHAPTER 2

It was just two days earlier that Jett Fox was at the New York offices of the Solace Counterintelligence Firm, briefing on the Casablanca assignment. Of course, no one on the outside knew this was what went on inside the building. The spy firm used a neighborhood bookstore called Solace Books on the upper east side of Manhattan as the front to their private espionage goings-on.

Inside the presidential suite, Fox sat across from Chairwoman Solace, Fox's boss and namesake to both the spy firm and the bookstore front. Chairwoman Solace was tall, and behind the desk her torso towered above the tabletop. Solace had fair skin, dark hair, and dark eyes. She was about twenty years older than Fox and had kept in immaculate shape for her age. She had a commanding presence that could bring a Muse concert to silence, a presence not unlike that of Sigourney Weaver or Demi Moore. The room didn't matter; if Solace was in it, she owned it. The dark eyes sat upon creases at the corners that held wisdom from decades working in counterintelligence. The bulbs watched Fox across the desk like two security cameras.

"Our client will contact you in Casablanca," Solace said. "I don't know the details of the case yet, but we were paid handsomely to remain in the dark until the client provides the specifics. Send the name of your hotel to the armory chief when you arrive so that I can arrange the meeting. Carry on as a tourist until you make contact."

Fox was annoyed to not know anything about a case before meeting clients, but Chairwoman Solace liked to challenge her operatives. Solace told Fox about her days in the CIA and that improvisation was a vital skill in espionage that she expected her agents to not only acquire, but also sharpen as they performed their assignments.

And so, Fox did as she was instructed. She went to Morocco and waited until Harry Pyne made contact at the swimming pool that afternoon. She was now in her hotel room preparing for that evening's official meeting.

Fox circled her electric toothbrush over her teeth and pondered how to approach the business dinner with Harry Pyne. This was a man who expected to own the room and the conversation. How might Fox steer it all back into her corner? Towing the line between wowing a client and staying focused on the message was not her strong suit. She felt her stomach tighten. She hated the salesmanship part of the job. She preferred action, and selling a client on her abilities seemed like a waste of time. It was a task best left to the benefactors who cared about the financial gains of private espionage.

Fox poured through the hotel room closet to find her stashed outfits. She thought to herself of the best message to send to Harry Pyne as they discussed the case. Pyne's eyes were subtle by the pool, but Fox could tell that he enjoyed the sight. Her outfit needed to tantalize without distracting from the work discussion. She needed Harry Pyne to feel like he was in control even though he had absolutely no control whatsoever. Fox smiled and came upon a black lace long sleeve dress with thigh high skirt. Yes, that was the one. She would have Harry Pyne in the palm of her hand.

She finished getting ready and slipped into the black lace dress. After careful inspection in front of the mirror, Jett Fox believed she was ready to wow Harry Pyne and move forward on solving a problem that had clearly troubled the government agent.

Fox hailed a cab and arrived at La Terraza a few minutes early. She greeted the host, and the two went through the pleasantries that had become routine. "Miss Fox, we are so happy to have you with us again," and so on and so forth. The host led Fox through the restaurant with walls adorned in Spanish treasures. A soundtrack of Spanish guitar ballads played over the speakers at just the right volume, loud enough to breathe life into the restaurant's immersive environment, but not so loud as to interrupt pleasant conversation. The host seated Fox at her regular table on the patio with a view of the sea. Fox's heart skipped a beat when she gazed upon the breathtaking twilight glow that reflected off the Atlantic coast onto Casablanca to signal the start of an eventful evening for the entire city. She never tired of the view no matter how many visits she paid to Morocco, and she had to pinch herself that her boss spared no expense.

To Fox's surprise, Harry Pyne arrived precisely on time. Gone was the casual clothing and replaced by a gray suit and navy-blue tie that matched his eyes. His curly brown hair had been combed neatly, and his face had been nicely washed to give a fresh pink hue to his skin. He acknowledged Fox and took his seat at the table.

"I've always enjoyed this restaurant," Pyne said. "I'm happy you chose it."

"What's your favorite part? The scenery, the music, or the food?"

"The food, of course," Pyne said. "It's so old-fashioned to visit a restaurant that lets you order whatever you want. It's how you know the chef loves her job. If she is willing to take on the challenge of a patron ordering something not on the menu, then she must have a genuine love of food."

The waiter appeared. He was well built with dark hair and eyes, brown skin, and a lovely smile. Fox looked over his impeccable features and spotted the name tag. His name was Achraf. He spoke English with a Moroccan accent. "May I start you with drinks this evening?"

Harry Pyne glanced sideways at Fox as if to insist she go first. Fox threw it right back to him. "The gentleman will go first."

Pyne smirked. "Bourbon on the rocks. And make it a double."

The Moroccan supermodel that happened to be their waiter that night turned to Fox. "And for the lady?"

"Vodka martini, dirty, straight up."

The waiter left and the drinks arrived shortly thereafter.

"Tell me a little about yourself, Mister Pyne."

He laughed. "I'm the one used to asking that question. It feels odd having it asked to me."

"Well then, play along."

"What's the point? If you're anything like me, you did a background check after we met this afternoon."

Fox smiled. "OK then, Mister Pyne. You studied oriental languages at Cambridge. You served a brief stint in Her Majesty's Royal Navy before they saw your potential as an intelligence officer. You made the move to MI6, and then everything after is heavily redacted. Oh, and you're an avid supporter of Reading football for some reason."

Pyne laughed. "Now for you. You lived in Brazil until you were 10 years old, which explains your accent. Your parents died and you were raised by your grandparents in Florida. My condolences, by the way."

Fox nodded to thank Pyne for the condolences.

Pyne continued, "You graduated *summa cum laude* at Yale. You were First Team All-Ivy League in volleyball. Oh, and you are an avid supporter of an American football team called the Miami Dolphins for some reason."

Fox laughed. "Touché, Mister Pyne."

She took a sip of her drink and decided it was time to discuss business. "So, tell me, what's the score? I get the sense that your case is a personal errand that you'd like to keep off MI6's radar. Is that right?"

Pyne hesitated and took a sip of his double bourbon. "It's a bit of both, if I'm honest. A friend of mine, a fellow agent, died on her last mission, and MI6 is doing nothing to follow up. They want to cut their losses from her investigation. I asked if I could take over from where she left off, but my supervisor felt I was too close and wanted only revenge. So I've been grounded, and MI6 aren't sending in another agent to investigate. Don't you find that odd? I won't stand for it, which is why I contacted your agency."

"You contacted us, but I get the sense that you don't particularly trust a private espionage agency."

"Of course not," Pyne said. "We're rivals on the best of days and enemies on the worst. And I apologize if this offends you, but you're not a spy. You're a mercenary. Without loyalty to any one government, it's not easy to trust you."

Fox felt annoyed. "Not easy to trust me? Mister Pyne, you fight for queen and country, a government-contracted serial killer. I have no such luxury. No license to kill. It takes true finesse to do the job the way I do it. You Brits are all the same. You believe you invented the game all because some naval communications officer wrote a series of spy novels aimed at thirteen-year-old boys."

Fox noticed an incredulous expression on Pyne's face.

"You expect me to believe you've never killed another person in the field?" Pyne said.

"I didn't say that," Fox responded. "I have no qualms about preserving my own life if the opposition leaves me no choice. But it's just that, a last resort, and I didn't do it lightly. The man I killed haunts me to this day. I didn't sleep for almost two months after I took his life. I do my best to carry forward and not let the past rule me, but I ponder the kill carefully and wonder if there was something more I could have done to avoid taking his life."

Pyne watched Fox. She felt his blue-gray eyes cutting through her.

"I respect your stance, Miss Fox," Pyne said. "I wish more operatives thought the way you do."

The handsome Moroccan waiter Achraf returned yet again. "Are the two of you ready to order?"

Pyne turned to Fox, who insisted again that the gentleman would go first. Pyne ordered, "Smoked salmon for starters followed by lamb cutlets and peas and potatoes. Might I also have asparagus with

Béarnaise sauce? And let's finish it with a slice of pineapple for dessert."

Fox raised her eyebrows. "I believe I've heard that dinner order before."

"You might have, yes, from one of those childish books you mentioned earlier." Pyne winked at her.

"Wonderful choices tonight, sir," Achraf said. "And for you, ma'am?"

"Roast chicken with *arroz cubano*, side salad, and a tray of toast with butter. And let's do strawberries for dessert."

"A lovely order," Achraf said. "We will have your food right away."

Fox smirked at Pyne, who chuckled. "What is it?"

"Just thinking that I learned something about you from your dinner order," Fox said. "You're a nerd for this spy business, aren't you?"

Pyne ignored the probe. "Tell me what it is you do, Miss Fox. I'm impressed with you, but this is a job that could get a bit dangerous. Are you properly trained in hand-to-hand combat?"

"As far as I know, yes."

"What about guns?"

"Yes."

"Cars? Skiing? Driving?"

"What are you on about?"

"I'm just curious about all you can do. You never know what you might need to know for any mission. It's good to have a wide range of skills."

Fox felt herself losing control of the conversation. Pyne was patronizing her, and she hated it. He was an infuriating man, bouncing back and forth between charming and appalling. Fox guessed that he had very few close friends.

"Mister Pyne, what I do is not so different from what you do. You play whatever role your government needs you to play. Assassin, card player, wine connoisseur. Likewise, every client needs my agency for a different purpose. One week, I'm a skilled martial artist. Next week, I'm a crafty jewel thief. In this case, you need me to be a detective and solve your friend's murder. And so I will be the best detective you've ever seen."

Pyne considered this. His blue eyes pierced Fox's soul.

"Alright, Miss Fox," he said. "Let's discuss the details."

CHAPTER 3

The food arrived. Jett Fox's mouth watered upon the sight of her roast chicken and *arroz cubano*. The thick tomato sauce crawled down the sides of the mound of white rice nestled next to the fried egg. She savored every bite, and intermittently slathered a slice of toast with butter. She ordered a second vodka martini. She then probed Pyne for more information.

"What was your friend's name?" Fox asked.

"Sharon," Pyne said as he drank from another double bourbon. "Sharon Graham. Wonderful operative. Saved England's hide more than once."

"And I assume the last place anyone saw her alive was in Casablanca?"

"Yes," Pyne confirmed. "I know only a little about her case. Something to do about diamond smuggling using race cars at Brands Hatch. It would normally be the sort of case designated for MI5, but the ministry of defense insisted we help out because of a possible link to terrorism with the diamonds being smuggled to the UK's enemies. Anyway, I didn't see the connection when Sharon told me about the assignment. That is, of course, until she died last month."

Fox noticed regret cross Pyne's face. The chiseled features, including the dimple in his chin, softened.

"I'm sorry for your loss," Fox said. "It's clear Sharon was important to you."

Pyne offered an appreciative smile. "Thank you. She was. This job rarely allows anyone to become close, but she was the closest thing I had to a best friend."

He straightened in his chair and continued. "Her investigation led her to Casablanca. She wrote a note on her tablet that she planned to observe a woman named Mickey Blaze."

"Mickey Blaze?"

"Yes," Pyne said. "Mykkelle Blaze. Goes by Mickey. I gather the spelling of her name was so extraordinary that she decided to go by Mickey instead. Must have had awful parents. I'd wager Mickey makes her sound more masculine for investors. She's an American from somewhere out west. Arizona or New Mexico. I can't remember. Anyway, Sharon noted that she planned to observe Mickey Blaze at Oasis last month. She left no details why, but it was the next lead in her investigation."

"I see," Fox said. "Fancy casino, the Oasis. Does Blaze own it?"

"No, but I did a little digging into Mickey Blaze, and it seems to be her favorite spot when she visits Morocco."

"What else did you find on her when you did a little digging?"

"Not much. She's wealthy, but not overly wealthy. She owns a racing team in the United States and has three drivers racing under her banner. I can see how Sharon picked her as a person of interest in the investigation, but her drivers have never appeared at Brands Hatch. So I'm having difficulty connecting her to diamond smuggling in the UK. But I can promise you that if Sharon identified her as someone that needed to be observed, then we should take her seriously."

"Has Blaze visited the UK recently?" Fox asked. "Her drivers may not race at Brands Hatch, but maybe she visits the track from time to time under the guise of scouting potential new drivers to bring to the States."

Pyne nodded along with Fox's theory. "She last visited the UK a few months ago when Brands Hatch re-opened the track to visitors after the pandemic. So it's possible that Sharon came across her name and face during the investigation at the track."

"And that's how she tracked Blaze here to Casablanca," Fox finished.

"Yes."

Fox thought for a moment and then answered. "If that much is true, then we should assume Mickey Blaze is a dangerous woman. She must have caught wind that Sharon Graham was following her."

Pyne's demeanor saddened again. "Deaths are rarely accidental in our line of work."

Fox felt like she had a clearer picture of the situation and what to expect. It was best not to guess too many details at this point so that she could remain open to any possibilities. The next step was to figure out how long she wanted to commit to Sharon Graham's case. Harry Pyne seemed intent on finishing Sharon's investigation, but that's not what he hired Fox's agency to do. How should she approach the case? Should she focus on the murder and get the proof needed for the local authorities to make an arrest? Or should she focus on stepping into Sharon Graham's shoes to finish what she started? Fox figured she would have that answer in the next twenty-four hours.

"I take it you picked this week to meet because you know Mickey Blaze will be in Casablanca?" Fox asked.

"Yes, she flew in this morning," Pyne said. "She's probably at Oasis right now."

"Do you have an idea of how long she stays in Morocco when she's here?" Fox asked. "I'm just getting a timetable for how long we have to monitor Blaze and get what you need to satisfy your supervisors about opening Sharon's investigation."

"I don't know that," Pyne said. "However, I can't imagine she would leave before tomorrow. Why fly to Morocco from America to stay only one night?"

Fox nodded. "I agree. I think we should take the night to get some rest and plan to watch her tomorrow night. What do you need to see from Blaze to convince your supervisors to put her back on MI6's radar?"

"Anything actionable. I'm not looking to tie her to a chair and get a confession to murdering Sharon

Graham, but I have a feeling before the night is over that Mickey Blaze will slip up in a way that gets me back in the game."

Fox was confident. She knew it would take most of the day tomorrow to get into character for meeting a woman like Mickey Blaze. After a few games in the casino, and a bit of alcohol, Fox believed she could get what she needed to help Pyne's case. She pondered the details and plucked at a strawberry from the dessert tray. She sank her teeth into the fresh strawberry and peeked toward the moonlit sea one more time.

CHAPTER 4

Jett Fox woke at six in the morning and immediately made her way to the hotel's fitness center. She boarded the treadmill and proceeded to burn off the lavish meal from the previous night. Six miles later, Fox switched off the treadmill and climbed down, panting and glistening with sweat. She felt embarrassed by running *only* six miles. The soft life had taken hold of her! It would be best to remember that this was a business trip, and her assignment was to learn all she could about the woman called Mickey Blaze.

Fox showered and dressed. She moved to the desk in her hotel room and opened her laptop. She logged into her company's database and ran the name Mickey Blaze. Her resources were limited compared to what she might get at MI6 or the CIA, but general search databases had become credible intelligence sources for gathering surface-level data on targets. Unfortunately, Fox found very little that Harry Pyne hadn't already told her the night before as she scrolled through articles and various public records. If Mickey Blaze was a criminal, she did an excellent job at hiding it, or, at the very least, distancing herself from crime. Fox felt encouraged because that meant Blaze was worth investigating.

There was more to Blaze's story than her business dealings. The gambling addiction and frequent visits to Casablanca told Fox a great deal about Blaze's personality. Blaze was a creature of habit, and meeting her in this city was the perfect chance to see her make a mistake. Harry Pyne was smart to postpone his investigation until this particular week, and Fox made a mental note to be as sharp as possible tonight. She had to make the most of this meeting. Whether it was a conversation to extract information or something smaller like out-dueling Blaze at cards, it was important to show Blaze that someone was on to her and that she would soon face her comeuppance.

Fox scrolled through her web search a little more to find talking points to direct the conversation. She wanted to ensure that the conversations with Blaze were interesting. She needed Blaze to believe the two of them could become good friends. Fox laughed to herself as she looked at the computer screen while slightly drifting off to one of her small daydreams. Approaching a person of interest was a bit like a first date, and it reminded her of all the times she poured over social media accounts before going out to meet the next failed romance. She felt a bit of melancholy as she thought of one person with whom she believed she was deeply in love. He was a man named Jeff, which was perfect. "Jeff and Jett" made for some adorable memorabilia. Her heart ached as she remembered him from her early twenties.

Fox snapped out of her sad trance and got back to work. She scrolled some more through the database and came upon a magazine article in *City Weekly*. Mickey Blaze was the cover story that week. This was the first decent picture Fox had seen of her. She gazed upon the picture of Blaze, her babyface features, high cheekbones, big brown eyes, blonde hair, and exquisite teeth through a charming smile. She hardly looked like a criminal mastermind. The magazine was regional to the west coast so it was no wonder Fox had never heard of Mickey Blaze before last night, but this was just the kind of article she could use to her advantage when they met tonight.

She read the article, which still had mostly the same information that Pyne gave to her at dinner. However, upon a further dive down the pages, Fox found interesting information. It was mostly a fluff piece promoting a woman in power and all of Mickey Blaze's trailblazing accolades in the racing industry. She started as an apprentice technician with an automotive company in its racing division. From there she worked her way up until one day she got on the track herself. It was her first chance to show off a prototype design that she had collaborated in designing with her supervisor. Rather than have one of the company's drivers get in the car, Mickey Blaze demanded that she be the one in the driver's seat. All of the important people eventually threw up their hands and had Blaze sign a waiver. She got in the car and blew them all away with the track's new lap record. The article had a direct quote from the director of racing operations at that time. He said he wasted no time once he saw the test lap. Mickey Blaze was special, and he had a driving contract drafted that day that turned Blaze from technician to driver.

Her driving career was short. She suffered an accident in a race shortly into her first season in the open circuit. She injured her leg badly and required a special brace to help her maneuver without a limp. She still wore that brace to this day. She said she considered it a blessing in disguise because it allowed her to move into management where she showed a much higher aptitude. Just four years after moving into a managerial role, she broke off from the company and started her own racing team, which she slowly built from the ground up.

Fox pondered the article for a moment. Harry Pyne either did not read this article thoroughly or he never found it in the first place. This article from *City Weekly* gave Fox her first insights into Mickey Blaze's personality. This was a woman who was forced out of doing what she loved because of injury, a savage irony after likely breaking through so many barriers just to get on the track. Management was great, but it wasn't her true love. So now she was chasing a dream that no longer existed, building an empire that didn't give her the satisfaction she craved. If Mickey Blaze was a criminal, she probably didn't realize she had fallen so far from grace until it was too late.

Of course, this was all conjecture on Fox's part. She had insight into Mickey Blaze's life, but she still had never met her. It was best to remain objective until their "chance" meeting at *Oasis*.

Fox saw an encrypted email pop into her inbox. It seemed to come from an official government email address in the UK. She clicked on the link and followed the annoying prompts required to retrieve the email. Finally, she had the real email. It was from Harry Pyne. He attached documents from the Sharon Graham murder, hoping that Fox could provide a fresh pair of eyes to the scene.

The images were brutal. Whoever killed Sharon Graham had stabbed her in the back and severed the spine. As if that weren't enough, the killer sliced Sharon Graham's throat open. It was an awful scene, and Fox clicked away from the picture as quickly as she could. The local police in Casablanca discovered the body on the beach washed ashore. So, Graham was disposed of at sea or possibly even killed at sea. The killer wanted to make her disappear and might not have planned on Sharon Graham washing up onto the shore of the very city where she was staying. Sloppy work, especially in the spy game, Fox thought.

Fox clicked on a different attachment. It was Sharon Graham's service record. Graham had a brief career in naval intelligence before moving into the secret service, achieving the rank of lieutenant commander. Most everything in the document was redacted, but just as Pyne had told her last night, Sharon Graham was highly respected among her peers and had performed admirably in her duties.

Fox clicked off the attachment and closed the laptop. No matter what happened tonight, she made a vow to keep Sharon Graham on her mind.

CHAPTER 5

Jett Fox chose a black velvet dress for the night. She observed herself in the mirror and felt satisfied by how she looked. She walked out of the hotel room to meet Harry Pyne downstairs. She stepped out of the elevator and spotted Pyne at the hotel bar nursing a bourbon.

"Getting started without me?" she said.

Pyne turned and said nothing. He simply gave Fox the 'up and down' and smiled. Fox felt herself involuntarily smiling back, and she hated it. So she simply did the same thing to Pyne, eyeing his muscular frame taut against the fabric of the black tuxedo, perfectly fastened black bow tie, and fashionable gold cufflinks. His blue eyes popped underneath the curly brown hair and above the squared jaw.

Pyne spoke, "It's like you're straight out of a Fleming novel with your black velvet dress and black hair." He pondered for a moment. "Is that how you got your name?"

Fox gently sat at the stool next to Pyne. She nodded. "I was one of those rare babies born with a full head of hair. Jet black hair. So my parents gave me the name and added an extra 't' at the end of it."

"I see," Pyne said. "Well then, here's to them." He raised his glass in the air and finished his drink. "What's the plan for tonight?"

"Find her, watch her, lose money with her, and see what we can get her to say," Fox said.

Pyne shrugged. "It might go faster if I just seduce the information out of her."

Fox's eyes went wide. Her face turned red. "Tell me you're joking."

"Not really. You American women all love a man with an accent, or am I supposed to just pretend you didn't fawn over the Moroccan adonis that served our dinner last night? Or that you gave me a heavy glance just now while seeing me in this tuxedo."

Fox didn't think about her next move. Her hand instinctively went up, palm open, and whipped across Pyne's cheek with the force of an aluminum bat against a baseball. The hotel bar went quiet, and Fox noticed the bartender debating with himself if he should intervene or not. Fox's handprint turned pink on Pyne's face. How was it possible that this man continually jumped back and forth between delightful and despicable?

"Forgive me," Pyne said. "Misogyny is not something I can erase overnight. I promise you I am working at it. It's a massive character defect, and I take full responsibility for it." He shook the glass of ice. "This certainly doesn't help, but it's not an excuse. I need to be better." Silence hung in the air a moment longer as Fox awkwardly sat in front of Pyne. "Good hit, though. Sharon hit me a time or two. You hit harder than she did."

Fox sighed and watched Pyne with a frustrated expression. "Just get up. Let's go."

The two rode in silence inside the economy rental car. Fox focused on the road as she drove with Pyne in the passenger seat. She dared not look too closely at him, but she felt an awkward churn in her gut. Finally, she glanced quickly to her side. To her surprise, Pyne was in good spirits. He sat casually in the passenger seat and noticed her glance at him. He gave her a crooked smile. She jerked back toward the road and huffed. Why did she let this man bother her so much?

"Miss Fox, are you going to have a problem working with me? I am sincerely sorry about my behavior at the bar."

And that was the problem, Fox realized. She knew he was sorry, and she believed him that he was legitimately working on his unseemly characteristics. It was up to her to be compassionate toward him and move on, and yet she still wanted to be upset. Fox cursed herself and changed the subject.

"I found something interesting earlier today about Mickey Blaze."

"Oh? What's that?"

Fox recited to Pyne the article she read about Blaze's brief racing career and instant rise to stardom on the business side of racing. The MI6 agent pondered it for a brief moment.

"That's a terrific find, Miss Fox," he said. "Have you decided how to approach her tonight using that information?"

"Yes," Fox said. "Mickey Blaze is a winner, and she respects other winners. She lost out on a professional racing career, and all it did was catapult her into an even more lucrative management business. Whatever she's playing tonight, I have to beat her. That will be the only way to gain her respect. And then we'll play the get-to-know-you game."

"I like it, and what do you want me to do?"

Fox had a cheeky thought come to her mind. It was an idea that would help the mission greatly while also offering catharsis for her anger. "Oh you, Mister Pyne? I'll have you thrown out of the casino for disrupting the lovely time I'm enjoying with my new friend, Mickey Blaze. And then we'll complain about you the rest of the night."

Pyne smiled and dipped his head. "That's... actually a great idea."

They were a block from Oasis when Fox pulled the car to the side of the road. Pyne needed no explanation as he opened the door and stepped out. He grinned at Fox with his hand casually resting on the frame of the door.

"Good luck tonight," he said. "Next time you see me, I'll be an irritating thorn in your side."

"You already are, Mister Pyne."

CHAPTER 6

Oasis stood just three stories high at the southeast quarter of Casablanca, surrounded by the Moroccan Desert to the east and quaint villas to the north and west. The casino was a gateway landmark for the highways going to and from the city. The building itself leaned in heavily on its name with golden sandstone walls and North African caricatures engraved into the stonework. All in all, it was an exclusive building with only enough rooms for guests with heavy bank accounts.

Jett Fox followed the short line of cars and limousines into the valet area. A man who looked to be in his early twenties opened Fox's door for her. He wore the customary red, white, and black of the valet staff. He smiled and motioned for Fox to step out of the car. Fox obliged and slipped a few bills to the man.

"Thank you!" The driver entered the car and carefully pulled away from the valet line and toward the parking area.

Fox carried herself with the confidence of an heiress as she made her way toward the casino entrance. She followed a man and a woman, who both looked to be in their late fifties or early sixties. They were well dressed and spoke to each other in French. Fox then heard the unmistakable sound of parrots. No, not quite. Fox turned to see four women a decade younger than she huddled together and squawking like cockatoos with French accents. One of the four women even had a similar hairstyle to a cockatoo. Fox grinned as she turned her attention forward. To be twenty-one again!

Fox became annoyed almost immediately when she heard a man speaking in a deep English accent behind her. "Hello, ladies. Might I join you this evening?"

The French cockatoos chirped in the affirmative as Harry Pyne snaked his way in between the four of them and wrapped his arms around the two in the center. "Drinks are on me, of course, but then I think we shall see which of you is my good luck charm at the roulette table. What do you say?" The cockatoo with the exotic hairstyle staked her claim to that role. Fox was appalled but also amused. It didn't take much for Harry Pyne to get into character.

The well-dressed men at the entrance opened the golden doors for Fox to walk through. She gazed around at the embellished foyer of white and gold and followed along until she reached the main gambling hall. There she saw the bustle of Casablanca nightlife as men and women enjoyed themselves in cocktails and the warble and clinks of the slot machines. She followed the walkway around the slot machines toward the eastern side of the gambling hall past craps and roulette to the live music. The band played upbeat jazz tunes that Fox didn't recognize, but she appreciated the band's commitment to carry the patrons back to a time before smartphones.

Fox moved on toward the back side of the gambling hall and the card tables. She had a hunch that this was where to find Mickey Blaze. Careful not to draw too much attention to herself as she gawked at patrons, Fox watched the card games unfold. From blackjack to poker to canasta to bridge, Fox did not see Blaze at any of these tables. Perhaps she wasn't here yet, Fox thought.

"A drink, ma'am?" Fox turned to see a cocktail waitress.

"Yes, thank you," Fox said. "Martini, dirty."

The waitress left and Fox continued her slow approach around the card tables. Five minutes passed and the cocktail waitress returned with Fox's drink. She handed the woman a few bills, including a generous tip, and she took a sip of the drink. She gave up on the card tables and began her second lap around the casino. At last, as she rounded toward the live music, Fox spotted the golden hair with a hint of bronze that she recognized from the magazine cover. Underneath the hair, Fox saw the big brown eyes, button nose, high cheekbones, and sparkling white teeth behind an exuberant smile while wearing a one-shoulder maroon dress. It was her, Mickey Blaze.

A man dressed in a black suit wearing an earpiece with dark hair slicked back with gel approached Blaze and greeted her.

"Miss Blaze! We are so happy to have you tonight at Oasis. What will be your game?"

The woman replied just as confident as Fox had imagined. "Craps, preferably a quasi-private table if you can spare it. I don't want just anyone joining my game. Only those you think will spend a lot of money."

"Ah, you must be feeling lucky this evening, Miss Blaze," said the man in the suit. "We will accommodate your request as always." The two of them began walking away from the noisy center back toward Fox's direction. Fox casually moved by the two of them without making eye contact. She listened in on the conversation every step of the way as their voices began to drown out over the noise. The two of them said nothing else of consequence, only the usual pleasantries between a business owner and a client. Fox walked a little farther until she was in the direct pathway of the band's speakers and no longer heard the two speaking.

Fox spotted Harry Pyne at roulette with his cockatoos. All four of them had drinks in their hands while Pyne fiddled with plastic chips and flirted. Fox emptied her drink into her mouth and moved around toward the card tables again.

It was now a matter of waiting until the right moment. Fox lost one hundred dollars too quickly at baccarat, a game she thought she understood from reading books but turned out to not understand in real time. She stood up from the seat, she tipped the croupier, and moved on. Enough time had passed that Mickey Blaze's craps table would be well on its way to a raucous evening.

Fox approached the table with elegance in every step. She eyed the woman in maroon holding the dice, surrounded by a few patrons who all seemed pleased and captivated by the game. The man in the suit with the earpiece spotted Fox and moved in front of her.

"Hello, ma'am, playing at this table is a minimum buy-in of fifty thousand dollars."

Fox gulped. That was two-thirds of her base salary for an entire year. The company would cover the expense, but her supervisor would be irate if she lost this game. She opened her purse and showed the stack of bills stashed inside. The man in the suit smiled.

"Come, join the table!"

He ushered Fox to the group. Blaze looked over, and she made eye contact with Fox for the first time. The two women sized up each other. Blaze was the first one to break the brief silence.

"That is a lovely dress!" Blaze exclaimed. "I knew I'd attract some big spenders to this table. Are you sure the buy-in isn't too high for you?"

Fox reached across the table and handed the stack of bills to the dealer. She smiled politely at Blaze. "Not at all. Let's play."

CHAPTER 7

The dealer pushed the stacks of five-hundred-dollar chips toward Fox while the stickman gathered the dice. The game was well underway, with the circle of players welcoming Fox into their game like children encouraging one of their friends to jump from the high dive into the pool for the first time. The individuals seemed to be in good spirits as they made bets. They hadn't lost too much money yet. The stickman gathered the dice and returned them to Mickey Blaze. Fox glanced around the table to get a sense of the players who had joined Blaze's table. They chatted among their small groups.

Fox stood to Blaze's right, with just one person standing in between them, a middle-aged gentleman with at least two days' worth of scruff lining his face. He smiled at Fox and nodded politely. He turned to Blaze and watched her with the curious infatuation of a man who had a crush on the shooter but was a bit too shy to do anything about it.

Blaze interrupted Fox's appraisal of the man standing next to her by introducing herself. "Mickey

Blaze, how the hell are ya?" She exuded the confidence expected from a multi-millionaire.

"Jett Fox, and I'm damn well, thank you." Fox preferred not to swear but wasn't opposed to it if it made her marks comfortable.

"Whoa! Cool name. Good to meet you, Miss Fox."

"Please, call me Jett. My mother is Miss Fox."

Blaze laughed. Caution signs went up in Fox's mind because she immediately liked Mickey Blaze and found her charming. In Fox's experience, most criminals had an uneasiness to them, no matter how hard they tried to hide it. She had met only a few who could mask the uneasiness. If Blaze turned out to be a killer, as Harry Pyne feared, she added herself to that exclusive list. Blaze just might be the better conwoman between us, Fox thought.

To Fox's right at the center of the table were a young man and a young woman who looked to be a couple. They stood close together and seemed comfortable with occasional bodily contact. They also looked to have the same amount of chips, and they had bets on the same numbers. They were clearly betting together. They either win together or lose together, Fox thought. Rounding the corner on that side of the table were two women dressed almost as well as Mickey Blaze. They spoke to each other in accented English. Fox surmised they were from the other side of the Strait of Gibraltar, one from Portugal and one from Spain.

Fox turned her attention to the last individual, a man standing directly opposite Mickey Blaze at the far end of the table. He was devastatingly handsome at first glance. He stood at average height, maybe a bit taller. He had brown hair that was neatly stylized with the exact right amount of gel. His face was bronze like he had spent the day in the sun. His eyes were a fierce hazel that sat upon high cheekbones, a narrow jaw, and a pointed chin. His frame was slender like a lizard. He dressed in all black with a green tie. Goosebumps formed on Fox's skin. She couldn't put her finger on it, but there was something odd about this man. He didn't interact with the other players. He barely made eye contact with the dealer or stickman. He seemed only interested in watching Mickey Blaze shoot dice.

Fox looked back to Blaze, who was ready to shoot. Fox made a modest bet on the pass line as Blaze wound up for her shot. The woman in maroon positioned herself for a strategic arc shot, launching the dice so that they made contact against the far wall with enough force to propel them straight down with minimal spin. The dice landed on five and two, and the players celebrated. Shooting seven, while also hitting the far wall, was a big deal, Fox thought. To keep the odds in the casino's favor, dealers get upset with shooters who do not make contact with the table's far wall after several shots. They want the dice to spin and take as much skill out of the game as possible, leaving things up to chance. However, Blaze performed a shot that was the best of both worlds.

She minimized the spin to increase the likelihood of scoring the number she wanted while also hitting the wall to make the dealer happy. Fox was impressed. Mickey Blaze was a tremendous craps player.

"That was an amazing shot," Fox said.

"Oh, you flatter me, Jett," said Blaze, as the stickman gathered the dice. "I'm terrible most of the time, but I'm feeling good about tonight."

Fox slipped her winning chips into the pile in front of her and left the bet pile as it was on the first shot. The players around her moved quickly as Blaze tossed the dice awkwardly toward the wall as soon as the stickman slid them to her. The dice clattered just in front of the wall and bounced up over the edge and onto the floor. The other players watched Blaze angrily. Many of them made hasty bets to try and keep pace with how quickly Blaze wanted to play. A craps *faux pas*, Fox thought. Patrons around any given craps table did not like playing with a shooter who rolled quickly. It led to bad bets and lost money. However, no one lost money this round with the dice going off the table.

Blaze sighed. "See what I mean. It was all luck. I'm a bit of a clutz at this game."

The handsome lizard man picked up the dice and handed them to the dealer. The dealer inspected the dice and handed them to the stickman. Fox saw her first opportunity to bond with Blaze.

"Who's the hot guy with the green tie?" Fox asked.

Blaze eyed him. "I don't know, but yes, he is hot isn't he."

This was Fox's chance to show off her own bit of confidence to Blaze. She called out across the table, "Hi there! What's your name?"

The man with the brown hair and hazel eyes seemed caught off guard. It was as if he hadn't expected someone to bother him while he played, which was peculiar since craps was a social game.

"Uh hi," he said. "Theseus."

Fox nearly laughed but contained herself. "Is it really?"

He nodded.

Fox turned to Blaze. "Oh, he's shy." She turned back to Theseus. "Hi Theseus. Do you want to bring your chips over here and play with us?"

Fox noticed his gaze skip quickly to Blaze and back to Fox. He was nervous, but not nervous in the way men usually get nervous around pretty women. No, there was something else, but Fox couldn't quite place her finger on it. Fox glanced at Blaze, who seemed to be avoiding eye contact with Theseus.

He answered, "No, I'm fine. Thank you."

"His loss, I guess," said Blaze, as she wound up for another throw. "In fact, dealer! I'd like to make an off-the-table bet. I'm going for nine on this shot." She intentionally bet against herself.

The middle-aged man in between Blaze and Fox spoke up. "Not for me!" His accent was French.

"You're hitting seven all night. No way that changes now."

The other players made their bets, including Fox. She maintained her chips on the pass line just like everybody else, except Theseus. He was the only one at the table who bet on craps. He tossed his chips to the dealer. Fascinating, Fox thought.

Blaze wound up for her third different shooting stroke. This time, she casually tossed the dice onto the table. The dice ricocheted off the back and landed on five and four.

Blaze jumped. "Ha! No way! Awesome!"

The dealer pushed chips to Blaze and Theseus. The slender man looked at no one. He simply moved the winning chips into his pile and tossed the same bet to the dealer for the next shot. The stickman gathered the dice, the dealer flipped the puck, and the other players slid chips to the dealer to bet on craps. Fox did the same. Blaze gathered the dice and delivered them across the table with force. The dice swung wildly through the air and landed off the table once again.

"Oh shoot! I'm so sorry again!" Blaze said.

Fox watched Theseus slither behind the table. He re-emerged and handed the dice to the dealer. Again, the dealer inspected the dice and deemed them appropriate. It was commonplace for shooters to fling dice off the table in craps. It happened often, Fox thought. The normal thing to do would be to get a new shooter. However, with this being a semi-private game and

Mickey Blaze likely the richest patron in attendance, Fox doubted the dice would change hands.

The wheels turned in her head. She watched Theseus with intrigue. Could it be possible? Had Theseus swapped loaded dice in and out of the game? If true, it was a clever ruse. It had no doubt been attempted many times by players over the decades, and to pull it off would require elaborate dice that could pass unmistakably as the house's dice. It would also mean using the ploy sparingly. But if Mickey Blaze and Theseus covered those aspects, then Fox believed they could pull it off.

Fox took out her phone and typed a text to Harry Pyne. "Need you now. Mickey cheating at craps. Find us. Fifty thousand dollar buy-in. Bring your girls." She sent the text and typed another one. "Oh and steal some house dice on your way."

CHAPTER 8

What was the reason for Mickey Blaze to cheat? She was beautiful and successful. She was a multi-millionaire, on the cusp of becoming a billionaire. She was less than a few positive ventures from crossing the velvet ropes into that exclusive club. Why would someone so close to that milestone risk cheating at a Moroccan gambling palace? Fox considered the possibility that the answer was in the question. Perhaps Blaze knew how close she was to achieving financial immortality and needed every advantage available to get herself across that finish line. She cheated at work, and it had spilled over into her playtime. Cheating at craps was just a symptom to a larger disease. Fox shook off the thought. She cursed herself for jumping to conclusions. She merely suspected cheating at this point. She still had to prove it.

Fox missed the result of Blaze's shot while deep in thought. But the dealer pushed chips toward her. Fox accepted the winning chips and pushed the original chips back to the dealer. Blaze was clearly a good shooter even without the loaded dice, and Fox intended to keep as much of her expense account intact that she could.

However, Blaze proved to be an unreliable shooter, and Fox quickly lost all the surplus she had gained. The couple next to Fox seemed agitated with each passing roll.

"Maybe it's time for a new shooter," the man said.

"Sorry, but this is Mickey Blaze's game," said the casino manager from behind the table. "We are happy to cash you out and you can play at any of our other tables, if you would like."

Fox had almost forgotten about the casino manager who had arranged this game for Blaze, and she worried about whether Pyne and the cockatoos could get into the game. Through all of this, Blaze continued making money while the others bled chips. The players won on occasion, but more often than not the players groaned their disapproval while Blaze continued winning. It was impossible for Fox to track the patterns in her game, and Fox began to seriously doubt her theory that Blaze cheated earlier.

Blaze then committed another craps *faux pas*.

"Well, these craps rolls have gone well! Hopefully I don't hit the number seven!"

One of the two women on the other side of the couple lost her mind. She shouted something in Spanish at Blaze. The man in the couple also spoke out. "You know we don't speak about that number while the puck is on! That's it! Cash me out. I've had enough of this game." The man and the woman both retrieved their chips and left the table. By Fox's calculations, both he and the woman had lost a net of $20,000 between them.

Was that part of the strategy? Would the casino not catch on to Blaze's cheating if she was merely winning money that others lost? Was the casino in on the cheat? That raised a million other problems. Perhaps Blaze came in to shill for the casino, an outcome more feasible than swapping loaded dice into the game. For now, Fox kept her focus on Blaze.

The man standing in between Fox and Blaze laughed at the scene made by the couple. "It's a silly superstition. Perhaps Mickey has the reverse curse inside of her."

Blaze moved back into her mechanical throwing motion, the one that Fox noticed her use at the beginning. She's not cheating on this shot, Fox thought. Whatever numbers came up would be a combination of chance and skill. Blaze arced the dice into the air. They careened off the wall with minimal rotation as they had done before, landing on the green baize with a soft thud. The numbers came up four and three.

The two Spanish women gathered their chips and left the table in disgust. It was an interesting dynamic that Mickey Blaze had created. Craps was normally a game where the players won and lost together. The players developed friendships through the camaraderie. However, Blaze seemingly wanted the players angry with her. She was playing against the others, something Fox almost never saw in craps.

Just then, Fox watched two new players being escorted by the important casino manager. The plan that she had been incubating began to turn in her mind. She needed to move closer to Theseus. As shifty as she could, Fox maneuvered her chips to the right and stepped near the two Spanish women, leaving space for the two new players to stand to her left. The players arrived at the table, two men. One man was slightly overweight, wearing a suit that no longer fit him like it once did. His hair was dark and on the verge of turning completely gray. His facial stubble suggested he hadn't shaved in at least a week. The other man looked slightly younger and wore an outfit that was almost in violation of that evening's formal dress code. They took their places to Fox's left.

The overweight man was the more boisterous of the two. He announced, "This is the hottest table in the building." His accent was English, but he was far from as refined as Harry Pyne. He tossed his fifty thousand dollars in cash to the dealer. He looked at Fox and licked his lips. "Hello there, love." Fox felt sick to her stomach.

Fox called up the table. "Miss Blaze, I believe this gentleman has a crush on you."

"Nope, he's all yours, Jett."

"Ladies, please, no need to fight over me."

The younger, not-so-well-dressed man spoke. "Oh would you shut up, Horace? Focus on betting and not humiliating yourself in front of women."

Fox then heard a sound she never thought she would be happy to hear. Four parrots screeched in unison, "Fifty thousand?!"

"Ladies, please, have you not been my good luck charms, tonight?" Fox turned around to see Harry Pyne rallying the troops. "You conquered the mighty roulette wheel with your French wiles. Now, I must ask you to help me again. What do you say?" The French cockatoos chirped their approval.

Once again, Fox scooched to the right. She was now placed at the rounded corner and standing closest to Theseus. Pyne took his place at the table and tossed his buy-in to the dealer. Pyne turned to Fox and introduced himself as if they were strangers.

"Harry Pyne." He offered his hand.

"Jett Fox." She accepted the offer and smiled. She felt two plastic boxes move from Pyne's palm to hers. They released the handshake, and Fox now firmly felt the grooves of the white dots on the red plastic.

She grinned and whispered to Pyne. "It's time to have a bit of fun with Mickey Blaze."

Before Fox could take any action with the house dice that Pyne had gifted her, she had to confirm that Theseus was swapping in loaded dice. That meant she had to bide her time and wait for Blaze to shoot off the table. She communicated as much of the plan to Pyne that she could, given the circumstances, but with Theseus being the anti-social player in a game as social as craps, it made the muted conversation with Pyne that much more difficult. Shy people tended to be the best listeners, Fox thought, and Theseus might very well pick up on the hushed conversation. Pyne reassured Fox that he understood the overall scheme. There would come a point where he needed to cause a distraction and that Fox would let him know when to initiate.

The game carried on, and the brand-new group seemed much livelier than the previous players. The older, overweight man, whom the younger one called Horace, lit a cigarette and played fast and loose with his chips. His companion made the opposite bet of Horace on nearly every roll. They were playing not to lose. This was shared money, the younger man making insurance bets to counter Horace's brazen gambling. It was a safe strategy, but it could only work for so long given the randomness of the dice. Fox surmised that they both would walk out of the casino that night with deficits.

Astonishingly, Mickey Blaze continued shooting spectacularly, hitting everything she wanted to hit. It further created doubt in her mind that Blaze was cheating and that the earlier action was merely a coincidence. After all, scoring nine on any roll wasn't uncommon. It was just incredible that Blaze called it as an off-the-table bet and managed to score it.

"She's an excellent player," Fox whispered to Pyne.

"I've noticed. Perhaps you were wrong about the cheating."

Fox rolled her eyes. "Just wait. She'll throw the dice off the table soon."

It didn't take long. Blaze found herself on a short streak of losing money. Fox watched her eyes carefully. There it was! The subtle hint of recognition. Anyone could have missed it. Blaze glanced ever so slightly to Theseus at the opposite end of the table.

"Here it comes," Fox said.

Blaze whipped the dice across the table as if she were throwing a discus. The red cubes bounced wildly off the green baize and over the wall toward the feet of Fox and Theseus. The slender man wasted no time. He crouched and reached for the dice. This was the tricky part as a spectator. Fox watched Theseus' hands. Quick on the draw, like an outlaw out of the wild west, Theseus scooped the fallen dice into his possession. His fingers twitched, and the two fallen dice vanished into his sleeves. Two new dice replaced them at his fingertips.

Fox confirmed what she saw to Pyne. Theseus stood up from underneath the table and handed the dice to the dealer. The dealer inspected them closely and again determined that the dice were authentic. The dealer handed the dice to the stickman, who used the stick to slide the dice to Blaze.

"She's going to roll a five and four on this shot," Fox said. "Make a faulty bet so that she doesn't think we're on to her."

Pyne addressed the dealer. "Off-the-table bet for me. Maximum bet on eleven."

Fox pretended to gasp. "Are you crazy? I like it. Maximum bet for me. Snake eyes." Fox tossed her chips to the dealer.

Horace's ears perked at the sound of Fox's voice. "Sweetheart, if you love crazy, then I'm your man!" He turned to the dealer. "I'll match her bet. Snake eyes for me, as well."

Horace's younger companion nearly spat in disgust. "Please stop embarrassing us, Horace." He made a maximum bet on the pass line. This was one of those instances that Fox predicted earlier where Horace and the young man would both lose. It was near impossible to counter-bet in craps even when loaded dice weren't in play, and now with a guaranteed five and four about to hit the table, Horace and the young man were set to lose a lot of money.

The man standing next to Blaze made a modest bet, and Blaze made the same off-the-table bet of nine that she made earlier. Blaze went through the charade of carefully planning her shot motion, and she unleashed the dice into a careful arc across the table. The dice bounded off the wall and turned up five and four as expected.

"Oh dear!" Pyne feigned disappointment. His cockatoos, however, were not pretending.

"What kind of a bet was that?"

"Are you sure you know how to play this game?"

"Don't worry, I still think you're handsome."

"Perhaps you should save the rest of your money for me?"

Horace eyed Fox after the shot. Fox tried not to look over at him, but she felt his gaze burning holes through her head. She reluctantly peered back. His face became eager.

"Oh don't worry about the money, sweetheart," Horace said. Fox cringed at his use of the word "sweetheart." This man was intolerable at best and an absolute creep at medium. She didn't want to think about his worst possible form.

Fox hurried onto the pass line and tried to ignore Horace's advances. It was time to work. Fox watched Blaze play as an idiot again, and the dice predictably rattled off the table. Fox paid close attention to Theseus. It was just like the last time he gathered the dice. This time, he swapped the loaded dice back into his sleeve and presented the genuine house dice to the dealer. Fox held back a smile. She was now ready to make her move the next time Blaze shot off the table.

She waited for the moment when the noise around the table reached a crescendo and then whispered to Pyne. "We're on. Next shot that goes off the table is the signal to get set. It's the shot off the table after that one where you cause the distraction."

Pyne confirmed non-verbally that he understood what Fox wanted. She could now only hope that her newfound partner understood the plan. She placed a lot of trust into someone she had only met yesterday.

CHAPTER 9

Fox eased her breathing and played the game like normal. She went over the plan in her head one last time. At some point in the next twenty to thirty minutes, Mickey Blaze starts bleeding chips. In an effort to slow the bleeding and get back to her winning ways, she purposely shoots the dice off the table to her partner Theseus on the other side. Theseus scoops up the playing dice and swaps them out for the loaded dice hidden in his sleeves. The dealer, believing the dice to be genuine, allows the game to continue. Blaze then makes her off-the-table bet of nine, and the trick dice "miraculously" come up as five and four to give her exactly what she wanted. Blaze then tosses the trick dice off the table on her next shot, and that's when Fox and Pyne spring into action. Pyne causes the distraction to bring all eyes on the table to him, and Fox tracks the loaded dice off the table. However, that leaves Theseus. The slender man has no interest in the kerfuffle above the table. He is only interested in getting the loaded dice into his possession to swap the genuine dice back into the game. Fox has no choice but to work some kind of magic on Theseus to distract him just long enough to steal the loaded dice and throw her own dice onto the floor in their place.

Fox grinned. She enjoyed the thought of pulling off this sneaky little prank. But now she had to focus and keep her deficit under twenty-five thousand dollars until she was ready to confront Blaze and embarrass her in front of the entire table.

The game passed along as it had all night. The cockatoos cheered when Pyne succeeded, and Blaze continued to make money while the others lost. She was an irritating shooter because she marvelously toed the line between brilliant and stupid. But, this was a semi-private game, and the players had to endure the high roller's idiosyncrasies. The puck flipped on and then back off once. Blaze rolled an easy eight to flip the puck on and then rolled a hard eight to flip it back off. Fox lost money in both instances, but at least Blaze did, too.

The worst part of the game was that Horace sexually harassed Fox whenever possible. Fox finally had enough of it. "Shut up or I will come over there and beat the hell out of you."

"Just stop already, Horace," said the younger partner. "I don't want you to get us kicked out of another casino because you can't behave yourself."

Frustration mounted, but before Fox lost her cool, Pyne whispered to her. "I know he's horrible, and I can't imagine what you're feeling, but hang in there. I'm going to use that incel as part of my distraction."

Fox calmed down. "Are you going to hit him?"

"Yes, but I'll save some of him for you."

Fox laughed.

"Are you flirting with that other woman?" The cockatoo with the crazy hair accused Pyne.

Fox's heart stopped. Had she gotten careless in disguising her conversation with Pyne? But to her relief, the English agent turned to the French woman and deflected as well as he could. "Nonsense, darling. I have eyes only for you. Now, what bet should we make on this shot?"

Fox hated how far the four cockatoos had set back feminism, but she was also amused by how Pyne played his role. She appreciated that he was quick on his feet, and he was proving to be a valuable partner in the field.

Blaze carried on the game, and Fox noticed after a few rolls that momentum had begun to swing away from her again. Blaze shot three more times, and Fox noticed frustration reach the woman's face. The brown eyes trailed briefly toward Theseus, the indication that meant Blaze was about to shoot the dice off the table. Fox braced herself. Blaze chucked the dice aggressively. They bounded off the table as predicted.

"Oh great, not again!" Blaze shouted. "Sorry!"

Theseus retrieved the dice, and Fox and Pyne glanced at each other quickly. The plan was in motion, and there was no turning back now. Theseus handed over the loaded dice. The dealer inspected the dice and once again believed they were the real dice. The stickman gave the dice to Blaze, and the game continued. Blaze made her off-the-table bet. She shot and rolled five and four. Blaze celebrated. The stickman reached for the dice.

"Hold on," the dealer said. "Let me see the dice again."

Fox felt her eyebrows go up. It's about time the dealer noticed, Fox thought. She glanced at Blaze. A look of concern formed on the shooter's face. Fox also glanced at Theseus. He held the same frowned expression. The dealer inspected the dice again. He seemed perplexed and eventually conceded. He handed the dice to the stickman.

"Play on," the dealer said.

Fox's stomach tightened. She felt the palms of her hands perspire. She watched Blaze closely. Blaze reared back and launched the dice across the table. And then all hell broke loose.

"Now you listen, old man, I saw you make another degrading gesture at the lady!" Pyne shouted at Horace as the dice were mid-flight.

The dice clambered at the lip of the table and ricocheted into the air. Fox glanced at Theseus, whose eyes watched the dice's every movement. Fox faked a trip over the carpet and collided into Theseus. She clutched at his shoulders and made sure his line of sight was locked onto her. Fox felt dice hit off the table and against her shins.

"Oh goodness I am so sorry!" Fox said to Theseus. He looked panicked.

The commotion behind Fox continued. "I didn't do anything!" Horace shouted. The sound of a fist ramming against a face followed. The patrons around the table gasped.

Fox scrambled. She lifted her shoe and felt two cubes safely underneath her. She then dropped the dice that were in her hand onto the carpet. "You are mighty handsome, though! I would say the fall was worth it." She hated herself for saying what she said. She moved back to her position at the table and saw Theseus move quickly at the floor. He swiped the dice from the carpet. Those dice traveled up his sleeve and were replaced by new dice at his fingertips, the same mechanic as Fox saw earlier. Fox crouched as quickly as she could, averting Theseus' gaze, and grabbing the two dice under her shoe. A smile formed over her face as the dice showed five and four. She came back up to see that all eyes were on Pyne and Horace.

"That's it! You two are done!" The casino manager motioned for the security guards to retrieve Pyne and Horace. The security guards moved in quickly and ripped the two men away from the game. Three of the cockatoos trailed behind the security guards. The fourth one watched them leave but turned to the table, standing over Pyne's chips.

"I'm going to take over him," she said. "The fool was playing with my money."

Fox felt her eyebrows go up again. Perhaps the cockatoos were not so dumb after all! And then, of all people, Blaze laughed. She said, "That's fine with me."

Horace's younger friend pulled Horace's chips over to his pile. "We were together."

The casino manager returned to the table. "Miss Blaze, if you would like to end this game, I understand completely. I leave it up to you."

She eyed the players around the table, lingering on Fox. Fox gave her a slight nod as if to say she was fine to keep playing.

"I think we're OK," Blaze said.

Theseus handed the dice to the dealer, and the game continued. Fox grinned. She had Blaze now. The loaded dice were tucked away safely, and Theseus would hand over legitimate house dice the next time the dice went off the table. One more part of the plan still remained, and it was the riskiest part of all. Would Mickey Blaze accept Jett Fox's challenge when that time came?

CHAPTER 10

Jett Fox tossed chips to the dealer. Although Blaze's playstyle had been erratic all night, the one constant that Fox noticed was that Blaze was talented with dice in her hand and that matching her bets would lead to success. She would have been the casino's worst nightmare had it not been for the fact that she deterred players from betting like she did with one craps *faux pas* after another.

There were now six players spaced around the table. Blaze sat at the head as the shooter with the same middle-aged man to her right that had been there since before Fox arrived. Fox noticed that the man had subtly attempted to flirt with Blaze, and she reciprocated the flirting. It's about time he decided to go for it, Fox thought. He had crushed on her all game. To the man's right was Horace's friend, who had taken over Horace's chips now that security had escorted Horace outside. To his right was the last cockatoo, a woman that Fox had come to respect as she claimed Harry Pyne's money for herself. Perhaps it wasn't Fox or Blaze but this cockatoo who was the greatest conwoman at the table. Fox stood to the cockatoo's right at the corner of the table with Theseus at the foot.

"I think a special mid-game-fight bet is in order," Blaze said. She tossed several chips to the dealer. "I'm shooting boxcars on this one!"

Blaze arced the dice and banked them off the wall in front of Theseus. The dice tumbled onto the green baize and turned up five and three.

"Oh blast!" Blaze said. She lost on the boxcars bet, but everyone else won money on craps. Fox went along as an unassuming player and bided her time until she could expose Blaze. She felt a sense of duty to put Blaze in her place and to show that someone was on to her. It didn't matter how many Sharon Grahams the woman hurt, another would come in to stop her eventually. And that was the crux of it, Fox remembered. She didn't choose to play against Blaze tonight because of some fascination with the soft life (although she knew she was tempted by the luxury of the rich). No, Fox went into the casino that night seeking justice for Sharon Graham. If proving Mickey Blaze cheated at craps was enough to nudge MI6 into investigating her, and thus achieve justice for the deceased, then Jett Fox will have done her job.

However, it all hinged on this final leg of the game. This round went as the previous three before it. Blaze shot unreliably, and the players slowly bled chips. But Fox managed to stay at her goal of not more than a twenty-five thousand dollar deficit. If she could hold strong until the dice inevitably went off the table one last time, then she could win back all the money she had lost while also exposing Blaze as a cheater. Of course, Fox's gambit would set off all sorts of alarm bells within Blaze. But if Fox's suspicions about Blaze's hubris were true, then everything should work out.

At last, Blaze lost some momentum. Fox watched the woman's eyes again for any sort of recognition. The big brown eyes darted toward Theseus ever so slightly as they had all night. It was time for Fox to put on her best charm and challenge Blaze to one last bet. Blaze unleashed the dice, and they bounded off the table.

"Oh my goodness! I can't believe I keep doing that!"

Fox watched Theseus perform his under-the-table ritual as the dice were swapped. Yes! Fox celebrated in her mind. Theseus had swapped out the house dice for more house dice, believing he had swapped in the loaded dice. He handed the dice to the dealer. He examined them and handed them to the stickman. He delivered them to Blaze. At last! Blaze now believed the loaded dice were in her possession.

"Well then, I think I'll make my off-the-table bet again. Maximum bet on nine!"

Fox mustered her courage. It was now or never! "I'd like to call your bet and raise you," Fox said sternly from across the table.

Blaze was confused. "Excuse me? That's not how this works."

"Well, why not?" Fox said. "This is your game, am I right? I'm sure the casino won't mind if we make things interesting. I'd like to raise the stakes on your bet and invite you to match it. Twenty-five-thousand dollars on a Don't Pass bet."

The others gasped. Don't Pass was a bet that the shooter would not score the point to flip the puck. Currently, the puck was on, and the point was nine. Betting Don't Pass in this specific instance was a direct challenge by Fox to Blaze. And considering the stakes that Fox suggested, the casino was guaranteed to split even on this shot no matter who won. In truth, this sort of challenge could never be made in a normal game. The circumstances of the game were what allowed Fox to get creative.

Blaze blinked. Fox saw beads of sweat forming on the woman's forehead. Fox began to doubt herself. Had she played this entire scenario too on the nose? Did Blaze see right through her? Surely, given the chaos that occurred when the dice were last switched, Blaze doubted that she had the loaded dice in her hand. Five seconds of silence felt like five years as Fox waited for Blaze's reply. Finally, the confidence returned to the millionaire.

"Oh you're on," she said, turning to the dealer. "Match Miss Fox's bet. Twenty-five thousand on nine."

I've got you now! Fox thought. She merely had to wait for the inevitable. How would she feel when Blaze realized what had happened? Fox maintained her composure, and she could feel Theseus' eerie presence next to her. She could tell that Blaze's partner knew something was amiss. However, Theseus tossed his chips to the dealer, sticking to the belief that Blaze had the loaded dice. The others placed bets with the momentum of the dice, assuming that Blaze would continue her current streak.

The loaded dice were tucked away with Fox. The bet was made. Fox had Blaze in the palm of her hand. However, even with the scheming, the sleight of hand, and Harry Pyne's brilliant distraction, the final shot still came down to chance. Blaze had played a spectacular game all night even without the loaded dice. She had bankrupted the others with those dice, but this time, the other players, Fox included, were set to make a lot of money. It would be a minor hit to Blaze's bank account. The hit to her ego was more important. It was now time for Blaze to shoot.

She rotated her wrist in the casual motion that she had used all night when the loaded dice were in hand. She flipped the dice across the table. They tumbled across the baize like pebbles skipping across a lake. The rotations halted, and the dice turned up to reveal four white dots on one cube and three white dots on the other.

The table erupted into the widest range of emotions it had all game. Fox ignored the commotion around her as a gigantic grin formed on her face. She stared at the two red cubes on the table with their dots showing four and three. And then she looked up to see Blaze standing aghast.

Blaze slammed her fists on the edge of the table. She shouted, "Impossible! How in the hell?! No! No!" Her eyes shot toward Theseus, and the rage carried across the table like a dragon breathing fire to protect its treasure. Theseus looked terrified for his life as Blaze slammed the table once more and stormed away from the game. The rest of the table cheered at her departure.

"Your winnings, madame." The dealer pushed fifty thousand dollars' worth of chips to Fox. She tossed five hundred-dollar chips to both the dealer and stickman. The dealer and stickman nodded their gratitude for the tips. Fox gathered the rest of her chips to cash out.

She turned to see Theseus watching her. He looked confused and defeated. Fox imagined the thoughts that must be going through his head. Somehow, he knew that Fox was responsible for Blaze's defeat, but he couldn't figure out how the woman standing next to him pulled it off. Fox gave a short, mirthless laugh and winked at Theseus.

CHAPTER 11

A week had passed since the adventure in Morocco. Jett Fox was back at her desk in the New York offices of the Solace Counterintelligence Firm. She stared at her computer screen in boredom. She scrolled through the emails from lawyers with process service requests. She had made the mistake three years earlier of getting herself on a private investigators' email chain where lawyers could easily send out requests to process servers. Her idea was to hopefully find diamonds in the rough, but it had not once panned out with anything useful. She didn't consider herself to be above doing classic private investigator work, but the Solace Firm had garnered global attention from most government intelligence agencies. Serving divorce papers to unfaithful spouses wouldn't come close to paying any bills. Still, she couldn't bring herself to have her email address removed from the mailing list, just in case. She clicked *Delete* on everything and sat in the uncomfortable office chair alone with her thoughts.

Casablanca had been an interesting case, but an unfinished one. Harry Pyne told Fox that he got what he needed to pique the interest of his superiors at MI6. In the world of spies, cheating at gambling was more than just a character flaw. They took it as an actionable trait in which a person was most certainly hiding something bigger. Pyne thanked Fox for all she did in exposing that side of Mickey Blaze. They had one last drink together at the hotel bar that night after craps.

"I'm afraid I won't be able to tell you how this case turns out," Pyne said, "but keep an eye on the headlines. I have a good feeling that Mickey Blaze's name ought to pop up in the near future."

Fox felt uneasy by what Pyne said. Did he mean to kill her in an act of vengeance for Sharon Graham? Might Fox scroll through the headlines on her news feed and see that Mickey Blaze died in a horrific accident? Her stomach turned at the thought. She knew the game. The intelligence community considered killing a government agent an act of war. Fox could only hope that whomever the British government chose to pick up Sharon Graham's trail was diligent in his or her investigation before choosing to pull the trigger on Blaze.

Fox and Pyne said their final goodbyes at the bar, and then Fox got on the first flight back to New York the next morning. She assumed she would never see the handsome Englishman again, and she was happy about it. However, the inevitable melancholy she felt upon returning home from an international case set in rather quickly. She stepped inside her one-bedroom apartment in New Jersey and nearly cried that she was no longer enjoying five-star accommodations in Casablanca. She flopped onto her couch and picked up where she left off on her streaming binge. She woke up incredibly early the next morning, prepared her lunch for the day, and drove her fifteen-year-old Japanese make commuter car through the Lincoln Tunnel to Solace Books on the Upper East Side. Fox shared a knowing glance with the woman stationed at the cash register for the bookstore and headed to the back where she made her way to the employee elevator and to her office a few floors up where the actual spy work took place. Somewhere in between working and driving back to her apartment in New Jersey, Fox spent three hours at the gym. She repeated this mundane routine for a week until now she sat in her office chair.

Fox turned to her computer screen and was determined to answer at least one of the unanswered questions. Who was Theseus? She couldn't get the slender man who helped Blaze cheat at craps out of her head. She opened the search engine and typed "Mickey Blaze and Theseus."

She got her answer immediately. Among several news articles, the first image that came up showed Blaze and Theseus at a racetrack. Theseus was dressed in the quintessential jump suit of a racer and holding a helmet. Blaze stood next to him smiling. The man's full name popped on the screen above the photograph: "Theseus Kastellanos." So the man who helped Blaze cheat was a racecar driver. Blaze employed him both legitimately and illegitimately. Fox remembered the look of terror on Theseus' face when he and Blaze both realized the loaded dice were not used on that final shot. His entire demeanor during the game had been strange. He feared Blaze. This suggested to Fox that the man had seen a side of Blaze that no one else had seen. Was it possible that Theseus knew Blaze killed Sharon Graham? Was he helping her cheat in the casino because he feared what she might do to him?

Fox read the brief bio under Theseus' name. "Theseus Kastellanos is a professional racecar driver currently competing as part of Blaze Racing Inc. in the Open Circuit Association. He is an up-and-coming driver with two years of professional experience. He previously raced on the amateur circuit for Wallaby Motorsport."

She spotted a more recent news article just under Theseus' bio. The article was posted five hours ago. She saw the headline, "Blaze Racing to host open circuit challenge in Los Angeles next month." The writer gushed about Mickey Blaze and how this was the former racer's first big event. After just a few short years of building the racing division, Blaze was ready to push manufacturing and sales. The race in LA was a chance to showcase the company's first model that would go on sale at the start of the new year.

Fox saw the envelope notification light up at the bottom of her screen to indicate that she had a new email. She clicked on it and saw a new email from her boss, Chairwoman Solace. No one in the building knew Chairwoman Solace's first name. She wanted Fox to come up to her office in ten minutes. She had a new assignment for her. Fox acknowledged the email and put her computer to sleep. That was just enough time to stretch her legs and have a little personal time. Nine minutes later, Fox stood in the elevator that took her to the next floor up. She stepped out to the reception area where she saw Solace's personal assistant, Eddie Muncey, seated behind his desk.

"Jett! How are you today?" He spoke with a thick New York accent.

"Hello, Eddie. I'm well. How are you?"

"The same, thank you."

Eddie wasn't traditionally handsome. He was medium height and surprisingly lurpy for someone who wasn't tall. He had a small gap in between his two front teeth, and his hairline was receding early for a man in his twenties. He had the youthful exuberance of Elijah Wood in his twenties, but he looked like Elijah Wood in his forties. Yet, he was well groomed and dressed nicer than any of the other men in the building. Today, he wore a long-sleeve white button-down with a solid blue tie in a double Windsor knot. Several sports trinkets lined his desk, including a New York Mets paperweight and a signed picture of Eli Manning.

"How was Casablanca?" Eddie asked.

"It started lukewarm but then heated up as the trip went on."

"Well, that's what happens with you trailblazers. The flames follow wherever you go."

Fox laughed. Eddie Muncey reviewed all field reports before submitting them to Chairwoman Solace. Eddie enjoyed a corny name pun, and so Fox knew Eddie was waiting for someone to set him up with a dumb Mickey Blaze joke. Fox also enjoyed the playful banter with Eddie. He was six years younger than Fox and hadn't been soured by the world just yet.

"How's your dog, Eddie?"

"Hyper as always. I should've gotten a bulldog instead of a beagle. I'm not sure I have the energy to keep up with this one."

"You live near a park, don't you?"

"My only saving grace, but he's still by himself for several hours a day."

"Your apartment must be a disaster every night when you get home."

Eddie laughed and nodded. He then pointed with his head toward the boss' door. "Chairwoman Solace said you could go in as soon as you got here."

"Thanks, I'll send you a postcard from wherever she sends me next."

Fox stepped up to the frosted glass door and opened it. She saw Chairwoman Solace seated at her desk. Solace held the same dominating existence she always did when Fox saw her, a woman in absolute control over any situation and with any guest.

"Have a seat, Agent Fox," she said. "I believe you know my guest."

Solace had garnered all of the attention that Fox nearly missed seeing she wasn't alone in the room. Across the desk from Solace sat the last person Fox expected to see today. She recognized the muscular frame, curly brown hair, and blue-gray eyes almost immediately. He dressed in a suit slightly less formal than the one he wore at Oasis in Casablanca. Blood and steam rushed to Fox's head. The man smiled at her.

"Hello again, Miss Fox."

Fox glared at Harry Pyne and then back over to Chairwoman Solace.

"You've got to be kidding me. What's *he* doing here?"

CHAPTER 12

Fox was incredulous. Any nice thoughts she had about Pyne helping her expose Blaze at the craps table had been replaced by irritation. She put up with this man just long enough to get her job done, but she never expected to see him again, let alone one week later in Chairwoman Solace's office. What could this entail? Solace mentioned a new assignment in her email. Was Harry Pyne a client once again?

Pyne cast a sideways glance to Chairwoman Solace with a sheepish grin. He said, "I told you she wouldn't be happy to see me."

Solace showed no emotion one way or another. She simply nodded for Fox to take a seat next to Pyne. Fox knew that Solace hated commanding anything a second time, so she sat down and reeled her emotions back in. Fox laughed inwardly at the idea that Pyne was back. Did the man irritate her? Of course. But when push came to shove, the man came through when she needed his help to embarrass Mickey Blaze at Oasis. As much as he bothered her, she knew that he was a serious man when it came time to work. That's all she could ask from him.

"I apologize for my reaction," Fox said. "I just didn't expect to see you back here so soon. Shouldn't you be off chasing Mickey Blaze?"

"That's exactly why he's here," Solace interrupted. She maintained composure and hardly moved a muscle while she spoke. Each word carried across the desk in a methodical manner. "Mister Pyne would like us to continue the Sharon Graham case."

Fox watched Pyne and saw pain cross his face temporarily before he straightened himself. Fox said to him, "I thought showing that she cheated at the casino would be enough for your supervisors to continue her investigation."

"It should have," he said. "Something's not right. I told them everything we did in Casablanca, and instead of sending an agent to finish the job, they grounded me... indefinitely."

"Did they not believe you?"

"They told me to drop Mickey Blaze as a suspect and turn in everything I had on her. No questions asked. Of course, I asked one more question, and that led to my suspension."

Fox was iffy on the protocols, but she understood what that meant and that it was quite serious to have Pyne in the United States at that moment.

"You're not supposed to leave the UK while you're grounded, are you?"

He smiled. "I'm risking a lot to be here, as you know."

"I've already worked out the contract details with Mister Pyne," Solace said. "We're going to treat this as a continuation of the first case. As much as I appreciate Mister Pyne's generosity to consider Morocco as a separate encounter, I believe that you should have known better than to consider Mickey Blaze a solved problem, Agent Fox. I expect my agents to show more initiative in the field, especially you. Mister Pyne hired us to solve Sharon Graham's murder, not to play craps with a crook."

Fox knew better than to argue with Solace. It was best to let the woman chide her and then take the next assignment graciously.

"Yes, ma'am."

Pyne spoke up. "In fairness to Miss Fox, I insisted that I had enough to convince MI6 to reopen their investigation into Mickey Blaze. Surely, I expected more from my superiors than to turn a blind eye from a woman who is connected at higher levels of bureaucracy than I thought previously."

"With respect, Mister Pyne," Fox started, "You insulted me and the firm throughout our brief time working together in Casablanca. Are you sure we're good enough for you?"

Pyne sighed. "I thought we buried the hatchet after the casino."

Fox thought of a selfish retort that would surely get her out of working the rest of this case. Something along the lines of "that's because I didn't expect to see you a week later." She'd no doubt anger Solace enough to be removed from the case. However, Fox took a deep breath and let the moment of frustration pass her by. No matter her feelings about Harry Pyne, she was interested in seeing this through to the end. Sharon Graham deserved justice, and Fox intended to get it for her. However, the next words out of her mouth were painful to say.

"You and I are good, Mister Pyne," Fox said. "Forgive my abrasiveness. What can I do to help?"

Pyne smiled and nodded. He then looked to Solace, possibly seeking guidance. It seemed as though he wasn't sure of the next step, either. Solace appeared annoyed. She was early Generation X, and the two millennials sitting in front of her clearly lacked the procedural aptitude that had been instilled in her since childhood. Or at least that's what Fox thought Solace was thinking.

"Agent Fox, what do we know about the night of the murder? Are we sure that Blaze was in Casablanca?"

Now it was Fox's turn to be annoyed. But, she learned early on working with Solace to take every one of her boss' questions seriously and to eliminate any smart aleck remarks.

"She was there," Fox said. "Interpol had nothing that Mister Pyne hadn't already provided to me. It was a brutal murder. Stabbed in the back and sliced at the throat. Body was dumped off the west coast, and then she washed ashore where the police found her. MI6 had already retrieved Graham's belongings from her hotel room before we were ever on the case."

Fox recited everything else she knew about Sharon Graham and Mickey Blaze, and Pyne confirmed everything she said. Solace showed little to no reaction to any of it. Decades working in espionage must have desensitized her to the grimmer details, Fox thought.

"Based on what you've told me," Solace started, "I agree that MI6 should have believed you. As you've suspected, Mister Pyne, someone within your organization is trying to protect Blaze. Someone important." She turned to Fox. "How would you like to approach this, Agent Fox?"

There was no attempt to see if Fox wanted to continue the case. To Solace, Fox was already on the job, and she wanted to hear plans for action.

"As it turns out," Fox said, "there's a big race in California next month. Mickey Blaze is hosting it."

Fox reiterated everything she read from her brief search earlier.

"I see," Solace said. There was a small pause in the conversation as Solace sat back.

Fox responded, "We could collaborate with a racing team to be our eyes and ears. I think we might convince them to let me join their staff in some capacity."

Solace shook her head and sat forward. "We're not the CIA or the FBI. Conscripting civilians is out of the question. We'll have to do this ourselves."

"What do you mean?" Fox asked, although she was fairly certain she already knew the answer.

Solace stared at Fox without humor. "Agent Fox, we have one month to turn you into a racecar driver."

CHAPTER 13

Jett Fox was beside herself as she left Chairwoman Solace's office. She had attempted dangerous feats in this line of work, but never had Solace asked her to do something so outrageous or so dangerous as this. A professional racer? Was it even possible to fake her way through something like that? There was no way. Fox was convinced this could not be done.

Before leaving, Solace asked Fox to check in with the company's armory chief. So that was Fox's next destination as she left the chairwoman's office and passed Eddie Muncey's desk. Fox entered the elevator and turned to see Harry Pyne charging down the corridor to catch up to the closing doors. Fox pressed the "close doors" button more rapidly and offered a cheeky grin to Pyne as the doors crawled closer together. However, the Englishman reached the elevator and snuck his arm into the crevice before the doors shut completely. Fox sighed.

Pyne turned and stood next to Fox. She looked at the man, who tilted slightly in his pose as if he were at a photoshoot for a magazine cover. He looked at her and smiled. He opened his mouth for a moment to say something but then stopped. He then started again.

"If you don't want the case, Miss Fox, I understand," Pyne said.

Fox remained silent for a moment. She then said, "I want the case. I'm sorry for being immature back there."

Pyne laughed. "I know I'm not the easiest person to like."

Fox thought the opposite. She hated how easy it was to like Harry Pyne despite his unlikable personality traits. But, she kept that to herself.

The elevator halted at Fox's floor and the doors slid open.

"I have a few things to finish today," Fox said. "Why don't you come back tomorrow, and we'll brainstorm?"

Pyne nodded. "I'll see you tomorrow."

Fox checked her email, which had stacked up with a few items of minor importance, such as chatter from the analysts. Nothing applied directly to her. Satisfied that there was nothing of importance, she typed "How to drive a race car" into the search engine. Unfortunately, every video that popped up was either targeted toward individuals who already knew how to race or featured braggarts gushing over themselves, which discouraged Fox that much more.

Fox saw that it was time to check in at the armory, so she made her way back to the elevator and pressed "G5" once inside. G5 required authorization, so Fox swiped her keycard across the panel, and the elevator whirred to life. The mechanical box dropped below the street surface until Fox's ears popped. The elevator stopped, and the doors opened to a world beneath the world.

Commotion smacked Fox in the face as the elevator revealed a concourse that opened up into a colossal laboratory. Fox stepped out into the vast space and was immediately greeted by a younger man in a white lab coat. He sat at his desk and appeared to be performing mundane work that didn't match the rest of the facility. He smiled and nodded at Fox, and he motioned for her to go on ahead into the lab.

Fox moved past the concourse and into the actual laboratory. It was an impressive structure that resembled a cross between a shopping mall and Santa's workshop. Several people in white lab coats were scattered across the room working on various projects, a perfect marriage of hardware and software. At one end the screech of a lug nut remover echoed across the ceiling. At the other end a lab worker typed at his computer. Everyone who worked in the armory wore either noise cancelers or earbuds.

In truth, Solace asking Fox to visit the armory was merely a formality. Fox came down to G5 almost daily to visit her work friend, the armory chief herself. Fox spotted her in the typical armory white lab coat. She was above average height, although not quite as tall as Jett Fox. Her dark hair that she kept short in a long pixie cut with side swept bangs sat upon a face with sharp features, pale skin, and brown eyes.

The armory chief held a semi-automatic rifle while wearing protective eyewear. She appeared to be tinkering with the weapon when she saw Fox. She spotted Fox walking through the lab and waved her over. She set the gun on the table and continued to tinker.

"A.C." Fox said. "How are things down here?"

"Better than bad, but worse than good," A.C. responded without missing a beat. "Here, put these on." A.C. handed Fox protective eyewear and noise-cancelers. Fox placed them on her eyes and ears.

A.C. maneuvered around the workbench toward the practice range and motioned for Fox to follow her. Fox followed and stood next to A.C. as she adjusted into a textbook firing stance, eyes locked on the scope and the rifle aimed at the target across the way. She exhaled softly and snapped her finger on and off the trigger in a rapid motion. The gun barrel popped with each short burst, but it wasn't even close to the sound that Fox knew the gun should make. Instead, the pops were low thuds that lacked explosive power. However, Fox noticed that the target at the other end of the practice range rattled and shredded with each shot. The low thuds then ceased and were replaced by a clicking sound that Fox definitely recognized.

"Damn, it jammed again," A.C. said.

"What in the world is wrong with that gun?"

A.C. smiled proudly. "Semi-automatic dart thrower. Built it from scratch. Looks like a legitimate rifle, but it's a mega-enhanced airsoft needler. It uses CO2 cartridges to fire wooden darts, but... I can't keep it from jamming. It's at least a year from being field ready. A little better for the environment than your standard rifle."

Fox scratched her head. "Are we going to war or something?"

"No, but you'll be glad we have one of these if we ever do." A.C. led Fox back to the workbench and locked up the rifle. "Solace briefed me on your next assignment. I know she's not one for jokes, but this is ridiculous even for my standards. You're entering the open circuit race in California next month?"

"It was either that or press credentials, but I don't think we can snoop around as media members like we could as a professional race team," Fox said. "Plus, they actually check up on you if you're in the media. A race team just has to qualify for the race, right?"

"*Just* has to qualify," A.C. snickered. "Do you even know how to race?"

"Cut me some slack, A.C." Fox said. "This wasn't my idea."

"All right, all right." The armory chief laughed. "I have some ideas."

CHAPTER 14

A.C. led Fox through the laboratory where Fox got a chance to see more of the armory's insane projects. Most had no practical use whatsoever, but A.C. argued that they did. Either way, they were fun to watch, and some would make fun office pranks, like the arrest chair. The armory had developed an unscented adhesive that could be applied to any office chair and instantly stick to anyone who sat in the chair.

Two lab grunts worked on this project together. One of them applied the glue, and the other sat down in the chair. The one who sat in the chair wore breakaway pants, and when he stood up rapidly, the pants ripped away with ease. He was already wearing a second pair of pants underneath his breakaway pants. Fox thought the whole demonstration was a joke, like these two lab grunts had become bored with their underground work and decided to have a bit of fun.

The more practical projects were ones that A.C. worked on herself. A.C. stopped at the clothing and fashion section on the way to the automotive section to show off one such design.

"I think you'll especially like this one." She motioned toward a medium-sized brown leather shoulder bag.

Fox waited expectantly. She smirked. "It's a purse. Oh wait, let me guess. It's a purse that also doubles as a grenade launcher."

"Close!"

Fox was being sarcastic, but A.C. hurriedly opened the purse.

"As you can see, unassuming inside like any other purse, but if you press here," A.C. tapped a corner of the purse, which gave a clicking sound. A panel opened to reveal several silver spheres. "Smoke grenade storage! Perfect for a quick getaway, if you need one."

Fox laughed. "Where are the hidden gold sovereigns and collapsible sniper rifle?"

A.C. frowned. "Joke all you want, Jett, but I'm trying to keep you safe out in the field. Here," she pressed against the purse's inner side. Another compartment opened. "Just enough room for your Beretta. And then here," A.C. traced her finger along the purse's outer base. There was a click followed by a stub that popped loose. A.C. pulled the stub from the purse to reveal the sharp steel of a throwing knife. "Got you covered for fight or flight. Oh, and there's one last thing," A.C. pulled up the straps and pointed to a specific area around the stitching. There was a small button. "This connects the purse to the armory's network. Speakers embedded all along the straps to record audio from up to fifty feet away. You can also clone cell phones and disrupt other electronic devices. A little more inconspicuous than using your own phone to do the same things. And, connecting your purse to the network will get it safely through airport security. A false image will appear on the checkpoint monitor. And this button on the strap will only connect the purse to the network with your thumbprint and mine, so anyone who steals your purse *won't* make it through airport security."

They made one last stop before going to the armory's automotive section. A.C. showed off a medium-sized mobile craft with seating for the driver and just enough room for a passenger seated behind them. It had two front skis and two spiked rear belts at the wheels.

"Snowmobile?"

"Not just any snowmobile," A.C. said. "A super snowmobile. Multi-barrel machine guns loaded at the front, one heat-seeking missile at the rear, and a spike drop on the underside to ward off any unwanted followers with unfriendly debris. It's the perfect vehicle to escape any explosive situation."

"Explosive situations in the snow," Fox corrected.

"Right."

"Aren't you worried people will say you're just copying popular fiction?"

"The classics are classics for a reason, Jett."

A.C. led Fox on through the armory until they reached the automotive section. The rich, dank smell of motor oil pressed against Fox's nostrils as soon as they rounded the corner to this section of the armory. Two mechanics worked underneath a sports car lifted ten feet into the air. They both acknowledged A.C. and continued working. A.C. walked past the repair area and stopped at a stationary driver's seat and steering wheel that were connected to three television screens about the same size as two side windows and a windshield of a car.

"Voila, your new car," A.C. said.

Fox smirked. "A driving simulator?"

"*Racing* simulator," A.C. said. "Until I can come up with a solid plan for how to keep you alive during the race next month, we'll have you doing practice runs on the simulator. Probably the only time in your life you'll get paid to play video games at work."

Fox laughed and then sighed. "The English agent who hired us might be snooping around down here tomorrow. I promised he could help us brainstorm some ideas."

A.C.'s demeanor changed. She smiled conspiratorially and raised an eyebrow. "*The* English agent? The one you've been talking about all week at lunch? What was his name? Henry? Marty?"

"Harry. Harry Pyne."

A.C. smiled even wider. "More like Wonder Boy the way you get when you talk about him."

"Shut up."

A.C. continued laughing. "And so, this case is part of your last one?"

"Yes, he didn't get the reaction in London that he'd hoped to get, and so he came back to see if we could take over permanently."

"Is that the *only* reason he came back?" A.C. teased. "Or did he just want to see a certain badass Amazon warrior?"

Fox rolled her eyes. "Harry Pyne is a misogynistic playboy who's so bored with his own life that he's come to ruin mine."

A.C. shrugged. "You brought him up, not me."

Fox sighed again. "So how does this simulator work? Just get in, drive, and type my initials next to the new high score?"

"It's a lot harder than it looks," A.C. said. "I bet it takes you at least ten tries to finish a race without crashing."

"Oh you're on. What are the stakes? Hundred bucks?"

"I was thinking of something bigger. How about if you can't finish a race without crashing, then you have to ask out Harry Pyne on a date while he's in New York."

Fox looked determined. "Fine, but if I finish a clean race in ten tries or less, you're buying lunch tomorrow."

"Deal."

Fox buckled into the simulator and booted up a course that most closely resembled the Los Angeles scenery she'd encounter next month at Mickey Blaze's open challenge. The video game graphics popped from the screen, and the speakers blared at the noise-cancelers over her ears. Fox ignited the simulated engine, and the seat began to rumble in a realistic way. The experience was so immersive in those opening moments that Fox felt like she was really on the racetrack.

She became even more immersed in the simulator as soon as she hammered the accelerator, and the seat bucked her backward. She felt the momentum with each turn and jerk of the wheel almost to the point that she became nauseous. The speeds felt like real speeds, and just as A.C. predicted, Fox clipped the back of another car and caused a massive wreck. "Race Failed" came up on the screen in big red letters.

This frustration continued for several races until finally Fox was on the verge of crossing the finish line. A.C. looked up from her work when she saw Fox having success on this latest run. Fox felt the adrenaline flow through her as though she were in an actual race. Small beads of sweat formed on her brow. But, Fox overcorrected the drift on the final turn and spun the car out of control, ramming through the barricade.

A.C. laughed at the crash. Fox sighed and looked up at A.C. with a defeated smirk.

"I still have two tries left."

"Uh huh, do you need me to call and make reservations for your date?"

Fox turned her focus back to the screen to begin her next race. This one went worse than the previous try. She didn't even make it to the final turn before she crashed into the opposing cars.

She sat at the screen waiting to start her final race. She was conflicted, obviously, because a part of her was most definitely attracted to Harry Pyne, but there was no way in hell she was going to let A.C. win this bet.

Fox accelerated gradually at the start of the race, matching the speed of the cars around her. She knew she didn't need to win the race; she first had to learn to finish a race cleanly. This took patience and discipline, which were two traits she failed to exercise in the earlier simulations. It wasn't as fun as trying to cut off her opponents and skip ahead to the leading position, but Fox thought the slow and steady race was somewhat cathartic.

She came up to the final turn and maneuvered for the drift. Three drivers sped along ahead of her and threatened to ram her through the barricade. Fox maintained her composure and slowed her pace so that she could finish the turn. More cars passed her until Fox was now in the back half of the pack. Let them go, she thought. She held the wheel firm to complete the amateur drift and accelerated out of it. She lost a lot of ground on the leaders, but that didn't matter. She finished the race cleanly in twenty-first place out of forty racers.

"Ha!" Fox shouted. "Buffalo chicken salads are on you tomorrow, A.C."

CHAPTER 15

Fox and A.C. sat outside in the veranda that overlooked the rest of Manhattan. Chairwoman Solace may have expected the absolute best from her agents, but the amenities she supplied at the office building made up for the grueling work schedule. One of those amenities was the veranda where the employees could relax and get fresh air. Working underground all day, the armory employees especially needed their veranda visits.

The two friends snapped off the plastic lids to their buffalo chicken salads. As if on cue, a pigeon fluttered onto the veranda railing. A cool breeze coursed across the building as Fox listened to the relatively quiet nature of the posh upper east side surrounding them. The wealthy denizens at the street level made their way to the various restaurants and shops. Fox turned her attention away from the ambiance and toward A.C.

"Harry Pyne should be here any minute," Fox said as she poured dressing onto her salad. "Please no matchmaker stuff."

"Oh you're no fun." A.C. poked at her salad daintily.

After a few minutes of eating and talking about their latest streaming binges, the doors from inside the building opened. A man dressed in the building's security uniform stepped through and held the door open for Pyne. The Englishman spotted the two women and smiled and nodded. Fox held up her hand casually to motion for Pyne to join them. Fox and A.C. both stood up.

"Hello, Miss Fox."

"Hello, Mister Pyne." Fox motioned to A.C. "This is the armory chief." She motioned back to Pyne. "A.C., this is Harry Pyne of the British Secret Service."

Pyne and A.C. shook hands. "A.C.? You go by the initials of your job title?"

Fox watched A.C. swoon. Her face flushed, and she smiled like a teenager. Fox swore the next words out of A.C.'s mouth might have been "You can call me whatever you want." However, the armory chief gathered her composure as she and Pyne sat down.

"A.C. are the initials for my name, too," she said. "My name is Alice Cooper."

Pyne laughed gently. "You must be joking?"

"No joke, I swear," A.C. said. "My parents met at an Alice Cooper concert, and our last name happened to be Cooper. They were going to name me Alice if I was born a boy or a girl. It didn't matter."

"So you've gone by A.C. since before you were the armory chief?"

"That's right."

Pyne laughed again. "Well then, the pleasure is all mine, A.C."

Fox noticed Pyne linger for a moment, clearly taking in the armory chief. Fox raised her eyebrows, and the corner of her mouth turned up. Fox wasn't surprised, of course. A.C. was gorgeous and being a huge techno-nerd played to her advantage in the dating world more often than not. The fact that she knew more about guns than most of her potential suitors was always a good icebreaker.

But enough about that, Fox thought. A.C. must have thought the same thing because she jumped right into her presentation.

"I explained to Jett earlier that Mickey Blaze's race at the Palisades is different from what she might normally see on TV," A.C. said. Pyne nodded as A.C. continued. "An open circuit challenge, like the one Blaze is hosting, isn't cut and dried like the open-wheel single-seaters of the Formula 1 series or the stock cars you'd see in NASCAR. The open circuit is kind of a throwback race where you can really put any car on the track that you'd like."

"So what, are we talking like *Fast and the Furious* racing? Or *Mario Kart*?" Fox said.

"Funny, but no, we still have minimum requirements our car has to meet to compete in the race," A.C. said as she lifted her work tablet from beside her salad. "We'll be going up against veteran racers driving some of the most expensive sports cars in the entire world. We don't have the budget to put you in a Lamborghini, nor do you have the experience to drive one and not end up over a cliff in Malibu."

Pyne laughed.

Fox turned to him and smirked. "Yes, I'm sure you'd love to see that."

A.C. continued, "I've made a list of some budget cars that should keep you safe during the race but that are also fast enough for you to crack the top forty in the qualifying round."

Pyne reached across for the tablet. "May I?"

"Sure thing!" A.C. said. She turned to Fox. "You should probably choose the same make as your current car. That will shave at least two days of training off our time crunch. Just like in the simulator, the key is just to qualify for the big race. We're not trying to win."

"How many Japanese cars do you have on the list?" Fox asked.

"Three," Pyne said as he handed the tablet back to A.C. "Might I suggest the Hanzo 468?"

"*I* would go for the Takahashi 72, myself," A.C. said.

Pyne grinned at A.C. It appeared he liked the challenge from the armory chief, and A.C. appeared to enjoy challenging him.

"I see, so you expect the Palisades to feature a course with more twists and turns rather than pure drag racing?" Pyne inquired.

"Not just that, but, as I said before, we're not trying to win this race, we're trying to keep Jett safe, and I think the Takahashi is the best bet for that."

"Safety first, sure," Pyne started, "but keep in mind that Miss Fox is on the track by herself for the qualifying round. With no other racers to distract her, we could afford more speed to make sure we secure the spot in the top forty."

A.C. leaned forward in her seat. She appeared excited to debate with Pyne. "That assumes the 468 can maintain its acceleration speed for the whole qualifying run. Let's say Jett gets those quick bursts out of the corners. Are they enough to close the gap with experienced racers who are not only driving better cars, but also getting the most out of those better cars?" A.C. stopped and considered Pyne's point of view. "If we had more time, then maybe the 468 is the better choice, but given that we have less than a month to turn Jett into a professional racer, the 72 gives us the best chance to hide any mistakes we make out there."

At a more immature time in her life, Jett Fox might have taken offense to the insinuation that she wasn't capable of handling the faster car. But, after years of working for Chairwoman Solace, Fox understood that A.C. just wanted to pick the vehicle best suited for the mission. At the end of the day, the race was a means to an end, and the riskier car might endanger the team's goals.

"I vote for the 72," Fox said. Pyne seemed surprised that Fox chose A.C.'s car. Fox added, "I'd like to *not* end up in the Pacific Ocean."

"Putting in the requisition now," A.C. said. "At least that's one box we checked off. Now to teach you how to race." A.C. turned to Pyne. "Any ideas there?"

"She can learn the basics in the simulator, but at some point, we have to get Miss Fox out on the track." Pyne turned to Fox. "You need that real experience of driving at speeds over one hundred kilometers an hour on winding roads with other cars on the track with you. It's something that doesn't translate to the computer."

"Believe it or not, but I've been in a car chase with people shooting at me," Fox said.

Pyne snickered. "And I'm sure your car looked like it, too."

Fox's jaw and neck cringed as she sheepishly stayed silent with a guilty grin on her face.

"He's right, Jett. You can't wreck the car. There's an unspoken understanding in racing culture that you keep it clean. All it takes is one negligent fender bender to blow your cover. Those are the kinds of things you have to learn if you want to pass as a professional driver." A.C. turned to Pyne. "And we'll get her on a real track soon enough, but for now she needs to keep practicing in the simulator until she's consistently finishing races without wrecking."

CHAPTER 16

A.C.'s requisition order processed quickly. The latest model of the Takahashi 72 arrived at the armory within two days. A.C. wasted no time getting to work on it to fine tune the car exactly how she wanted it. Meanwhile, Harry Pyne returned to England to avoid suspicion and hoped to return a week later, and Jett Fox continued her training on the simulator.

Fox stepped out of the elevator and into the armory for her daily race training. She spotted A.C. in the automotive area under the hood of the 72. She called down to a mechanic positioned underneath the car and spoke in technobabble that Fox only slightly understood. A.C. was dressed down for the physical labor. She wore a denim jumpsuit with a few oil stains, and she wore a red bandana over her hair. She saw Fox and waved her over.

"Here's your new car."

The car itself wasn't the belle of the ball, but it wasn't an eyesore either. It had a practical style with its chrome paint job and sleek curves. Fox noticed the interior, compact in the back with only enough room for bags. It would be a tight fit for anyone with enough patience to sit back there. As if A.C. read Fox's mind, she commented on the back seat.

"The idea is to remove these seats altogether to give you more room up front," A.C. said. "We'll install a single seat with harnesses and try to make the stick shift as simplistic as we can."

"Simplistic is good, but I'm guessing you'll need gear shifting to become second nature to me," Fox said.

"If you had no stick shift experience, this whole thing would be virtually impossible."

"Then I guess I should thank my grandfather for buying me a manual transmission as my first car."

"Definitely." A.C. returned to the 72's hood. Fox followed. "We'll get you better acquainted with the car after we make the interior installations. Chairwoman Solace submitted our application for the race. Apparently, one of her many LLCs was a believable option to sponsor a race team. She didn't need to create a new one. That's lucky, right?"

Fox considered. "Maybe. On one hand, an existing LLC looks better for business history if Mickey Blaze were to look into it. On the other hand, it's easier for her to latch onto something that might connect the LLC to any off-the-books espionage activity."

"Do you think she'll look that deeply into us?"

"If Mickey Blaze is who we think she is, then yes, but I'd also wager that she'd want us in the race anyway, and she'll just try to kill us there."

A.C. ignored Fox's unceremonious death declaration. "Well, as long as you know what to expect."

The rest of the week went just like that. Fox spent hours in the armory practicing on the simulator while A.C. modified the 72 into a proper racing machine. Practice hours on the simulator dipped into Fox's weekend, as well, but she afforded herself some time away from the mission to keep her sanity.

Fox took in a terrible off-off Broadway play set in the 90s about a woman and her search for love in the era of dial-up internet, but her true love was a fellow teacher at the high school where they taught. The male lead looked an awful lot like Steve Zahn, and Fox was distracted by that for the duration of the play. It took several hours at the gym to sweat out that miserable experience.

"If it was a parody, it wasn't very funny," Fox said to A.C. the following Monday.

"Yuck, give me a dumb *Marvel* movie any day over trying to be cultured." A.C. glanced over the Takahashi 72 and admired her work. As promised, the interior had been completely replaced with a single seat and harnesses. She shut the hood, appearing pleased with any work done to raise the car's racing specs. "OK, I think it's ready for a test run!"

"Great!"

Both women's phones buzzed. They looked down at their phones to the message from Chairwoman Solace.

"Race application approved. Meet at my office in an hour. AC, get clean before you come up. No grease on my floors. Agent Fox, Harry Pyne just landed back from England. Get him up to speed before the meeting."

"Duty calls," Fox said.

"See you at the meeting," A.C. added.

Fox went to her office to file away any mundane office work. She fired off a few emails with analyst reports and referring clients to available private investigators. There was one analyst report in particular that caught Fox's eye. It was a report of the FBI looking into the disappearances of children across the country. The children in question all disappeared around the same time. It was normal to see something depressing come across her desk, but Fox noticed this one because the children were all between the ages of ten and twelve and came from foster homes. It meant that there was no one on the other side who could pay ransom money to get those children back.

There was nothing that could be done about it right now, and so Fox moved the report into a folder on her desktop labeled "Come Back Later." If this was still an open FBI investigation after the Mickey Blaze mission, Fox would undoubtedly look into it.

This was the ugly side of working in the private sector. The firm needed money, which meant that most of its clients were the rich and elite. Fox could only make time for the people who really needed the help when she could afford it. It broke her heart, but she had to put the missing children on the backburner until she completed the Mickey Blaze mission.

She came across one more analyst report that hooked her attention, and this one was relevant to her current mission. This report gave credence to what Harry Pyne told her in Morocco, that British domestic security believed criminals were using racing teams at Brands Hatch to smuggle diamonds. In this particular report, there were rumors of an unidentified diamond mine somewhere in the Canadian Rockies, but no one could substantiate the claims when pressed, and the area was too vast to commission a team to look into it. The report of an unidentified diamond mine didn't directly relate to the information she had, but Fox took note of the correlation.

"Hard at work I see."

Fox looked up from her computer to see Harry Pyne standing in the doorway. She smiled, "Harder at work than you these days."

"Ouch." Pyne laughed. "For the record, I was grounded, but there were plenty of MI6 office tasks that required my expertise."

"Oh? Such as?"

"My supervisors thought it might be a great idea to have me on the graveyard shift for a few days, checking in with the station heads across the world. It's not quite the switchboard nonsense of the 50s just to make a call to Hong Kong, but it took me back to my navy days. It was kind of nice to get back in the trenches with that sort of work again."

"We do something similar here. When we're not out in the field, we're expected to log at least two weeks of cash register duty in the bookstore downstairs every year to help out the part-timers."

"I see. So the woman downstairs?"

"Agent Stonecreek. She's kind of my work rival. We don't talk much to each other at the office, or ever really."

"How fortunate for her." Pyne winked, but there wasn't quite enough sarcasm in his voice. "How many bookstore days have you done this year?"

"I did one day back in January and then another day a few weeks ago," Fox said. "I might have done more that week if you hadn't hired us to meet you in Morocco."

"You're welcome."

Fox rolled her eyes and changed the subject. "A.C. has the 72 all ready for a test drive. Chairwoman Solace rented a track upstate for the next two weeks, so we'll head up there tomorrow. Did Solace let you know we're meeting at her office in the next little bit?"

"Yes, and that you'd get me caught up on anything I've missed the past few days."

"You're caught up. Just the car and the practice course."

"How's your sim driving going?"

"Good! But I'm ready to get out on a real track."

Pyne tilted his head. "We'll see."

Fox rolled her eyes again as the two of them strode to the elevator.

CHAPTER 17

The elevator doors slid open, and A.C. was already inside on her way up to the meeting with Chairwoman Solace. She looked taken aback when she saw Harry Pyne, and her throat flashed red.

"Oh hey!"

"Hello, A.C." The elevator doors closed, and Pyne continued. "Hey, after this mission is over and I'm back in good standing with MI6, I'd like to introduce you to our quartermaster. You have some impressive designs in the armory, and I think you have a good shot at a government contract, if you're interested."

A.C. responded, "Oh that would be great! I'd love to see some of the stuff you guys build over there. Do I have to sign an NDA?"

"Well of course," Pyne laughed. "We can't have you sharing our ideas with the CIA."

"Right, because you know we'll just make it better over here."

Pyne was speechless but amused.

A.C. continued, "Come on. Think about it. *The Office*. The American version is way better than the British version."

"*American* version, how crass," Pyne said. "*The Office* is a UK original, and the American knock off is nothing more than that. A knock off. Next, I suppose you'll tell me that Ethan Hunt is better than James Bond."

"Ethan Hunt *is* better than James Bond," A.C. said.

Pyne cringed. "Oh this ought to be good."

"Ethan Hunt is a bona fide genius with an eidetic memory, but he still has the emotional intelligence to work within a team. James Bond is a vain man child."

Fox smirked as the two of them argued with each other. They were both smiling as they argued, obvious flirtatious undertones to their disagreements. Fox was amused. She made it fairly clear that she had no plans to pursue a romantic entanglement with Pyne. Had A.C. taken that to mean she had permission to pursue her own? Interesting, Fox thought.

The elevator halted and the doors opened to the waiting room. Fox shared her usual pleasantries with Eddie Muncey, and then Eddie ushered the three of them inside to meet Solace inside the presidential suite. She had the television turned on to sports highlights.

"Not your usual viewing," Fox said.

Chairwoman Solace grinned ever so slightly that it almost freaked out Fox. "Believe it or not, Agent Fox, you can learn more about your targets on a station like this than you might realize. The FBI once set up a sting outside Yankee Stadium during the 2003 World Series. It didn't make the news because they were helping MI6 capture a British fugitive. But, the reason they got on his trail in the first place was because one of the junior agents at the FBI was watching *SportsCenter* and happened to see him in the highlight reel. And the fugitive kept going to games until the FBI finally set up the sting at the World Series and arrested him."

Fox remembered that World Series. Her hometown Marlins beat the Yankees in that World Series. It happened within a few years after moving to Florida to live with her grandparents. She watched the television screen as a basketball player leapt over a defender from just inside the free throw line and slam dunked the ball through the hoop. "I'll keep that in mind."

"The real reason I have it on is because Mickey Blaze is supposed to make an announcement about the Palisades race," Solace said as she held up a glossy information packet. "Here's the itinerary and everything else we need to know. I went through it already. Our application was accepted, but it doesn't mean we're in the race just yet. They want to inspect our car, and they'll also want to put you through a medical evaluation, as well, Agent Fox. And of course, you'll need to score a qualifying time in the top forty."

"A.C. reminds me every day."

Solace turned to A.C. "That's why I'm putting you in the field for this mission."

"What?" The armory chief's eyes went wide.

"Agent Fox needs a pit crew as part of her cover. I don't want anyone touching our car without your direct supervision."

"But Chairwoman, I—"

Solace cut her off. "I know you've never been in the field, but every once in a while, a mission comes up that requires an agency's quartermaster on location. I read the report on the modifications you've made to the Takahashi 72, and I don't trust anyone else to even breathe on our car unless you're there looking over their shoulders."

A.C. swallowed hard. "Yes, ma'am."

Fox noticed A.C. shaking. "It'll be OK, A.C. Don't worry about the undercover aspects. Just focus on the car, and leave the theatrics to me." Fox glanced quickly at Pyne and then back to A.C. "Pyne is very good at cover stories and deflecting attention away when covers are in jeopardy. You should've seen him in Casablanca. I'm sure he'd be willing to teach you a few things if you have any questions."

"Did you just call me Pyne? Are we finally good enough friends that you're not calling me *Mister* Pyne anymore?" Pyne said the word *Mister* in an exaggerated accent that sounded neither American nor Fox's subtle Brazilian-accented American.

Fox held up a finger to Pyne. "Don't push it."

Pyne turned to A.C. "I'm happy to help with anything you need. I'm playing the role of our PR manager, so anyone who might bother you has to get through me, and trust me, they won't."

Solace stepped in. "I'm not coming to LA with you three, but I'll come upstate and watch training over the next few days. Mister Pyne, I'm guessing you have to go back to England in a few days, as well?"

"Yes, and I won't be back until we fly to California."

Pyne opened his mouth to say more, but Solace stopped him. "It looks like Mickey Blaze is up." Solace turned up the volume on the television.

Blaze took the podium dressed in a pristine black business suit and dark red blouse. She let her blonde and bronze hair hang about freely, and she smiled at the members of the media who had gathered for the press conference. Her beauty radiated off the television screen just as it did at the casino in Casablanca. Mickey Blaze was truly America's sweetheart.

Just to her right, she was joined by her top racer and partner in crime, Theseus Kastellanos. The slender lizard-like frame sent chills down Fox's spine. He smiled, too, but his smile seemed more strained than Blaze's smile.

"Good afternoon!" Blaze started. "I have a quick statement, and then I'll be happy to take as many questions as you'd like to ask. First, let me just say that we at Blaze Automotive and the Blaze Racing Team are incredibly excited to host The Open Circuit Challenge at the Palisades in three weeks' time. The top open circuit racers from around the globe will be here for the opportunity to compete for a total purse of ten million dollars, with two million dollars of that purse set aside for our first-place winner." Audible murmurs went around the media members. "And of course, we're excited for any newcomers who might make their open circuit debuts in our race. Although," Blaze paused and turned on the playful banter, "I've seen the list of veterans who entered the field, and I don't like the chances for our newcomers."

There was some laughter among the audience. Blaze giggled as well. Fox remembered from her game at the casino that Blaze had a mastery for psychology and how to control the audience. Her big brown eyes helped her as she kept friendly eye contact with the members of the media.

Blaze continued, "Now, the reason I invited you all here today is because I have an incredible announcement. Blaze Racing is gaining one new driver for the Palisades race. Of course, you all know Theseus Kastellanos, a man who has catapulted himself into the star attraction of Blaze Racing. He is still my number-one guy, but he'll have a little more competition out on the track." Blaze paused and looked across her audience. "Professional racing was always my passion. It's something that was stolen from me early in my career, and it's something I've never relinquished as my dream. After consultations with some of the finest medical professionals in the world, I received a resounding 'yes' to a question that's burned my soul for far too long. Will I ever race again?" The audience gasped. "I am coming out of retirement, and at the Open Circuit Challenge in three weeks here in beautiful Southern California, I will make my grand return to the driver's seat."

CHAPTER 18

The presidential suite inside the Solace Counterintelligence Firm had gone silent, aside from the commotion on the television. Media members flooded Mickey Blaze with question after question as Jett Fox and the others watched the screen. Finally, after several minutes, Chairwoman Solace turned off the TV. The others turned to face her.

"Well," Solace said. "That was unexpected."

"It certainly makes our jobs more difficult," Harry Pyne said.

"What do you mean?" A.C. asked.

"This is no longer just some throwaway race where Blaze can sell a few extra units of her new car," Pyne said. "This is now a national news story. The place will be crawling with the media."

Fox considered as she sat down at the desk across from Solace. "She knows we're onto her."

Solace watched Fox and simply nodded for her to go on.

"This whole press conference," Fox continued, "it's a dare. She knows we're onto her, and she's daring us to stop her."

"I wouldn't be so sure," Solace answered. "You might be right, but it's possible Blaze always planned to re-debut as a driver at this race. Go into the mission with the possibility she knows you're onto her, but don't assume she knows everything. You'll betray your own cover if you engage her with sub-text. It's a good way to get yourself killed."

"Understood."

Fox passed through the Lincoln Tunnel and back to her apartment that night and sank into her couch. Her heart raced at the thought of sharing the track with Theseus Kastellanos and Mickey Blaze, two people that likely wanted her dead once they put it all together that Fox was the investigator sent to expose them. Then there was the question of why. It wasn't enough to prove that Mickey Blaze killed Sharon Graham. What was the motive? Was it diamonds as Harry Pyne suggested that first day in Casablanca? Was it something else? What criminal enterprise required the services of a woman in the automotive industry?

Fox moved to her bedroom and tried to sleep, but she was restless. She thought about other possible motives. She also thought about the report the analysts intercepted concerning the FBI's investigation into missing children across the United States. She would much rather work on a case like that, and perhaps the perks of the private sector were worth sacrificing to have a chance at doing work that actually mattered.

Surely an apprenticeship under an ex-CIA operative was enough for Quantico to take a look at Jett Fox.

There was also her grandfather's mysterious past that she could lean on. Although never a government operative himself, Walter Fox consulted more than a few times. That was how he ended up in Brazil during the Cold War. He fell in love with a Brazilian woman, Jett Fox's grandmother, and bore a son, Jett's father. Eventually, after their son had grown up and started a family of his own, Walter Fox wished to return to the United States, and he and his wife moved to Florida. Fox's parents remained in Brazil. After all, that was where they grew up. They had no desire to follow Fox's grandparents to the United States.

Tragedy struck. Following the sudden deaths of Fox's parents in a horrific car accident, Walter Fox hastily returned to Rio de Janeiro to gather Jett Fox and bring her to Miami. Thanks to legacy immigration laws within the United States, the government awarded citizenship to Jett Fox almost right away. It was a simple matter of proving her lineage.

Some considered it cruel irony that a ten-year-old child who had never lived in the United States could become a citizen so easily, but as Fox grew up, she intended to maximize her privilege to its fullest potential and never take anything else for granted. She worked twice as hard as her classmates to score astounding grades, and she became fluent in English, Portuguese, and Spanish by the time she was sixteen years old. As she grew in stature, she became a natural outside hitter on the high school volleyball team. With her grades, exceptional performance on the volleyball court, and Ivy League legacy as the granddaughter of Walter Fox, Jett Fox earned an athletic scholarship to Yale.

A buzzing on the nightstand shook Fox out of this history report in her head. She looked over to see a text message on her phone. It was a reminder from A.C. about what time to meet for the trip upstate. Fox sank back on her pillow and closed her eyes. Somehow, her mind went blank just long enough to fall asleep.

The next day went about as routine as expected. Fox met with Chairwoman Solace, Harry Pyne, and A.C. for the trip upstate. Solace added a last-minute passenger, her assistant Eddie Muncey. Fox was surprised by the addition of Eddie because he didn't normally leave the office, but given that Solace planned to spend a few days with the team upstate, it made sense to have an assistant with her for the trip. The team packed into the SUV as Solace's driver pulled away from the bookstore. The SUV headed west into New Jersey and then Pennsylvania before crossing back over the New York state line a few hours later. From there, it was more or less a straight shot through rural New York to Syracuse before turning west and arriving at their destination in Rochester, New York along the Erie Canal.

The SUV made two brief stops along the way, and there was quite a bit of chit-chat for the six-hour drive. Pyne and Eddie bonded over their discussion of European football. Pyne was pleasantly surprised that an American had such extensive knowledge of the Premier League. Fox and A.C. went through their usual checklist of talking points, but they skipped over some of the more "lady problem" topics that might gross out the men in the car. A.C. talked about tattoos she would like to get and where on her body she would like to put them, and that triggered the attention of Pyne and Eddie, of course. When the conversations between all four of them intersected, it was usually about alcohol or work or stories from college that weren't inappropriate. With Chairwoman Solace in the SUV, every conversation ended abruptly any time someone considered crossing the line to discuss things that were a little more racy.

But at last, after about six hours on the road, the SUV passed a decorative red sign with white and gold lettering. "Welcome to Rochester." This city in northwest New York halfway between Syracuse and Buffalo had all the charm of a harbor town with its bridges, quaint shops, and forested backdrop. It was late afternoon by the time the SUV rolled through the city limits, and Fox watched a tour ferry on the canal float to a stop as passengers disembarked. Several individuals rode bikes along the bridges, and an older couple walked their labradoodle. The SUV passed through the center of town and continued a few blocks until it came upon the hotel where the team would stay for the next two weeks.

Muncey divvied out the room keys after he got the group checked in. Fox and A.C. went up to their room and each crashed onto her own double-sized bed.

"We should hit the gym," Fox said.

"Uh what?" A.C. was appalled.

"It's good for you. Come on."

"But we just got here. We've been on the road trapped in that steel box for six hours."

"More of a reason to get out and stretch our legs!"

"Twenty minutes to relax first." A.C. closed her eyes and wrapped her arms around a pillow. "Throw on an episode of *New Girl*. The one where Jess is being unreasonable."

Fox rolled eyes and relaxed her body. "Fine. Twenty minutes."

Just when Fox might have begun to fall asleep, A.C. woke her up.

"Hey, I had no idea that Eddie Muncey was into you."

Fox sighed. "I know. He's very sweet, but he's not so subtle about his crush. I'm worried he's getting the wrong idea."

"Well, you shouldn't lead him on."

Fox sat up and turned to A.C. "I'm *not* leading him on. I like talking to him. He's a friend."

"Then you better make it clear to him because I saw the stars in his eyes."

Fox smirked. "The same stars you have in your eyes for Harry Pyne?"

A.C. opened her eyes and dropped the pillow. "Hey, you know what, we should go to the gym."

CHAPTER 19

The following day after arriving in Rochester, the team made its way twenty miles south into the forest to Monroe County Municipal Speedway. The parking lot was empty except for two vehicles parked near the employee entrance. Surrounded by thick forest in all directions, it was indeed a ghost town where Jett Fox could nail down her training without distraction.

Chairwoman Solace led the way, followed by Eddie Muncey and Fox. Harry Pyne and A.C. stayed with the SUV until the semi-trailer truck arrived with the Takahashi 72. A man who looked to be in his forties wearing a red polo with the Speedway's logo on it approached Muncey. He looked happy to see the team.

"You must be the race team," the man said.

"Hello," Solace said. "You must be the manager. Nice to meet you. I believe you've spoken with my assistant on the phone."

Eddie shook hands with the Speedway manager as they hurried through pleasantries.

"Our truck should be here in a few minutes," Solace said. "Is there anything you need to go over with us before we start training?"

"Just a few things, but the county office sent over all the paperwork you signed, so you're welcome to get started right away," the manager said.

Fox took that literally. Or, at least, the persona she wanted to portray took it literally. "I'll head in and inspect the track. Get a feel for it before the truck gets here."

She brushed past the manager without waiting for permission. Chairwoman Solace took the cue as she spoke to the manager behind Fox's back.

"You'll get used to her. All the talent in the world but the manners of a mastiff."

Fox grinned at the remark. They slid right into their characters. Fox knew that she wasn't just using these two weeks in Rochester for race training, but she was also using these two weeks to practice the social performance expected of her during race week in California. The mission hinged on Fox's ability to sell the notion to Mickey Blaze that the chance meeting in Los Angeles was merely coincidence.

Fox marched through the tunnel into the stands and looked out upon the Speedway's racetrack. It was modest in size, no larger than some of the smallest tracks used in NASCAR. She didn't know for sure, but she guessed that the total length of the track was around three-quarters of a mile that featured tight turn radiuses on either end and straightaway parallel stretches. It was a course designed to test a driver's hard-braking ability into turns and smooth accelerations out of them. It captured the spirit of the street course that Fox would face in Southern California. She pictured the scene: Rather than the Speedway's protective walls, she envisioned the oceanside cliffs in Malibu, and instead of stands and a press box on the straightaway, she saw a beachside sprint toward the Ferris wheel at Santa Monica Pier.

She heard footsteps behind her as she looked back to see Solace and Muncey coming down the steps.

"The truck is here," Solace said. "I want you on the track in thirty minutes."

"Yes, ma'am."

Solace turned on her heel and walked away, but Eddie lingered. Fox motioned for him to join her. He stepped up to her carefully. Fox questioned herself whether it was the right idea to tell Eddie what she was thinking concerning their friendship. On one hand, she didn't want to make assumptions about what he was thinking, even if he didn't hide his crush all that well. On the other hand, it was better to get her feelings out in the open before Eddie got his hopes too high. She opted for the latter option.

"Hey, I need to tell you something, and I'm sorry if it's a little awkward," Fox said.

"OK, shoot."

"I just want to make sure that it's clear we're friends, and that you don't get the wrong idea between us," Fox said. "If I'm completely off-base here, let me know, but I've seen a few things from you that might hint you think there is more going on between us than there actually is, and if I've led you on at all, please forgive me."

Eddie reluctantly smiled and threw his hands up. "Say no more. We're good." He extended his hand. "Still friends?"

Fox smiled warmly and shook Eddie's hand. "Still friends."

Eddie glanced out at the track and cringed. "Don't crash."

Fox went into the trailer and changed into the racing jumpsuit provided by A.C. She emerged from the trailer and stepped into the pit area where A.C. already had the Takahashi 72 primed for this first practice session. Fox's heart rate picked up ever so slightly as she approached the car with a helmet in hand.

"OK, let's do a few laps around the track to get you used to the car and the road," A.C. said, "and then we'll have you really let loose."

Fox scoffed. "No more wasting time! Let's burn rubber!"

A.C. rolled her eyes as Fox climbed into the 72. The interior was almost unrecognizable from when she saw it on that first day. A.C. had taken every safety precaution imaginable as Fox slipped her arms through the harness straps. She buckled the harness, and A.C. leaned in to double check that Fox was in securely.

"I feel like I'm preparing for a shuttle launch," Fox said.

A.C. ignored her. "Let's test the speaker and microphone in your helmet." A.C. put on her headset and spoke into the microphone. "Test, test."

Fox heard A.C. clearly through the speakers. She gave a thumbs up. "I read you, Armory Chief."

A.C. was satisfied with the electronics. "OK, fire up the engine, and let's get started."

A.C. slammed the door shut and jogged to the pit area. Fox turned the key, and the 72 roared to life. She shifted gears to gradually pilot the car out of the pit area until at last she was on the track.

"Just take it easy for a bit and get used to the road, Jett."

Fox knew A.C. was right, but she was anxious to push the limits on the 72. She pressed and yanked on the gear shift to accelerate into the tight turn out of her snail's pace. She rounded the turn and came across the backside straightaway, adjusting the gear again to accelerate further into a sprint.

"Jett, slow down!"

"Come on, A.C., let's see what she can do!"

Fox maximized the acceleration and came upon the opposite end tight turn. As she expected from her first observation of the course, this was a true test of her ability to hard brake into the turn. She slammed her foot down and attempted to turn just as she practiced in the simulator. The tires screeched underneath her as the 72 did its part to maneuver with Fox's inexperienced racing skills. Sure enough, Fox was unable to carry the hard-braking maneuver through to the end as she slammed into the barricade and came to an abrupt halt.

There was silence in her headset. Fox expected a scolding, and frankly she deserved it. The team had only one shot at this. There wasn't enough room in the budget for a new car. However, instead of a scolding, laughter came through the headset. A.C. was *laughing* at her.

"Got that out of your system? Are you ready to listen to me now?"

Fox laughed into her helmet back to the armory chief. "Yes, I'll listen. Sorry, A.C."

Fox moved the car back into the correct position and steadily moved forward. She circled the track a handful of times to get used to the way the car handled the road, and she felt much more comfortable. Each pass gave her an opportunity to see how she might tackle the challenging turns at either end.

"Last caution lap. When you hit the starting line, open it up."

"Copy that."

Fox picked up speed on this final lap. She coasted down the backside and came upon the turn where she rammed into the barrier. She took the turn smoothly and felt the slingshot effect of her turn onto the front-side straightaway and the starting line. She shifted and accelerated and closed in on the starting line. She watched the line disappear underneath the car, and pressed the pedal to the metal in the literal sense.

The first test came upon her in an instant. She hadn't quite maximized her speed yet, and so she braked into this turn more easily than she had at the opposite side of track earlier. This allowed her to maintain some of her speed for another slingshot effect that gave her a great burst out of the turn onto the straightaway. The 72 sizzled by the forested scenery and speedway advertisements until she reached the turn that gave her dire trouble early on. Her pulse pounded, and she braked earlier than she did the first time she took the turn. She avoided the barricade completely this time, but she noticed that she lost considerable speed taking the turn as safely as she did.

"Too soon on the brakes," A.C. said. "If you passed five cars in the first turn, all five of them just passed you back."

Fox wasn't so sure she enjoyed the live commentary from the armory chief. She picked up speed again coming out of the turn and crossed over the starting line to where she could maximize her speed. Her velocity was higher now than it was at the start of this simulated race, and she eyed a spot on the road where she estimated she needed to brake. Fox passed that spot and slammed the brakes. The tires screeched again, and she cranked the wheel to drift the turn. The car seemed to move exactly as Fox had hoped, and it looked as though she might accelerate out of this turn with her best time yet. However, there was a sharp thud on the passenger side rear, and it jolted the car until the front collided with the barricade.

"OK that's enough for now. Come back to the pit area, and let's assess the damage and talk strategy."

Fox sheepishly pulled the 72 into the pit area and shut off the engine. She exhaled deeply into her helmet and unbuckled the harness. She stepped out of the car as A.C. and Pyne approached. Pyne scratched the back of his head while A.C. rushed to the passenger side to inspect the areas where Fox collided with the barrier multiple times.

"A bit harder than the simulator, isn't it," Pyne said.

Fox grinned. "So it would seem." She looked around for the other two members of their team but saw neither of them. "Where are Solace and Eddie?"

Harry Pyne pointed at the press box. "Bird's eye view."

Fox nodded. "All right, let's hear your critiques."

"No critiques," Pyne said. "We're throwing you into the fire on this, and you've handled it gracefully."

A.C. moved around the car to Fox. "The *first* collision was your fault because you were trying to show off, but the second one was mine. You took my advice after the drop in speed, and it got you into trouble. We need you to be comfortable with the turns first before we try to master them, and that's on me."

Fox patted A.C. on the shoulder. "Sorry about the first one."

"Let it be a lesson, Agent Fox." The three of them turned to see Solace and Eddie approaching from the press box. "Your initial profile of Mickey Blaze suggested she struggled with hubris and impulse control. What I saw just now made me think you're not all that different from her."

Fox took the criticism from her boss and nodded. "Ma'am."

CHAPTER 20

The new training strategy paid off for Jett, Fox and A.C. Fox became more comfortable in the car with each passing day until finally, on the last day that Harry Pyne and Chairwoman Solace would be in attendance, Fox felt like she was ready to show the team that she could make the hard-braking turns.

"You're sure you're ready to open it up?" A.C. asked through Fox's headset as Fox made one final practice lap around the track.

"Let's do it. Tell Pyne and Solace it's on."

Fox shifted and accelerated out of the final turn toward the starting line. She maximized the pace as she crossed the line and hit the peak in the straightaway final third as the abrupt U-turn loomed large in the windshield. She'd been on this track for half a week now, and she kept her eyes on a patch near the road that she chose as her hard-brake signal. She reached that point and slammed on the brakes, cranking the wheel to drift. The tires screeched as the rear of the 72 whipped around. In an instant, Fox had the car facing the opposite direction toward the straightaway as she moved her foot back to the gas. The 72 burst through the slingshot with incredible handling as Fox was sprinted along the track's far side.

"Yes!" A.C. shouted into the headset.

Fox stayed focused. She did it once, but it wouldn't matter if she couldn't complete the full lap. She spotted a similar patch near the road as she did at the opposite end of the track. Repeating her movements exactly, Fox seared the tires as she rounded the corner and fired out of a cannon on the other side to successfully slay both turns at maximum velocity.

"Way to go, Jett! Are you coming in for a pit stop or doing more laps?"

"Five more laps. Let's make sure it's not a fluke."

Fox flawlessly sped through all five laps. Her accomplishment wasn't a fluke. She pulled into the pit area with the whole team waiting on her.

"Never had a doubt," Pyne said. "Graduates from Yale, Cambridge, and MIT. I knew we could figure out a way to turn you into a professional racer."

Solace watched Fox like a proud mentor, but she kept her composure and hardly betrayed even a smile. "Well done, Agent Fox. I'm satisfied with how things are going so I'm returning to Manhattan tonight. Eddie will oversee the remainder of the training." She turned to Eddie. "Keep an eye on them." With that, Solace turned on her heel toward the speedway's exit.

Eddie looked back to the crew. "You'll hardly know I'm here. I just have to let her know if there are any emergencies that need her attention. Other than that,

I'm just here to make sure we shut it down on time every night."

Pyne clapped Eddie on the back. "Nonsense, you're part of the team, and I say tonight we have a bit of fun. After all, it's my last night in the States until we meet up in California in two weeks. What do you say?"

"OK, sure thing!" Eddie said. "Where are we going?"

"I guess it depends on if we want to go somewhere classy or wild. What will it be?"

"Classy, for sure," Fox said. "I'm too old for anything wild."

"Me too," A.C. agreed.

"Honestly, me too," Pyne said.

"Yeah, yeah, rub it in that I'm the baby of the group," Eddie said, "but I'm down for classy, too."

"Very good. I believe there's some kind of party at the Port of Rochester tonight. Family friendly."

They packed up the 72 into the trailer and drove back to Rochester. At the hotel, Fox and A.C. got ready for the evening, and A.C. needed help picking an outfit for the evening.

It occurred to Fox that since this was Pyne's last night in the States for the next few weeks, it was possible that A.C. might make a move on the English spy. If that were the case, Fox was currently helping A.C. pick an outfit to best entice the Englishman. She cringed at the thought, but she also cursed herself for feeling jealous. A.C. was her friend, and if she wanted to make a move on Harry Pyne, then Fox owed it to her to be supportive and helpful.

"Try this," Fox said. "It'll really make your brown eyes pop."

It was a green and yellow ensemble that indeed made the armory chief's eyes come alive. A.C. inspected herself in the mirror with the same careful consideration that she gave the Takahashi 72 at the racetrack. She smiled, pleased with the outfit that Fox helped her choose.

Fox wore a tan leather jacket over a white blouse and maroon jeans with boots that matched the jacket. The two women shared the mirror to finish getting ready and moved downstairs to meet up with Pyne and Eddie. The two men were already in the lobby when Fox and A.C. arrived.

The group went out to explore Rochester in all of its northwestern New York glory. They walked along the port just as the sun began to set behind the Genesee River. The "party" was more of a festival, but not quite up to that level either. There was live music, children running rampant, and an impromptu volleyball net set up on the small river beach. Fox was tempted for a game to relive her glory days, but she was really tired that evening after spending several hours at the Municipal Speedway.

Eventually, the group found their way to a dance club, and although they originally intended not to get wild on this night, there was an itch as the four of them stared at the doors.

"It might actually be fun, for just a bit," A.C. said.

Fox smiled. "I can already feel the headache in training tomorrow."

The loud music turned out to be exactly the buffer the group needed to dissipate any semblance of this being a double date. Pyne coached Eddie on approaching strangers with confidence and charm, and Fox and A.C. thwarted pick-up attempts by other strangers.

Fox gave her usual drink order to the bartender. "Vodka martini, dirty, straight up."

Some local dressed in plaid overheard the drink order and approached Fox. "That was a hell of a drink order. Hi, I'm Jeremy. And you are?"

"Xenia Onatopp." Fox spouted out the first Bond girl that popped in her head. The bartender handed the martini to Fox. She took a sip.

"That's a crazy name. And who's your friend?"

Without missing a beat, A.C. responded, "Holly Goodhead."

Fox spit out her drink and laughed uncontrollably. Pyne and Eddie found their way back to Fox and A.C. They were laughing, as well.

"Did you boys have fun chasing the *chicas*?" Fox said.

The DJ slowed things down quite a bit, and everyone looked at each other. This was a moment of truth. Fox had put up her guard with Harry Pyne since day one. A.C. had been quite open with him, and the two of them had grown a little closer that whole week in Rochester. If he asked one of them to dance, who would it be? He looked at A.C. and smiled at her.

"Would you like to dance?"

A.C. smiled and enthusiastically accepted. Fox felt a sting to her heart. Why did she feel that way? She knew this would be the outcome. Harry Pyne was placed with two options, two women of equal beauty and brains. It only made sense that he chose the woman who had been friendly to him and made her intentions clear from the start.

Fox pondered her own feelings. They were funny. Fox was surrounded by three remarkable individuals, but she just didn't feel the "it" factor with any of them. Fox enjoyed conversing with Eddie, but she wasn't physically attracted to him. A.C. was perhaps the biggest catch of them all, but Fox preferred to have her as an ally on that battlefield rather than a target. Fox didn't believe she was attracted to women, but if she were ever to cross the picket line, it would probably be with someone like A.C. Although, that could have just been the alcohol speaking to her brain. And then there was Pyne. Fox respected him as a professional, but she already knew that he'd get on her nerves far too much in a romantic relationship. What she felt for him was nothing more than lust.

Fox watched Pyne and A.C. on the dance floor at the beginning of a possible courtship, and she was happy for them. She turned to her friend, Eddie, and decided to stop thinking about love.

"What are you drinking tonight, Eddie?"

"I don't know, beer?"

Fox laughed. She got the bartender's attention. "A beer for my friend, and another martini for me."

The next ten days passed uneventfully. Fox, Eddie, and A.C. woke up every morning and shared breakfast at the hotel restaurant. Fox exercised at the gym. They'd carpool to the speedway for race training, and Fox improved her craft on the track every day to the point Eddie and A.C. were convinced that she could pass as a professional racer for one weekend.

It was time to pack up and leave Rochester, and Fox felt a bit of melancholy as the SUV pulled away from the city. It was hard to admit, but this work trip was downtime, and the real work was about to begin. Nerves racked within Fox as she prepared for the inevitable confrontation with Mickey Blaze. She savored every bit of this respite because she knew very well that she was headed toward the most dangerous mission in her entire life.

CHAPTER 21

Shining sun, cool ocean breeze, and traffic backed up on the 405. Yes, Jett Fox already received the full Southern California experience less than an hour after her plane landed at LAX. The driver hired by Chairwoman Solace said very little as he crawled along behind the line of cars on the freeway. At least the gas-guzzling SUV had all the amenities fit for a professional athlete, and Fox would be lying if she said she didn't enjoy playing this character.

Fox's phone buzzed. It was a text from A.C.

"Did you land yet?"

Fox typed, "On my way. What's the hotel like?"

Fox watched the dots on the screen as A.C typed a message. The message popped up. "Overkill. You'd think we were movie stars, not a racing team."

The driver pulled the SUV off the exit onto the famous Wilshire Boulevard. There was a billboard at this exit promoting the Open Circuit Challenge with Mickey Blaze's face plastered onto it. The driver weaved around Wilshire Boulevard and into Beverly Hills until finally they arrived at the Brentford Hotel. Fox couldn't believe her eyes. This hotel was even fancier than the one in Morocco, and it was clear that Solace spared no expense for this cover story. With its intricate ornamental garden and cobblestone driveway at the front leading up to the valet service, to the high arches and detailed textures on the exterior, it was a stunning sight.

I doubt I'm getting a split of the commissions on this job, Fox thought.

The driver pulled up to the valet service, and a man walked up right away to open the passenger door for Fox, which she hated. She smiled politely and looped her arm through her all-purpose armory handbag. She got out of the SUV and walked around to the back to grab her suitcases. The same man who opened her door tried to reach for her bags.

"No, no thank you, I've got it," Fox said.

Just then, Fox noticed rustling in the bushes. She turned in that direction just in time for a slimy man wearing a fedora to pop out of the bushes holding a camera. He pointed the lens at Fox, which was followed by the snapping sound of several pictures taken. Fox ignored him and pulled her luggage together until she heard a second man say something to the man who snapped the pictures.

"Oh wow, is that Anne de Paula, the supermodel?"

"No, but it looks like her, though."

Fox was both appalled and amused. She'd never heard that one before, but admittedly it was flattering to be compared to *her*. Still, duty called, and Fox pressed the secret button on her handbag strap to connect it to the armory network. She maneuvered the handbag accordingly as she adjusted her luggage and waited for the appropriate response from the two men.

"Hey, what the hell?" the man said. "My camera just went haywire! Oh no! All my pictures are gone!"

Fox smiled menacingly with her back turned to the two men. She shook off the experience and went inside following her first-ever run in with the paparazzi.

She saw A.C. inside, and the two reunited. A.C. traveled on the ground with the semi-trailer truck, and Fox could only imagine how dreadful of a trip that must have been, traveling literally from the Atlantic to the Pacific. She left the day after they returned to Manhattan from Rochester. They greeted each other, and A.C. gave Fox a recap of the trip as Fox stood in line to check in.

"It gave me plenty of time to come up with some new gadget designs for the future," she said. "I think I was completely miserable in Indiana, but I got better by the time we were in Iowa. And then I was miserable again in Colorado and crossing into Utah. And I'd never been to Las Vegas before, but we didn't stop long enough to enjoy it."

Fox retrieved her room key, and the two of them went upstairs. Fox was on high alert from the get-go. This wasn't like Rochester. This was like Morocco. She inspected her room with the instinct of a spy, and A.C. assisted just like they were trained. They tore apart electronics, inspected any spot that could potentially be a secret hiding place, and ensured that the armory received the signal from Fox's handbag. Satisfied that the room wasn't bugged, they relaxed.

"When is Harry flying in?" Fox asked.

"I talked to him right after I talked to you. His flight got it in about a half hour after yours did. He should be here soon."

"Good, then we have time to make sure everything is ready before the welcome party in Calabasas tonight," Fox said.

A.C. nodded. "I have my room set up as a remote armory. As long as you have that handbag, I can disrupt anything electronic at Mickey Blaze's estate."

"How close will I need to be to clone Mickey's phone?"

"At least five feet. I'm guessing that means you'll have to talk to her."

"It was inevitable. Hopefully I can convince her that our little game of craps in Morocco was merely happenstance, and that the meeting tonight is entirely coincidental." Fox inhaled and exhaled deeply. "It's also been more than a month since we saw each other. Maybe she won't remember me, or at least won't remember how she knows me."

There was a knock at the door. They both straightened at the sound. Fox slipped the Beretta from its hiding place in the handbag and went to the door. She opened it carefully with the gun at the ready and saw Harry Pyne dressed in a light blue polo and khakis with a pair of sunglasses hanging casually from the middle button below the shirt collar. She opened the door the rest of the way and let him in.

"High alert," Pyne said as he shut the door behind him. He motioned toward Fox's pistol. "I do say, it's beginning to feel like a mission, although that's a woman's gun."

"And I happen to be a woman."

Pyne saw A.C. and smiled at her. Fox realized that they hadn't seen each other since they danced together two weeks ago in Rochester.

"Good to see you again, A.C."

"Here." A.C. stood up and handed Pyne a small device. It looked like a microchip. "Put this in the heel of your shoe." She turned to Fox. "You don't need one since you have the handbag." She turned back to Pyne. "This is so I can track your movements this week."

"I didn't realize we were already at that point in our relationship," Pyne said cheekily.

A.C. ignored him. "If you two get separated, I can put you back together quickly in case either of you runs into trouble."

"What's the play tonight?" Pyne asked.

"I'll clone Mickey's phone while you keep up our cover," Fox said. "You're going as my press agent, remember? I need you to schmooze with sponsors and make me look good. But not too good. We don't need the attention."

Pyne nodded, adjusting into work mode. Fox remembered how quickly Pyne could get himself on task from their brief work stint in Morocco. In fact, this night reminded Fox a lot of that night at the casino.

"I think I understand the character," he said. "There's a certain bashfulness coupled with eagerness, an agent who wants to prove himself with an unproven commodity. Yes, I can handle that." He tilted his head. "Are you nervous to talk to Mickey Blaze?"

"A little, but I'm good," Fox admitted. "I just need some laps in the pool to calm down."

They still had a few hours before they needed to leave for Calabasas. Fox went to the hotel pool, which wasn't occupied at the moment. She climbed into the water and went through several reps of each swim stroke until her arms and core burned. The water calmed her as she'd hoped, and she lay on her back to float after the exercise. She got out and looked at her phone to see she had been swimming for a little over an hour. She dried herself and went back to her room to dress for the night.

Fox needed a look to capture Mickey Blaze's attention while also setting herself apart from the woman who would become her adversary once more. How could she mimic Blaze's style while also making it better? Fox smiled, she had just the look. She picked a single-shoulder white dress with golden trim and thigh-high skirt just above Fox's knees. It was similar to the maroon dress that Blaze wore in Morocco but with a color scheme suited for an Amazonian warrior. She stylized her hair so that the jet-black locks fell down at her shoulders. Fox inspected herself in the mirror and was satisfied with the look. She looped her arm through the armory handbag just as her phone buzzed with a text from A.C.

"Put in your earpiece."

Fox did as instructed and spoke into it. "Big Sister to Little Sister. Come in, Little Sister."

"I read you, Big Sister."

"What about you, King George?"

Fox could practically hear Pyne's eyes rolling through the earpiece. "Presented and composed."

"I'll meet you downstairs in twenty minutes."

Fox double checked all of her equipment. She safely secured the Beretta in its hiding place in the handbag. Circuitry in the handbag was charged. Throwing knife. Check. Smoke grenades. Check. Finally, she poured herself a vodka tonic to calm the nerves. She sucked on the lemon and placed the half-full glass on the table, throwing the lemon into the trash.

Fox and Pyne rode in the back of the SUV for the hour-long LA commute from Beverly Hills to Calabasas along the 405 until merging onto the 101 and heading west around the Santa Monica Mountains and Topanga State Park. Keeping with his "try hard" sports agent persona, Pyne dressed down less fashionable than he normally would for such a party.

"As you said, I am playing the role of someone who will get some attention from people out of pity or politeness, but ultimately they'll want nothing to do with me because I'm not at their level."

"That is quite intuitive. I'm impressed."

At last, after moving at a snail's pace to travel thirty miles in an hour, they arrived at Mickey Blaze's compound. The sprawling estate consisted of Mickey's mansion at the center surrounded by ornate statues and gardens, a horse stable and run on the western side of the property, and a miniature vineyard on the opposite end. It was the sort of vineyard one had for a hobby rather than a business. The mansion itself may as well have been a castle. Its grandeur stood above everything in town, even a town as posh as Calabasas.

To add to the mystique that Blaze was some sort of royal inviting the commoners into her home, there were press outside the mansion on either side, as men and women walked a literal red carpet up to the entrance of Blaze's castle. Of the twelve people she saw enter the mansion ahead of her, no fewer than eight of them were big time celebrities that made her jaw drop.

"I think we might be in over our heads, Pyne."

"Now, now, Fox, it's all about how you carry yourself. Sure, you might not be Robert Downey Jr. or Scarlett Johansson, but that hardly matters. Walk up those steps and ignore the cameras. They are beneath you."

A.C. came alive in their ears. "Hold on, are there celebrities at this party? Who's there? Who's there?"

"Later, A.C." Fox said. "I'll tell you everything. Stay focused right now."

The driver stopped the SUV in front of the lengthy walkway toward the mansion's entrance. Fox took a deep breath and exhaled slowly as the driver got out and opened the door for her. Fox stepped out and was pounded by the *clickety-clack* sound of cameras snapping her picture. But, Fox was a pro. She glided up the steps just as Pyne instructed, ignoring the photographers every step of the way. She overheard a few of them mention they didn't know her, and that made her happy. Perhaps she could knuckle down and do her job tonight, after all. Pyne strode a few paces behind, her pretending to talk on his cell phone. The photographers paid no attention to him. The space he gave to Fox seemed to perfectly suggest that he was with her as a business associate and not an equal.

"Nice job," Fox said to Pyne as they walked through the doors into the mansion.

Fox gasped at what she saw next. The massive corridor gave way to a foyer two stories high. There was a painting on the ceiling from end to end featuring the soft blues and whites of the sky at mid-day. The walls were constructed of granite as they cascaded down toward the sparkling white tile. A massive staircase sat on the far side, leading up toward a second-floor patio that overlooked the foyer. There were six different routes to take away from this room into the other rooms of this modern-day palace.

A man dressed in a tuxedo approached Fox and Pyne. "Ah yes, thank you for verifying your invitation at the gate. If you'll follow me, Miss Blaze would like to address the guests before anyone gets too rambunctious." He laughed softly to himself. Fox smiled and returned a fake laugh of her own.

He led them through more of the house, and it was much of the same spectacular design and space as the foyer. Mickey Blaze had several pieces of art and ancient relics that likely belonged in a museum. Extracting them from her was a quest for another day. The man from the foyer led them to the back patio where he opened the door and invited Fox and Pyne to mingle with the rest of the guests.

If the inside of the house was impressive, the backyard was magnificent. A multitude had already gathered in the massive backyard that featured a half-size football field, a swimming pool, several gazebos, and a collection of vintage cars parked in front of a stage where a DJ had already begun playing contemporary music. Fox recognized too many movie stars, supermodels, and other various celebrities to count. And, of course, there were the professional racers, her competition for the week.

Fox was in awe at the grandeur of the estate. Opposite from the swimming pool and near the half-size football field, Fox spotted a pond that ran parallel. And inside the pond she saw several things that she could have sworn were animatronic at first, but then realized they were real. Pink animals with medium-sized beaks and long legs grazed at the pond.

"Flamingos?!" Fox couldn't believe her eyes, but the flamingos were real. Fox spotted four flamingos in total, and the partygoers watched them with curious amusement.

At last, the stage at the far end of the yard came to life with the voice of a recognizable emcee from reality television. "Ladies and gentlemen, your host for the evening, Mickey Blaze!"

Fox and Pyne turned their attention to the stage as Blaze revealed herself and accepted the microphone from the famous emcee. The audience applauded. Blaze dressed in an emerald-colored dress with a black jacket over the top. Her blonde and bronze locks of hair fell casually at her shoulders as she smiled at her audience.

"Thank you all for coming tonight. I don't want to take too much of your time, but I had to get up here and give thanks to everyone who helped make this event possible." Blaze yammered on for about a minute. "So, enjoy yourselves tonight, except for the drivers. We have qualifiers tomorrow." The crowd laughed. "Thank you again, and enjoy the party!"

Blaze turned to exit stage left as she waved at people in the crowd with the sincerest smile that she could muster. Fox was impressed by how well Blaze could work a crowd. As Blaze made her way to the steps, she looked right at Fox. The recognition was almost instantaneous. Blaze stepped down from the stage and kept her eyes glued on Jett Fox.

"Make yourself scarce, Pyne. Dorothy and the Wicked Witch have a lot to talk about."

CHAPTER 22

Fox worked her way toward the stage, veering away from Mickey Blaze's watchful eye and in the direction of the vintage cars. She stopped in front of a forest green 1953 Jaguar C-Type, a truly magnificent race car of its era. This particular refurbishment sparkled under the stage lights. Blaze came up beside Fox, and the two of them stared at the British car for a few seconds without saying anything.

"Marvelous, isn't she?" Blaze asked.

Fox forced a smile. She also clicked the strap of her handbag to connect to the armory network.

Fox heard A.C. in her ear. "Got the phone. Cloning it now. Keep her talking as long as you can."

"It's beautiful," Fox responded to Blaze. She extended her hand to Blaze. "Juliana Ferreira. I've been anxious to meet you, Miss Blaze. You throw an amazing party."

Blaze cautiously took Fox's hand. Doubt briefly crossed her face. She likely questioned herself whether this was the same woman she met in Casablanca over a month ago. The game of craps was brief, and Blaze met so many new people every day. Maybe this woman was not Jett Fox, the mysterious gambler who bested her.

"Ah Miss Ferreira! Yes, I saw your name on the qualifying roster. A newcomer to the scene. Very nice. I always hope to have newcomers make the top forty at every race week. It's nice to get new blood around here."

Fox cringed at Blaze's use of the word "blood." It seemed like blatant disrespect coming from the mouth of a suspected murderer. However, Fox shoved her disgust aside and kept up the facade of this Juliana Ferreira character that she had concocted.

"Then I should thank you for accepting my team's application. This is a tremendous opportunity for us to show what we can do."

"We'll see if you're still thanking me after going toe to toe with these ruffians." Blaze motioned around the party, nodding particularly at the professional drivers. "Tell me, what made you decide to take the leap to street racing? From what I remember in your application, you're primarily a track racer back east."

"The prize money." Fox was being cheeky, and Blaze offered a courtesy laugh. Fox continued, "In truth, a race like this is a great chance to build our brand at the lower level. I'm sure you understand that. I know that my chances of even qualifying are slim to none, but an open challenge like this is something we can use to sell tickets to a race in Tucson or Albuquerque."

Blaze offered a crooked smile. She was from the American Southwest, and Fox wondered if Blaze took that last line as a challenge to her roots.

"Beauty, brains, and talent," Blaze said. "You are the total package, *Miss Ferreira*." Blaze bordered on disdain as she spoke the fake name. "I'd say only half the drivers here have an understanding of the business side of our sport, and the other half aren't as keen as I am, but you...there's something interesting about you."

"That is a tremendous compliment coming from *the* Mickey Blaze."

"I aim to please. Now, if you'll excuse me, I have other guests to see. Enjoy the party, Miss Ferreira."

A.C. shouted into Fox's ear. "Hold on, Jett, I'm not done cloning her phone!"

Fox hurriedly kept the conversation going. "One last thing before you go, Miss Blaze."

Blaze held up a hand. "Please, call me Mickey. My mother is Miss Blaze."

Blaze's eyes went cold, and Fox knew right away that the jig was up. This was the exact exchange they had when they first met at the casino in Casablanca. Still, Fox intended to maintain some manner of pretense to their conversation. She smiled at Blaze.

"Just between the two of us, woman to woman, can you tell me a little about the car you're driving in the race on Sunday?"

Blaze humored her. She motioned toward the Jaguar. "I'll be accused of being too derivative, but the exterior is inspired by the 53 C-Type. It's my favorite race car in history. It was tricky to blend the modern style with the throwback curves, but what can I say? I'm an artist. V8. Nine hundred horsepower. Zero to sixty in 2.1 seconds. Oh, and the color is just like your hair. Jet black."

Fox's heart dropped. Pretense was finished. She was now violating Chairwoman Solace's warning to not engage Blaze in sub-text. However, she saw no other choice but to hold her ground and challenge the racing magnate. Fox thought of Sharon Graham's investigation, how it all started and why it might have ended. It was time to let Blaze know that she was closing in on her.

"Oh, I wouldn't worry too much about being derivative. I believe it was Mark Twain who said it's better to have old second-hand *diamonds* than none at all."

The tiniest hint of worry crossed Blaze's face at the mention of "diamonds," but she corrected it. Fox flashed a smile at the small sign of discomfort.

"I certainly hope so," Blaze said. "This is a big week for my company, and I'd hate for anything to crap on it."

Fox could hardly contain her smile at this point. "In my experience, you can count on bad luck as much as you can count on loaded dice."

Blaze's nostrils flared. Her cheeks burned red. She did her best to compose herself, but Fox had gotten to her. "Well, I have enjoyed this small talk between us, but I really should see my other guests. Again, enjoy the party, and I look forward to seeing you in the qualifying heats, *Miss Ferreira*."

She walked away, and Fox waited until she was out of earshot before addressing A.C.

"Did I keep her talking long enough?"

"Yes, we got her phone, and oh boy you really made her mad. She's texting Theseus Kastellanos right now to keep an eye on you. Apparently, you made quite the impression on both of them. She referred to you as the woman from the casino, and Theseus knew exactly who she meant."

"Well, it's nice to be remembered."

Suddenly, a gentleman in an expensive tuxedo with perfectly groomed medium-length brown hair, fashionable facial stubble, and dark eyes approached Fox. He had broad shoulders, square jaw, and high cheekbones. He smiled at her to show off a flawless set of teeth.

"Hello, you were just speaking to Mickey Blaze," he said in a thick Spanish accent.

"Yes."

"Allow me to introduce myself," he said. "I am Luca Monreal. I am one of the drivers. I don't believe I've had the pleasure."

Admittedly, Fox didn't know anything about him, but this man was stunning. He stood slightly taller than

Fox, and even through the tuxedo she could tell that the man was ripped.

"Of course, Luca Monreal!" Fox said. "I am a huge fan. My name is Juliana Ferreira. Rookie driver hoping to qualify for the circuit in this race."

"My goodness your accent is *magnifica*. So unique. I cannot tell if you are native to the United States or somewhere else. Portugal, perhaps?"

A.C. chimed in her ear. "This guy's legit, Jett. Pro racer just trying to hit on you. Might be a good distraction to keep Theseus away."

Fox smiled at the handsome Luca. "Born in South America and raised in the United States."

"And now you are joining us as a professional driver. Wonderful. Forgive me for being so forward. You are a fellow competitor, but I was struck by your beauty."

This guy may be legit, but is he for real right now? Fox thought. She gained an iota of respect for Mickey Blaze and what she accomplished to get to a point where she was considered a driver first and a woman second. And yet she was willing to throw that all away for whatever criminal activity she was performing behind the scenes.

Just then, Fox spotted Theseus' slender frame slithering through the crowd in her direction. She had to make a split-second decision, and she hated the role that her character Juliana Ferreira had to play next. However, she could think of a worse way to spend ten minutes than rounding first base with this hot Spanish race car driver.

"Walk me to the pond, will you, Luca? I'd like to see the flamingos."

"Of course. It would be my absolute pleasure."

Fox waited until Luca turned his head and then rolled her eyes. She shot off a quick text to A.C. "Muting my mic. Don't be alarmed."

Fox slipped her arm through Luca's arm and latched on as the Spaniard led her from the stage across the half-size football field until they reached the pond. The flamingos seemed oddly content with partygoers staring at them. They waded through the water and paid little attention to the human beings. One of them bent over and splashed a little water at the others with its beak. Just then, Fox heard an unmistakable English accent bellowing in salesmanship. She looked over wide eyed to see Harry Pyne speaking frantically at a group of bored patrons. Fox bit her lip to keep from laughing.

"Ah! There she is now. Miss Ferreira! Miss Ferreira! Come over here real quick."

"Friend of yours?" Luca asked.

"My agent. Excuse me for a moment."

Fox approached carefully, as scripted. "Dudley, what did I tell you about bothering the guests? I said you could come tonight if you behaved yourself. And now you're embarrassing me in front of the entire party." She turned to the guests. "Please excuse us." She pulled

Harry by the suit collar. "Dudley, if you do something like this again, you are fired. Do I make myself clear?"

"Oh yes, of course, Miss Ferreira. Please forgive me. I couldn't help myself. I'm just trying to build your brand. Ferreira to the moon! Remember?"

"Go have a drink and disappear. I don't want to see you again for the rest of the night. And for the last time, leave these people alone!"

It wasn't exactly a Broadway performance, but Fox and Pyne shared a knowing look trying not to laugh at themselves. Pyne departed into the crowd, and Fox heard him order his usual double bourbon from a server. Fox returned to Luca at the pond.

"You handled that well," Luca said. "I remember when I had an agent like that. You should fire him and get on with a premier agency."

"Maybe one day. Maybe if I win the race this weekend!" Fox put off an exaggerated expression to indicate she was joking, and Luca chuckled.

"I enjoy your confidence. I will destroy you in the race, I'm afraid, but tonight I bask in the belief that you, Miss Ferreira, could topple any one of us on Sunday."

"And don't you forget it."

Fox spotted Theseus lurking among the crowd and felt a shiver go up and down her spine, but not the good kind. She ignored Blaze's henchman and turned to the Spaniard. He gave her a good shiver. This one's for you, Sharon Graham, Fox thought. She reached out and cupped his cheek with her hand and then pulled herself in for the kiss. They melted into each other's lips passionately for several minutes, and just as Luca rounded first and attempted to stretch a single into a double, Fox pulled his hand away and ended the make out session. They came up for air, so to speak, and Fox noticed that Theseus had disappeared.

Fox gently stroked Luca's scruff. "Thank you, Luca, I enjoyed that. I'll see you at the qualifiers tomorrow."

The Spanish race car driver seemed confused as Fox got up and left him by himself with the flamingos. Fox found Pyne and motioned for the two of them to leave.

As they headed toward the exit, Fox looked up at the balcony of what appeared to be the master bedroom. Blaze stood at the railing and watched Fox carefully. They made eye contact as Blaze took a sip from her drink. Blaze remained stone faced but did not break eye contact.

CHAPTER 23

Jett Fox noticed her heightened excitement level as she lay in bed that night. The flight from New York, LA traffic, a confrontation with Mickey Blaze, and an annoying game of cat and mouse with Theseus Kastellanos piled up into a sensory overload, and Fox found it difficult to fall asleep.

Against the headwind of her swirling brain, she managed to distract herself long enough with a daydream about the Ivy League Volleyball Championship during her junior season, which ended with a disappointing defeat to Princeton. It all came down to the final match of the season with Princeton and Yale at first and second place in the standings, respectively, a winner-take-all contest to decide the league champion. Somewhere during the ramblings of that memory, around the time where Princeton scored the final point to win the match, Fox fell asleep.

She couldn't place exactly what happened, but commotion stirred, and suddenly her eyes snapped open. Dreary from the sudden awakening from her REM cycle, Fox glanced around at the darkness of her hotel room. There was no explanation as to why she reacted the way she did next, but instinct took over. She pressed through the haziness of being half asleep and found herself at full attention. What was it that caused her to hone her senses so drastically?

Fox's heart rate quickened, breathing uneven and fast. Terror pulsed through her entire nervous system. Whatever it was that caused her to wake up abruptly from her sleep caused panic to surge into her body. Her forehead and chest were drenched with sweat. She could barely see anything in the room. Even the hotel hallway light from the doorway wasn't enough to make out anything.

She heard a small elastic clapping at the foot of her bed, like a phone set to vibrate. She slowly reached over to the nightstand and felt her phone in the same place she left it before falling asleep. So, the noise at the foot of the bed was not her phone. What on earth could it be? This only caused more panic to sear over her entire body. She wasn't alone in this hotel room.

Paralyzed by fear, Fox remained absolutely still as her intruder finally made its presence known. She waited for a shadowy figure to show itself, possibly with a knife, standing over her bed. Maybe even someone crouched to her side that would pop up and attempt to strangle her with fishing wire. But, no. The intruder was no one of that sort. Instead, Fox felt a subtle tug at her sheets. And then, the creeping wriggle of some kind of creature sent more jolts up Fox's spine as she neared the breaking point of her terror.

She kept still, stifling the screams that she desperately wanted to shout. The creature slid across the bottom of her bed until Fox felt its scaly, tough exterior on her foot. Every tiny hair follicle stood up straight from Fox's skin as the creature dragged its legless body over her foot and up her leg.

Panic. Sheer utter panic swept over Fox. There was no mistaking the intruder's identity. The elastic clapping like a vibrating phone. The scaly skin. The sweeping crawl of its underside muscles contracting over her frame. There was a rattlesnake in Jett Fox's bed.

She raced through every memory she had regarding snakes between her childhood in Rio de Janeiro and her adolescence in Miami. Fox had received more than a few lessons about snakes during her life. However, this was her first time applying any practical use to those lessons. The rattlesnake was already upon her, so any attempt to leave the room was out of the question. Fox found herself in the last resort stage of dealing with snakes: no sudden movements.

Fox fought against every instinct that screamed for her to leap from the bed. Pools of sweat dropped from her face and down to her throat, and the sweat on her torso swamped her T-shirt. The snake crawled farther up her leg until it came to the hem of her shirt. Please do not go underneath my shirt, Fox pleaded to herself. She wanted to scream so badly, but she remained silent and still.

The number one thing she knew about snakes was that they were nature's introverts. Snakes wanted to be left alone, and they were more likely to leave humans alone as long as they were given the same courtesy. It wasn't foolproof, but at the current moment her best chance to keep the venomous viper from biting her was to let it explore.

Thankfully, the rattlesnake went over the hem of her T-shirt and not underneath, but now she could feel the reptile's overbearing gaze as it creeped along her torso. Fox's heart pounded heavily. It pounded so hard that her entire body vibrated with each beat. Could the snake feel that? Of course it could. It was only a matter of time before the creature felt threatened and injected its venom into Fox's veins.

The rattlesnake worked its way up Fox's belly until it crossed over her chest and came to the edge of the bed sheet. This was it. Fox could see just enough in the darkness that she would be able to get a good look at whatever popped out from underneath the sheet. The snake stopped for a long moment, and Fox wondered about an alternate scenario. What if the snake curled up and turned her bosom into a bed for itself? Fox decided that situation was much worse, and she'd prefer the snake bite her if it came down to those two options. It was better to spend a night in the emergency room than a night with a rattlesnake sleeping on her chest.

Mercifully, the snake moved again. It continued its path up her body until finally Fox felt the crease at the bed sheet lift. A bulbous head with two glowing orbs on either side of a long snout shoved its way from under the bed sheet toward Fox's soaking throat. It took everything Fox had to keep from trembling. Never in her life had a situation tested her constitution to this point, and Fox might have been amazed at herself had she not been scared beyond the ability to acknowledge her accomplishment.

The glowing orbs watched Fox intently. A small tingle nipped at her throat, and Fox recognized that the snake used its tongue to drink from the pool of sweat. She had very little patience left in her, and if this snake didn't move away soon, Fox was sure to get herself bitten by the serpent because of anxiety. The rattlesnake slowly moved its head in the direction of the window, and finally its body began to crawl again. It moved away from Fox's throat and toward her arm. Fox felt another tingle wrench her nerves as the snake glided from under the bed sheet and down her shoulder. At last, the snake was at the edge as she watched the bulbous head dip over the mattress. Fox held back another shriek as the snake's spine-chilling rattle thundered in front of her.

There was a distinct thud against the carpet as the rattlesnake reached the ground. And that's when Fox burst out from under the sheets and raced for the door. She smacked the light switch and temporarily blinded herself amid the bright beam of the ceiling. With one quick look back toward the bed, she didn't see the snake and had to assume it was still firmly in its position on the carpet on the other side of the bed. Fox wrenched the door open and stepped into the hall. She shut the door behind her and let out every bit of sound that she was forced to hold back while in the bed, a combination of shrieking, yelling, and a breakdown into hysterical tears as she shivered from head to toe and swiped at her own body like the snake was still on her. She collapsed to the floor and clutched her legs, still simmering from the experience.

A.C. and Harry Pyne emerged from their rooms with worry on their faces as they spotted Fox curled up on the hallway floor. The two of them rushed to her.

"What happened? What's going on?" Pyne said.

Fox spoke sounds, but she struggled to piece together a sentence. She finally said, "Snake. Inside. Don't know. Still alive."

"Snake?"

"Are you saying there's a snake in your room?" A.C. asked.

Fox nodded hastily as her body shook.

"Ra… rat… rattlesnake." Pyne and A.C. looked at each other and back at Fox. "It was on me. Cou… couldn't move."

It took several minutes for the moment to pass. Pyne had a bottle of expensive champagne in his room that he was saving for a romantic encounter, but he brought a glass to Fox to help calm her nerves. A.C. got on the phone with a local snake wrangler, but she emphasized that they needed to approach the hotel quietly and that she would let them in through the back away from prying eyes. Pyne poured himself a glass of the expensive champagne and sat down on the floor next to Fox.

"Do you think they followed us back from the party?" Pyne asked. He skipped right to the part where they both already knew the snake wasn't in Fox's room accidentally. Fox said nothing. She just looked at Pyne with an expression as if to say "yes, duh." Pyne forced a brief smile and frowned again. He said, "Sorry."

A.C. came back through the hallway twenty minutes later with a woman dressed in an unbuttoned plaid shirt, jeans, and a baseball cap. She carried a plastic bucket and a four-foot pole with steel tongs at the end.

"This is Carrie," A.C. said. "She's the snake wrangler."

"I hear you found a rattlesnake in your room," Carrie said.

"More like the rattlesnake found me," Fox said.

A.C. opened the door for Carrie, and the snake wrangler stepped in. "Hold the door open for me. This will take just a minute."

Fox was still too on edge to look inside the room, but she heard the footsteps of the wrangler as she walked through the fancy room.

"There you are," Fox heard Carrie say. "It's a rattlesnake, alright."

Fox heard the pinching of steel as Carrie wrangled the snake with the tongs. There was a soft thud of plastic as Carrie must have dropped the snake in the bucket. Sometime during the capture, Fox heard the snake wrangler confirm that it was a female snake. A few moments later, A.C. stepped out of the way as Carrie emerged with the white bucket. Fox could see the outline of the snake in the bucket through the glare of the hallway lights.

"How in the world did a snake get all the way up here?" Carrie asked. "I've seen some crazy stuff. People do insane things when they're drunk, and they need me to come catch the wild animals they think they can control, but I've never seen a rattlesnake get all the way up a hotel like this on its own."

Fox recounted the tale exactly as it happened. Carried nodded in understanding.

"I'm impressed. Most people would've tried to capture the snake on their own or even tried to kill it. You definitely shouldn't kill these guys. They don't understand the situation they're in, and it's actually a crime to kill them unless your life is in absolute danger. And you shouldn't try to catch them on your own. You did exactly what you should've done in that situation, and thank you for that. Still, it's crazy that she got up here. I don't know how that could've happened."

Despite the entire encounter, Fox had calmed down enough to where she could have a conversation. "You're right. I don't think our little friend got up here by herself." Carrie seemed dumbfounded by the implication. Fox could imagine the thoughts swirling through Carrie's head. She followed up her statement, "Let's call it a prank gone wrong, but at least no one got hurt."

Carried shrugged and walked toward the back stairwell with the rattlesnake bucket in tow. A.C. paced in the hallway and stopped in front of Fox.

"I'll check Mickey's text messages. Maybe she sent a coded message to someone to have this done to you."

"Of course she did, and we already know which text she sent," Fox said. "It was the first one to Theseus when she told him to keep an eye on me. Now we know what keeping an eye on me means."

CHAPTER 24

Fox stayed with A.C. the rest of the night. The two of them woke up the next morning knowing full well that they had to put the midnight visitor incident behind them because today was the qualifying round. Sure, it seemed silly to go through with the race when Mickey Blaze had crossed the line and sent an assassin to kill Jett Fox, but they knew that maintaining this race team cover had small rewards that would ultimately make their jobs easier.

They arrived at the Palisades by mid-morning. There was a bustle, as to be expected. According to the itinerary, each team was required to arrive one hour before its scheduled qualifying run, but it couldn't arrive earlier than that. If the team wasn't precisely on time, it forfeited its place and was immediately disqualified from competing in the race.

"So in other words," Fox started, "even if I survived a rattlesnake attack, a trip to the hospital would have gotten us booted from the competition. Got it."

Fox and Pyne sat in the SUV as A.C. spoke to them on speaker phone from the semi-trailer truck. "They have to squeeze a hundred and twenty qualifying laps over the next two days. Each team gets only twenty minutes to set up, run practice laps, complete the qualifying lap, and then get off the track. If any team is even one second over that twenty-minute time limit, they're disqualified. While the team in front of us is on the road, we'll have that time to get our car off the truck and into the queue."

Pyne was suspicious. "So, forty minutes total? They can eliminate half the field just from these rules alone."

The Palisades was a classic racecourse that hosted numerous stock car and open-wheel single-seat races every month. Stretching 2.4 miles, the Palisades was only slightly shorter than the world-famous Daytona International Speedway and thus featured one of the longest laps in the United States. While the Open Circuit Challenge would be a street race on California Highway 1 from Santa Monica to Malibu and then looping back to Santa Monica, the qualifying heats were held on the actual Palisades track.

Fox knew that this actually helped her more than hindered her. Each team was qualifying under the same conditions, and with the lack of practice time at the Palisades, the qualifying times were likely to be slower than usual. Fox planned to use that to her advantage by being more aggressive in her lap.

Fox and Pyne sat quietly watching the efficiency of each team move in and out of the track. It was a well-oiled machine, and Fox hated to admit it, but Mickey

Blaze deserved the credit. She was the master of her craft.

A.C. spoke through the phone as Pyne held it in his hand. "Are you guys seeing this?"

"Everyone is on task," Fox said. "It's a bit intimidating. I hope we can mimic it."

"I know we're all big picture people, but right now we need to completely focus on this qualifying lap. Our turn is coming up."

Fox and Pyne looked at each other. Fox sensed an uneasiness in the armory chief's voice.

"Are you OK, A.C.?"

No response.

Pyne spoke next. "A.C., if you're having doubts, we should discuss them now. We won't get another chance."

A.C. sighed. "I'm OK. Just a little scared of all the people. I've never had to do something like this before."

Fox saw an empathetic smile appear on Pyne's face. "Just put all your attention on the car. You won't have to talk to anyone. Leave that to me."

A.C. exhaled more confidently this time. "Got it. All attention on the car."

The semi-trailer truck pulled up to the unloading area just outside the track as A.C. and two other mechanics exited the truck and moved toward the rear to get the Takahashi 72 out of the trailer and into the tunnel. Chairwoman Solace's driver pulled the SUV to the side as Pyne and Fox opened the doors and darted toward the tunnel. Fox went into the locker room and changed into her racing jumpsuit within a couple of minutes and went outside to where Pyne was directing traffic and playing a buffer between A.C. and anyone who might talk to her.

A.C. tugged Fox at the shoulder and yanked her over to the race car. She handed the helmet to her, and they ran through their pre-race routine that they practiced more than a few times in upstate New York. Out of the corner of her eye, Fox spotted Theseus Kastellanos watching her from a distance. He looked incredulous as he saw Fox in her gear, or alive for that matter, Fox thought. She gave the rival racer a knowing look.

"Give me two seconds, A.C."

"We don't have two seconds."

Fox approached Theseus, and they stared at each other for a moment. She took in Theseus' gecko-like frame, admiring his bronze face and hazel eyes. Under completely different circumstances, Fox might have imagined what Theseus looked like by the swimming pool and not wearing a shirt, but she let the moment of weakness pass her by as she instead focused on the fact that this man tried to kill her. Fox was the one to break their icy staredown. "I received a wonderful gift last night. Give my regards to Miss Blaze for being a tremendous host."

Theseus showed the only emotion that Fox had seen him show since she met him: panic. However, that panic quickly turned to smugness, as if Theseus was trying to save face. "Good luck in your qualifying heat today, *Miss Ferreira*. I plan to welcome you to the circuit properly on Sunday."

That can't mean anything good, Fox thought. It was the first time Fox had heard Theseus speak two complete sentences, and she heard a Mediterranean accent flow from his mouth. Fox smirked and turned on her heel back to the car. A.C. looked annoyed, but Fox ignored her and got in the Takahashi 72. She strapped into the safety harness, and A.C. spoke into the headset. Fox confirmed to her that everything worked properly.

"The team ahead of us just finished its qualifying lap," A.C. said. She walked ahead of the 72, and Fox could see her lips moving in sync with the voice in her headset. "I'm on my way to the pit area. The marshal will lead you out." She gave a thumbs up. Fox returned the gesture.

Two minutes passed. A man in a green vest signaled for Fox to pull forward slowly through the tunnel. Fox did as instructed. The shadow of the canopy enveloped the windshield until she came out the other end onto the racetrack.

"OK, head into the pit exit, and we'll do one last check before your practice laps," A.C. said.

Fox waited patiently inside the car, only the low hum of the 72 and her breathing to keep her company. The pit crew that Chairwoman Solace and A.C. had assembled worked swiftly through a series of checks. A.C. then chimed in Fox's ears.

"We have enough time for three practice laps and one slow-down lap," A.C. said. "After the slow-down lap, come to a full stop at the starting line. Green flag is permission to hit the gas."

"Copy that."

Fox drove the 72 out of the pit area and rounded toward the starting line. She hit the gas after the starting line to initiate her practice run.

The Palisades track was superior in every way to the Monroe County Municipal Speedway, and Fox had a bit of difficulty adjusting to the LA track's sophistication during her first practice lap. A.C. told her not to worry, but Fox didn't believe her because of the tone in her voice. A.C. confirmed her suspicions after the second practice lap.

"These are taking longer than I expected so this will have to be your slow-down lap. Come to a complete stop at the starting line on your next pass."

"Copy that." Fox dared not argue with her right now.

This was one of those moments where Fox remembered what A.C. and Pyne said back in New York. She remembered they told her that the little things were going to blow her cover as a driver, not the big things. Something that should seem so simple as coming to a complete stop at the starting line wasn't actually that straight forward, and Fox was aware of the moment and what the track operators and fellow drivers might think if she messed up something this easy. She rounded the final turn and positioned the car at the starting line, slowing gradually along the final stretch until she came to a complete stop. Fox heard A.C. exhale relief into the headset. Fox nearly laughed.

"Get ready. Green flag coming up."

Fox watched the tower near the starting line and saw green fabric whip back and forth. She released the clutch and accelerated with a screech of the tires through the starting line.

"Good launch point. Keep it up."

Fox followed the armory chief's commands exactly as she made her first long turn on the massive Palisades track. Fox had total focus on the road in front of her, and the 72's handling ability canceled out minor mistakes that Fox made with the wheel. She now understood that A.C. was right to suggest this car. Through all the training and now this qualifying lap, Fox not only respected the 72, but she also loved it.

"This is the trickiest part of the track. Hard brake in one-hundred feet and then a quick burst to slingshot the remainder of the turn."

Fox followed the instruction, and the 72 did the rest of the work. She reached the final turn and performed another hard brake. A quick shift of the stick and maneuver with her feet, and Fox burst out like a pro, heading straight for the finish line. She whipped past the line, and she heard A.C. let out a pleasant cheer.

"Fantastic run. Now let's hurry and get out of here."

Fox drove the 72 toward the exit area to find the truck. She parked and unstrapped the harness. A man from the pit crew opened the door for her as she stepped out, and he immediately stepped in and shut the door. He drove the car onto the ramp, and the truck driver retracted the ramp. Fox was impressed with her own team's efficiency as the truck was on its way out of the Palisades just before the twenty-minute time limit struck.

That's when Fox caught sight of Mickey Blaze, dressed for work instead of play in a sleeveless black blouse and white slacks. She watched Fox carefully and then approached her.

"Impressive run, *Miss Ferreira*," she said.

Fox nodded. "Thank you."

There were people of note watching the two of them interact, including members of the media. Fox wanted to get out of this situation as quickly as possible.

"Say, we're having a luncheon at my estate tomorrow," Blaze started, "it's something of an empowerment luncheon for women in sports. I'd very much like it if you could join us." She motioned toward the track. "After a qualifying time like that, you're sure to be an up-and-coming attraction to keep an eye on."

Fox smirked. "You'll have to specify what you mean by keeping an eye on me. I'm afraid someone might get the wrong idea, and then I'll have strange visitors at my hotel room in the middle of the night."

Blaze returned a mirthless chuckle. "Come to the luncheon tomorrow. Eleven thirty a.m. Can I count on seeing you there?"

"I'll be there, Blaze."

CHAPTER 25

The Brentford Hotel pool area featured one of the best views in Beverly Hills, especially at sunset as the orange glow turned into a shade of purple with the lights of the downtown Los Angeles skyline toward the southwest, and the Pacific Ocean directly west. There was a swanky hotel bar at the pool area, and it was full of patrons at this time of the early evening. It was the ideal place for Jett Fox to exercise in the morning and afternoon when the visitors were sparse, but at the moment it was better for blending in among the crowd of socialites who made their way down from their rooms before going out on the town to do all the unspeakable things rich people do at night.

Fox, Pyne, and A.C. nursed their signature drinks at a table close to the pool and overlooking the spectacular western view. Fox had her vodka martini, Pyne had his double bourbon, and A.C. had a glass of red wine. Fox pondered one of her usual questions. Did she drink too much? Maybe. Today had been a rousing success, a qualifying time that would likely see her into the top forty for the big race on Sunday. However, she didn't feel celebratory, and that made her question whether she should be drinking. No one liked a drinking partner slipping into a *vin triste*, the gloom that follows too much alcohol.

Fox couldn't get Mickey Blaze off her mind. Why did she want her at a "women in sports" luncheon? Was this some sort of trap? Did Blaze intend to kill Fox in the quiet of the Calabasas mansion and then dump her body into the Pacific Ocean just like she dumped Sharon Graham into the Atlantic? There was a harrowing idea. She ran through these thoughts with her two companions.

"It's possible," Pyne said, "but it's also just as likely that she sees you as a legitimate rival, and she has a role to play for the public. Now, you too are in that role."

Fox nodded and finished Pyne's thought. "She can't afford a scandal this close to the race. She knows we did well enough to crack the top forty, and she has to play nice."

"She is crafty on the phone," A.C. changed the subject as she scrolled through her own phone. "I'm going through her text conversations right now. Other than last night when she was furious and sent Theseus to keep an eye on you, there's nothing in here to indicate criminal activity."

"No coded messages?" Fox asked.

"Maybe, but deciphering coded phrases is hardly my area of expertise. I'm an engineer."

Fox grinned. "You mean this isn't a CW show and that you don't have a PhD in whatever the plot needs that week?"

"Nope, but I can make a homemade bomb in about twenty minutes using Styrofoam as the main ingredient."

Fox glanced around for a moment just to make sure no one heard A.C. say that. The ambient noise from the bar and pool covered up their conversation fairly well, but it was probably best if they kept the homemade bomb talk to a minimum. She held out her hand and motioned for the phone.

"Let me take a look."

A.C. handed the phone to Fox. It was a true glimpse into Blaze's busy life. She had more than two hundred unread emails, thirty unread text messages, and just less than ten missed phone calls. In an odd way, Fox gained even more respect for Blaze because it was clear that Blaze was making these people wait for her. There was no urgency on Blaze's end to respond to any of these people. She was the boss, and she would get to them when it suited her.

Fox shook off the thought. She felt disgusted giving credit to Blaze. She looked over the names of the people who had texted her. It was a combination of nicknames and abbreviations with a few full names.

"What about the names?" Fox asked A.C.

"It's just like with anybody else. Nicknames and abbreviations for people she knows closely, and then full names for people she doesn't."

"And we have the real people associated with these phone numbers?"

"Yes, but no hits in criminal databases. They're all clean. Most of the names match up with the nicknames and abbreviations. However, there are five active conversations in her texts with people that don't match the names she has them listed under in her contacts list. I looked into those five people the closest."

"What do we know about them?"

A.C. grinned. "They all appear to be *torrid love affairs.*" A.C. became melodramatic in her enunciation of the phrase.

"You're kidding me."

"Look for yourself."

A.C. pointed out all five text threads. Fox went through them, and they were indeed steamy. From detailed descriptions of sexual acts to dramatic tension in which Blaze argued with her lovers, the text threads could light up the romance section of any bookstore. Fox did her best to push all that aside and look at the text threads with the eyes of a criminal investigator. If she were trying to find coded messages, what might be key phrases in these text threads to indicate Blaze's suspected smuggling? Fox handed the phone to Pyne.

"There's a pattern, and I wonder if Blaze chose scorned lovers as the coded messaging on purpose because there's a clear beginning, middle, and end that makes disguising the messages easy."

Pyne looked through the texts for a moment, and his eyebrows raised. Fox and A.C. shared a knowing look and looked back to the Englishman. The sides of his mouth turned upward with his eyebrows. He handed the phone back to Fox.

Pyne cleared his throat. "I saw the pattern, yes. She says something similar to all of them."

"She has a *rendezvous* planned with this one tomorrow night. She has this contact listed as Landon Pettigrew. Who is that really?" She handed the phone to A.C.

A.C. scrolled quickly. "That phone number belongs to a woman named Hannah Stevens. She's a banker right here in LA."

A banker, interesting, Fox thought.

"Who's up for a stakeout tomorrow night? We'll learn something either way, and it's the only lead we have so far that might hint at Mickey Blaze's secret life."

"A.C. and I will get everything ready for the stakeout while you're at Blaze's mansion for the luncheon," Pyne said.

"Good plan." Fox turned to A.C. "I hope you don't mind, but I'm going in without the earpiece. I'm confident Blaze isn't going to try and kill me again until after the race on Sunday."

"That's fine. Use your handbag as a panic signal, just in case. Keep the bag turned off, but if you feel like you're in danger, connect it to the network, and we'll come running."

Fox entered her hotel room, and she felt the previous night's terror creep back onto her. She reminded herself that she was a professional, but fight or flight had taken over her senses. She didn't want to be inside this room, and so she went down the hall to A.C.'s room and knocked.

"Still thinking about the rattlesnake?"

"Obviously."

Fox moved inside and fell asleep on the couch instantly. She woke up the next morning before the sun had come up completely. The gray sky teased one of California's famous overcast mornings, and there was a sharp chill in the air as Fox stepped onto the patio and looked out on the calm view of Beverly Hills. Fox commenced with her morning routine as she changed into exercise clothes and went to the hotel gym where she spent two hours. The sun broke through the overcast by the time she finished at the gym, and she went up to her room to shower and change for breakfast. She met up with Pyne and A.C. They talked casually about the plans for the day, which included setting up for the stakeout and getting Fox ready for the luncheon with Mickey Blaze and her friends.

"It's a networking event with titans of the sports industry," Pyne said as he ate from his poached egg and avocado toast. "Blaze is smart. She's doing to you exactly what I would do to an enemy that was getting too close to finding the skeletons in my closet."

"No sweat. I can play along with Blaze's little game. I'll kill her with kindness. Or rather, Juliana Ferreira will kill her with kindness."

Fox considered what to wear to the luncheon. The other women were likely to wear business casual attire, and Fox should try to blend in. She opted to keep it as neutral as she could imagine when she picked out the parts for her outfit. She dressed in a white long sleeve blouse, gray herringbone blazer, and black suit pants. She hated the outfit in every way, which was a good thing in this instance.

"It's an event for women, but we all have to dress like men," Fox said as she met with A.C. and Pyne downstairs.

"You're not kidding," Pyne said. "I'm certain I have that same jacket in my closet back home."

Fox rolled her eyes. "You're not helping, Pyne."

"You look fine," A.C. said. "Have fun with the sports ladies. We'll have everything ready for the stakeout when you get back."

Fox climbed into the back of the SUV as Chairwoman Solace's hired driver veered along the same path from Beverly Hills to Calabasas until they arrived at Blaze's mansion a little less than an hour later. Fox was twenty minutes late for the luncheon by design, and there were other women ahead of her who walked up the steps toward the front door. This put Fox at ease as she got out of the SUV and walked up the steps herself. The exact same doorman who greeted Fox at the party two days earlier was the one to greet her again. He led her through the impeccable house to the backyard where at least two dozen women gathered underneath a gazebo near the pool.

She felt completely out of her element here, and the challenge was to regain some manner of composure. After all, she had to leave Jett Fox at the door and become Juliana Ferreira, and Juliana Ferreira was very much in her element among this elite group of two dozen Chairwomen Solaces. Fox steadied herself and plastered a genuine fake smile onto her face.

CHAPTER 26

Mickey Blaze stood out as the peacock among the tweed of business casual women gathered at the gazebo. She wore a single-breasted plum dinner blazer, matching slacks, white blouse, and a golden scarf underneath the buttoned dinner jacket. Fox thought the outfit was truly hideous, but the woman who wore it did so with gusto and confidence.

Blaze saw Fox and casually waved her over to the small group where she stood. Fox confidently marched up to them and returned a winning smile.

"Ladies, I'd like you to meet Juliana Ferreira," Blaze said. "I don't want to spoil the results of the qualifying round too early, but you should expect to see Miss Ferreira in the field of forty at the race on Sunday."

There were three women standing with Blaze, and they all greeted Fox. One was most definitely a WNBA player that Fox recognized, Samantha Jaxon. She was the best dressed of the three, clearly channeling her years of press conference experience into an outfit that slayed the luncheon's theme. She stood a few inches taller than Fox, which was impressive considering Fox cracked six feet herself. Blaze introduced them, and Fox shook Samantha Jaxon's hand.

"Pleasure to meet you," Fox said. "I'm a big fan."

"Thank you." She turned to one of the other two women. "This is my agent, Jessica Brown."

Fox shook hands with Brown. She was exactly what Fox expected of a sports agent. She was confident and loud.

"Juliana Ferreira? I don't believe I've heard your name before, but it's nice to meet you."

Blaze interrupted, "Yes, well, *Miss Ferreira* is as wily as a fox, but I'm sure she'll get big exposure this weekend."

Fox offered a sideways glance to Blaze, and the two made heated eye contact. Brown's voice brought them back to the conversation.

"Well, if you're racing this weekend, then I'm sure you're about to become a household name." Brown offered a business card to Fox. People still did that? Fox thought. "If you need any help navigating your newfound fame, just give me a call. My firm is excellent at helping up-and-coming superstars. In fact, I like to have my clients do a bit of cross promotion. Maybe you'll even work with Miss Jaxon here, if she'd like."

"Of course, whatever you need, Miss Ferreira," Jaxon said. "I look forward to watching you in the race on Sunday."

The third member of this small group seemed a bit shy compared to the others, and Fox knew right away she would get along great with this woman before even meeting her. She was dressed in an unremarkable blouse underneath a plaid sweater vest, neutral-colored skirt, and high socks. Her hair was combed but still a bit messy, and her glasses were sitting upon frames that were not stylish. Her soft complexion around her eyes suggested that she and this woman were close to the same age.

Blaze introduced her. "This is Rhiannon Misrasi, a reporter for Sporting Times Network. She has a daily column on the network's website, and occasionally she does a spot on the network's competition debate show."

"Hello." Rhiannon Misrasi nervously extended her hand and smiled. Fox smiled warmly back to her and shook firmly. If there was one thing Fox knew without a shadow of a doubt, it was that shy people attached themselves to anyone outgoing because outgoing people carried the majority of the social burden for them. Shy people were also incredibly interesting once they felt comfortable enough to open up. Fox believed she and Rhiannon could become close friends by the time the luncheon ended.

"Nice to meet you, Rhiannon. Do you have a niche sport that you cover, or do you cover everything?"

"A bit of everything," she responded.

"Are you covering the race on Sunday?"

"Yes, I'll be there. I'm actually writing about Mickey Blaze's return to the track, and we have a big feature planned following the race."

"Oh, that's perfect. I'm sure you'll have something interesting to write about, good or bad." Fox turned to Blaze and winked. She turned back to Rhiannon. "Tell me, Rhiannon, do you have any insider information on the NFL?"

"No more than any other reporter," she said. "Why do you ask?"

Fox offered an exaggerated sigh. "Oh I just keep waiting for the Miami Dolphins to show improvement, but every year they keep letting me down."

Rhiannon laughed. "I'm from Buffalo. I know all about teams letting me down."

"Oh you poor thing. That is truly a cursed sports town." Fox had an idea. "That would make for a funny column. Have you written anything like that about Buffalo sports?"

"A few years ago, yes. If you'd like, I can send you a link."

"Yes! Please do."

Fox sidled up next to Rhiannon as if she expected her to get out her phone right now and copy the link. The reporter hesitated but realized what was happening and got out her phone. Blaze, Jaxon, and Brown maneuvered away from the two of them and carried on their own conversation. Rhiannon found the article, and Fox gave her the safety phone number that would send the text to the armory network before spitting back the text to Fox's real phone number. Just then, Blaze got up in front of the entire party and asked everyone to take a seat.

Fox sat down at a table and was immediately joined by Jaxon and Brown. There was a fourth spot, and Fox looked to Rhiannon and motioned for her to take it. Rhiannon smiled and did so. Once everyone sat down, Blaze spoke for a few minutes about women's empowerment and how they were all shattering glass ceilings together. Fox knew she was supposed to care about these kinds of speeches, but she was a woman of action, and these luncheons and other similar events seemed counterintuitive to the messages shared at them. It didn't help that Blaze was dressed like she should be sitting in a luxury box at Staples Center deciding which of the Los Angeles Lakers to trade away. Or maybe it did help, and that was the point. Fox snapped out of the thought as Blaze ramped to the conclusion of her brief speech.

"So, enjoy the meal, and please mingle!" Blaze said. "Hopefully you'll all make a new friend or two before the day is over."

Fox took this as an opportunity to poke at her new friends at the lunch table to see what might come up about Blaze. "Wasn't that mind-blowing a few weeks ago when Mickey announced she was medically cleared to race again?"

Samantha Jaxon spoke. "Amazing, but we'll see how she performs. I've had plenty of teammates over the years who were never the same after they came back from lengthy injuries. Maybe it's different in racing. What's your opinion, Juliana?"

Fox still wasn't used to anyone referring to her as Juliana Ferreira, but she rebounded as quickly as she could to answer Jaxon's question. "I'd assume she's been practicing in secret for months, and she never would have announced the comeback if she weren't already sure her motor skills were top notch. This is Mickey Blaze we're talking about, after all."

"I wouldn't be so sure about that," Brown chimed in. The sports agent leaned forward conspiratorially. "Just like Samantha's had teammates, I've had clients who tried to push their way back into playing too soon after serious injuries. Although sometimes I was the one who pushed them!" Brown laughed hysterically at her own dark humor. No one else at the table laughed. Although, Jaxon offered a courtesy chuckle. Fox did *not* like this sports agent.

However, Fox found it interesting that Blaze made an effort to speak to these two women, Jaxon and Brown, before the luncheon started, and neither of them had much confidence in Blaze's ability to race on Sunday. It was probably nothing, but Fox took stock of it. Blaze had doubters, which may have contributed to the proverbial chip on her shoulder.

Waiters appeared and placed avocado salads in front of everyone, the first course of the luncheon. Fox licked her lips at the delicious-looking salad of avocados, cucumbers, tomatoes, and onions topped with oregano and garlic. She smelled olive oil, vinegar, and honey that topped the salad, and she took a bite quickly. It was just as delicious as it looked and smelled. They also poured wine into everyone's glasses, and the waiters explained that the wine was grown right here in Mickey Blaze's own vineyard.

Fox smelled the wine before drinking it and swirled it around in her glass. Her lunch companions might have thought she looked like a snob as she did this, but Fox was checking for poison. There was a grim thought, Mickey Blaze committing mass murder at a women's empowerment luncheon.

Rhiannon turned to Fox. "I hope you don't mind me saying, but your accent is quite unique. Where are you from originally?"

Fox considered how much of her backstory to share. There was probably no harm in sharing the truth with these three women, but it was also possible that all three of them were assigned by Blaze to specifically get information out of Fox. She knew to tread carefully here.

"I was born in Paraguay and immigrated to the United States while I was in elementary school," Fox said. She opted for a half truth: right story, wrong birthplace.

"Come to think of it, you look very familiar," Jaxon said. "Did we ever play against each other? Did you play basketball in college?"

"I didn't, no."

Brown added, "What about other sports? Your height and build, you must have played *something*."

Fox felt uncomfortable with the questions. Even the best cover stories could fall apart with the simplest of prods, and Juliana Ferreira wasn't exactly a far cry from her real-life persona. Thankfully and surprisingly, the reporter thwarted the questions.

"I'm sure Juliana trained to drive professionally most of her life," Rhiannon said.

Fox picked up on the cue. "It's true. From working at my uncle's auto shop to amateur racing, semi-pro races back east, and now the Open Circuit Challenge, it's been a grind. I didn't have time to try out anything else."

The waiters returned and gathered the salad plates. They lay the next course of the luncheon, fish tacos. Fox scrunched her face at something so unrefined as fish tacos being the main attraction of an event for rich people, but they were delicately constructed and artistically presented as if the chef were inside the mansion with a television crew demonstrating how to turn the fish taco into affluent cuisine.

"Where did you go to journalism school?" Fox asked.

Rhiannon set down her fish taco. "Harvard."

Fox hesitated when she heard the answer. Given their similar ages and Rhiannon's work as a sports reporter, there was a slim chance that Rhiannon Misrasi had seen Fox play college volleyball for Yale while she was a cub reporter at Harvard.

"Harvard educated, very nice."

"I don't like to brag about it because it might come across as obnoxious. Most of my classmates are a little too proud of themselves."

Fox knew the feeling, and she wondered if there were times she was ever too obnoxious about her own Ivy League education.

There was a rustle and a sigh across the table as Jaxon took off her shoe and adjusted it. "Sorry about this. I hate wearing platforms. I'm already six-foot-three. Why do I force myself to wear these? Jessica can tell you how much I trip when I wear them."

"It's true. For someone so athletic, you're kind of a clutz."

All four at the table laughed.

"It's worse when you get all serious to make sure I'm OK. Just laugh at me next time."

"You got it."

The waiters returned a third time to remove the fish taco plates and present the dessert plate, pina colada grilled pineapple slices. Fox noticed that most of the women stood from their tables and began to mozy around the extravagant backyard with their plates of pina colada pineapple slices in all manner of chit-chat. Fox felt full so she hardly touched the dessert. That's when Blaze appeared at the table.

"Ladies, I hope you don't mind, but can I borrow Juliana for a moment?"

Irritation crept over Fox's neck. She glanced at Rhiannon, who watched her carefully. However, it wasn't the look of someone in the know. No, Rhiannon watched Fox with curiosity, almost as if she recognized that Fox was irritated and wondered why that might be.

"You have my number, Rhiannon," Fox said as she stood. "In case I don't see you before you leave, let's keep in touch." She winked at Rhiannon, who seemed to give Fox a knowing nod. She'd have to wait until later to see if they were truly on the same page, but at least for now Fox thought she had an ally in Rhiannon Misrasi.

Fox walked alongside Blaze across the yard toward the stable past the flamingo pond. Blaze waited until they were out of earshot from the other women.

"I wondered when we would play our cards in this little game of ours, Miss Fox. Oh wait, excuse me, Jett. I know how much you hate being called Miss Fox."

Fox had a decision to make, and she had to make it quick. Should she double down on the cover story or give it up and see what Blaze had in store for her? Neither option sounded appealing.

"I'm really sorry, Blaze, but Jett Fox was a fake name I created that night at the casino." Fox had opted to protect Juliana Ferreira and the racing cover. She reasoned that this was the choice Chairwoman Solace would have made.

"Is that so?" Blaze was unconvinced as they stood just outside the stable. Blaze entered first, and Fox carefully followed.

The stable was modest in size, a stable for someone who enjoyed horses as a hobby as opposed to a career. However, even for an amateur stable it was kept clean and smelling fresh. There were two horses in the stalls, a palomino and a chestnut.

"I apologize for the deceit in Casablanca," Fox said. "I was out there on vacation, and I heard you would be at the casino that night. I wanted to meet you, but I didn't want to seem like some racing sycophant." It was a hollow excuse. She doubted Blaze would take the bait. "Your horses are adorable, by the way."

Blaze smiled briefly and talked about them without excitement. "Thank you. The palomino is a stallion named Outlaw, and the chestnut is a mare named Scarlet."

"Do you ride them or just have them?"

"Oh no, I don't ride them, but I spend as much time with them as I can. I like to watch them race each other in the corral. Outlaw is a bit faster than Scarlet." Blaze turned to face Fox, appraising her. "You humiliated me that night in Morocco."

An involuntary proud grin forced its way onto Fox's face. "It was all in good fun."

"How did you figure it out? The loaded dice, I mean."

"It wasn't easy. I wasn't sure you were using loaded dice until I made my move to swap them out."

"The distraction by the Englishman."

"Guilty."

Blaze's mouth smiled, but her eyes did not. Fox suddenly became aware of her surroundings. They were inside the stable away from prying eyes. If Blaze were to kill her, this would be a situation where she might get away with it. Fox had tipped her hand numerous times over the past few days in California, and there was no way Blaze bought the Juliana Ferreira story. Chairwoman Solace was right about how Fox should have handled her interactions with Blaze, and Fox cursed herself for ignoring the advice.

"Credit where credit is due," Blaze said. "I might have done the same thing if I were in your shoes. You certainly got my attention."

"In hindsight, I should have just told you who I was and that I planned to enter your race," Fox said, "but I couldn't help myself. I've always been a sucker for a game of misdirection."

Blaze raised an eyebrow, and her mouth turned upward into a crooked smile. She then relaxed. "Well, you got the better of me in Casablanca, but I'm afraid you won't have the same luck at the race on Sunday. First place is as good as mine."

Fox felt relieved by Blaze's sporting challenge. "Oh we'll see about that. I know my chances of winning aren't great, but I might surprise you."

Blaze mirthlessly chuckled, as she was accustomed. "Tell you what, *Miss Ferreira*, if you can finish in the top fifteen, and judging by your qualifying time, I think that's a fair goal, I would be happy to form a mentorship with you. We're both women in a sport dominated by men. The media expects us to be allies, but I think you have a thing or two to learn. Impress me this Sunday, and we'll talk."

Blaze stormed away, "accidentally" shoving Fox aside with her shoulder as she marched past her. It was clear to Fox that Blaze didn't buy the story, but Fox stuck to the cover, and so Blaze played along.

"Oh, clumsy me," she said.

"It's all right," Fox said in response. She glared at the back of Blaze's head as she left the stable.

CHAPTER 27

Fox and Pyne sat in the parked junker car across the street from the address of the scheduled "date" between Mickey Blaze and "Landon Pettigrew." It was a fancy restaurant in Hollywood with tinted windows to keep people exactly like Fox and Pyne from peeking at the patrons. The two spies were a half hour early so they brainstormed alternatives.

"If it's really a date, then I don't want to watch anyway," Fox said.

Pyne nodded in a fatigued display. The bags under his eyes had grown dark, and he sighed as he lay back against the passenger seat. Fox considered bothering him about it, but she opted to let it go. A.C. jolted them both to life as her voice came through their earpieces.

"I'm sending you a picture of Hannah Stevens from her employment profile at the bank. I'm not sure how up to date it is. She might look totally different now, and she might disguise herself."

The photograph popped up on Pyne's phone in the mount on the dashboard. Hannah Stevens looked average with her medium-length blonde hair, glasses, and work attire. She had no defining characteristics that would make her memorable. Fox had to study the picture for longer than she normally would to memorize the face.

"Were you able to find anyone named Landon Pettigrew among Hannah Stevens' known associates? Facebook friends or anything like that?" Fox asked.

"No, and the phone isn't part of a group plan that belongs to Stevens, either. It's her phone, and she makes monthly payments on it. I'd say it's definitely Hannah Stevens on the other end, and Landon Pettigrew is just an alias that Blaze uses to protect her identity."

Pyne spoke in an exasperated tone. "So we're looking for two blonde women in Hollywood. Wonderful."

Fox studied Pyne. It wasn't the usual sarcasm that came out of his mouth. The MI6 agent was genuinely tired, and Fox was worried.

"Are you OK?" Fox asked.

Pyne turned to her. "I'm fine." Fox raised her eyebrows at him. Pyne rolled his eyes and continued, "OK, I'm exhausted. I think all the trips back and forth between London and the States are catching up to me."

"You can go back to the hotel if you want," Fox said.

Pyne considered. "I'd hate to do that to you, especially when we're *this* close to figuring out why Sharon Graham died."

Fox laughed to herself because of Pyne's contradiction. He was using the guise of being helpful to hide the fact that he was here for personal reasons. And he was too tired to recognize it.

"How about a compromise? You sit there and take a nap, and I'll wake you up if I need you."

Fox watched his face. It was clear that he hated the idea, but he was also tired enough that the temptation sounded appealing.

"Fine, you have a deal."

"Sing him a lullaby, A.C."

"No! No lullaby."

A.C. laughed. "Are you sure? I know all the lyrics to *Space Oddity*."

Pyne laughed. It was the sort of belly buster laughter that only came when someone was tired. A.C. laughed with him through the earpiece.

Ten more minutes passed. It was getting closer to the time mentioned in the text. Pyne's eyes were closed, but his breathing was normal. He hadn't fallen asleep yet. She left him alone and turned her attention to the restaurant. Who did she expect to see that might give a clue as to what to do next? Would Blaze or Stevens show up and risk exposure if the operation went poorly? Or was this a face value lovers' retreat? She watched the restaurant carefully, taking stock of every person that walked inside and outside. They were all dressed quite well, and she made up stories for all of them, whether they were aspiring actors meeting with producers or screenwriters gathering to share ideas. This was Hollywood after all!

Fox checked the time. It was exactly the time of the scheduled encounter. Her stomach turned with nervousness, or maybe it was the fish taco from Mickey Blaze's party. Either way, she watched the restaurant with bated breath.

In a cruel twist of bad luck, an unmarked semi-trailer truck whistled by her window and obstructed the view to the restaurant momentarily. It stopped in the middle of the road, and Fox knew she'd have to get out of the car if she wanted to see anything. Did she dare? If Mickey Blaze was watching, that would destroy the stakeout instantaneously. Just then, a limo pulled up behind the truck, and the door opened. A woman with blonde and bronze hair stepped out. Fox leaned forward to get a good look. The woman turned slightly, and that was all Fox needed to see.

"I have eyes on Blaze," she reported to A.C. at the hotel room armory. Pyne woke up from his nap. Blaze waited until there were no cars coming, and she crossed the street to the restaurant. She met up with a handsome man who looked like he just stepped out from one of the nearby movie studios, and they kissed each other.

"Fascinating," Pyne said.

Fox turned back to the limo. It accelerated forward at a steady pace and followed the semi-trailer truck through the stop light, keeping the same pace as the truck up a hill. It was decision time. Should Fox stay at the restaurant and wait on Mickey Blaze or follow the limo? Without consulting with Pyne, Fox turned the key in the ancient junker's ignition and accelerated forward. It turned out she didn't have to consult with Pyne because he was on the same page. He monitored the limo as closely as Fox did. A.C. chimed in their ears and wanted a status update. Pyne responded to her.

"Blaze is the decoy." Fox smiled. They were in sync, and there were few better feelings than teammates who could read each other's minds.

"We're following her limo, which is following a semi-truck," Fox said.

"What do you mean Blaze is a decoy?"

"She met up with a man at the restaurant," Fox said. "They're having a romantic dinner at the restaurant so that she gives herself an alibi in case this all goes up in flames. She'll have text messages to prove that she planned to meet up with her *boyfriend*, and now she has eyewitnesses who can say they saw her at the restaurant."

"It's a master stroke," Pyne said. "This whole time we thought it was either a date or a scheme. We never considered that it was both."

"A.C., are you picking us up on your map?"

"Yes, I've got you. Your handbag and the microchip in Harry's shoe both have strong signals."

"Perfect. I have no idea what's about to happen, but be ready to call the cops and send them to our location."

Pyne's exhaustion had faded away. He was fully alert and grinning. Fox sensed his anticipation. He had waited months for this moment, to find out why his friend died and why his supervisors sat on their hands investigating it. With a bit of nuance coupled with some luck, Fox hoped to get him some answers tonight.

Just as Fox suspected, the limo continued to follow the truck. She kept her distance just like she was trained and used Pyne as a navigator. They were on the road for quite a while as the limo and truck turned onto the 101 and headed north. Fox followed for several miles until the vehicles turned off and ventured through the side streets and into the San Fernando Valley. The streets became less crowded, and Fox worried that it would be easier to spot her following the limo. Fox and Pyne said nothing during the trip unless it was about the two vehicles they followed. The semi-trailer truck turned left into a parking lot, and Fox stopped short two blocks away and turned her own car off.

Fox opened her handbag. She retrieved the Beretta from its hiding place and secured it into her belt. She then opened the bottom panel and grabbed three smoke grenades. Finally, she snapped the throwing knife out from underneath the handbag and secured that onto the other side of her belt. She turned to Pyne.

"You're driving now. Be ready to pick me up."

Fox didn't wait for an objection. She got out of the car, crossed the street, and made her way up the two blocks toward the parking lot where the truck and limo had turned. She wasn't surprised to see that this part of the Valley where they had decided to park was dead at this time of night. They would have chosen it for this exact reason as Fox walked up the street without spotting another individual.

Fox reached a cinderblock wall at an alley and heard commotion on the other side. She looked around the alley and found an old, rusted oil drum perched against the brick wall and carefully climbed it. It was all she needed thanks to her six-foot frame as her head poked out the other side and revealed an auto mechanic's shop where the semi-trailer truck was parked. She got out her phone and recorded the show.

Several nondescript men and women opened the trailer and unloaded an unimpressive car onto the pavement. A woman got into the car and coasted into a stall inside the auto mechanics shop and shut off the engine. The truck obstructed Fox's view of the auto mechanic's shop, so she climbed down from the oil drum and moved it down the alley. She carefully climbed the rusted oil drum again and stood over the cinderblock wall. She had a perfect view inside.

Fox spoke quietly so that her voice could get lost among the mechanical sounds. "It's a chop shop. They're dismantling a car that was delivered in the truck." She looked back in the direction of the limo, which remained lifeless parked alongside the truck. She turned back to the shop and saw the mechanics tearing the car apart piece by piece with mammoth proficiency. They slowed significantly once they reached specific areas of the car. Fox heard a voice command them.

"As soon as you find one, report it. No one is going home until I have every piece accounted for."

Fox followed the voice and saw a woman dressed in a business suit. She was in her mid-forties, slightly overweight, blonde hair, and she wore glasses. Fox remembered the picture she studied at the restaurant, and she nearly cried from the relief that following her hunch paid off.

"Hannah Stevens is here."

Pyne exhaled slowly. "That is fantastic news."

Fox waited as three people at the front of the car dismantled the brake pads and scoured them. One of the men raised his hand, and another man came to him with a tray and tweezers. The man holding the brake pad pointed to a spot, and the man with the tweezers carefully extended the tool and latched onto a tiny object that Fox couldn't see from her position. Zooming in with her phone didn't help.

"I might have to move in closer."

"Be careful."

Fox scanned the area. She had two options. The first option was to move around the alley and come in from the property on the northern side of the building. Fox currently stood on the rusted oil drum on the west side of the auto mechanic's shop. The second option was to climb over the wall back at her original spot before she moved the oil drum and then get on top of the semi-trailer.

She pondered for a brief moment as the commotion inside the shop continued. Fox finally opted for the second option. She climbed down and lifted the oil drum back to its original place. She climbed back up and looked over the wall at the limo. Convinced that no one was in it to bother her, she lifted herself over the cinderblock and down into the auto shop parking area.

She stayed crouched to make sure no one heard her and then darted toward the truck on the opposite side of where the workers hacked away at the car. Moving her feet as nimbly as she could, Fox hopped onto the trailer gap and kept her body level with the trailer. She hopped again to grab hold of the ledge and hoist herself up onto the trailer roof and crawled into a flat position. Once her entire body was pinned onto the roof, she waited a brief moment to make sure no one saw or heard her do any of this. That's when she crawled forward to the edge and looked down into the auto shop. *Now* she had the view she wanted.

Fox arrived just in time to see a woman raise her hand as she held the engine gasket. The man with the tray approached her, and she pointed to three different spots on the gasket. There was no mistaking what Fox saw: the brilliant shine, the perfected cut, and the excitement lingering inside Fox's heart. The man lifted the artifact from the gasket with the tweezers as the auto shop light allowed it to twinkle.

"Diamonds."

CHAPTER 28

The sparkling gemstone was unmistakable. As Fox spoke the word "diamonds" as quietly as humanly possible, Pyne and A.C. both gasped.

"Are you serious?" Pyne asked.

"Yeah."

Fox spoke the confirmation softly and couldn't elaborate because of proximity. However, all three of them knew what it meant. Sharon Graham was right all along. She was right to identify Mickey Blaze as a person of interest. She was right to volunteer for the cooperative role between Special Branch and MI6. And now, as Fox watched the man with the tweezers place the three diamonds from the gasket into the tray, she knew that Harry Pyne was right to go rogue and pick up his deceased friend's case. Specifically for Jett Fox, this discovery gave her everything she needed: motive, means, and opportunity. Blaze murdered Sharon Graham, and Fox covered all the critical elements necessary to pin a legitimate accusation against her.

"I have your footage uploaded to the armory network," A.C. said. "Get back to your original spot."

Fox turned herself around quietly and crawled toward the trailer gap. She listened carefully with every movement to make sure that no one inside the chop shop heard her. Easing herself over the edge and onto the trailer, she bent her knees as she landed to help soften the thud. She repeated this process to drop onto the pavement and then pranced to the cinderblock wall as she leapt and used the momentum to grip the edge and heave herself over the brick fence and into the alley.

She crashed onto the other side a little too heavily as the crunch of the gravel beneath her echoed through the air. She froze. It was the loudest she'd been, and she waited for any recognition on the other side. It never came. The group continued to work on the car. Fox carried the oil drum once again to the spot with the best view of the auto shop and climbed atop it. She peered, but this time she left her phone in her pocket. She had all the footage she needed, but now it was time to see where the group went next.

An hour passed as Fox moved up and down between watching the shop and hiding from any potential passers-by. Hannah Stevens and her army of miscreants had dismantled the entire car. The man with the tweezers placed one last diamond into the tray, and just when Fox thought the process couldn't get any more tedious, the man handed the tray to Stevens, and she began counting the diamonds. She placed each one into a briefcase with velvet lining as she counted. The auto workers stood close by as men with guns watched them closely, making sure to not let any of them leave until Hannah Stevens accounted for every diamond. Another half hour passed, and Stevens gently closed the briefcase.

"You're all excused. Next shipment is in three months." Stevens stood up with the briefcase and walked toward the limo. Fox got down from the oil drum and hustled to the spot closer to the limo. She wanted to confirm that Stevens actually got in the limo. She perched again and gazed over the barricade and saw the banker climb into the limo with the briefcase in hand. The door closed, and the driver moved around to his side. He climbed in and ignited the engine. Fox jumped down from the wall and hustled down the alley.

"Pyne, get ready to drive. We're following the limo."

Fox broke into a sprint down the street until she heard a car exiting the auto shop parking lot. She stopped suddenly and got to cover. The limo pulled onto the street and turned in the opposite direction of Fox.

"I have them, and I see you. Cross the street and I'll pick you up."

Pyne started the car, and Fox crossed the street just in time for him to pull up next to her. She got into the passenger side as Pyne drove forward. They passed the auto shop casually and carried on at a steady pace, keeping the limousine in sight as it made its way through the Valley toward the highway.

"So why didn't you have me send the cops to the auto shop?" A.C. asked.

"I want to see where this thing ends," Fox said. "Sharon Graham's working theory with Special Branch and MI6 was that the diamonds were smuggled to enemies of the UK, whoever they might be. It makes me wonder if Hannah Stevens has one more stop before she calls it a night."

That piqued Pyne's interest. "You think Hannah Stevens is taking the diamonds to one of Blaze's criminal partners tonight?"

"It's time to rattle the cage. If Hannah Stevens is making a delivery, we're going to make sure that delivery doesn't happen."

That began an excruciating journey around Southern California. Pyne complained about "America's traffic laws" as they weaved around the Valley and headed east toward Glendale. The limousine pulled over temporarily as Fox and Pyne watched it from a distance. They worried that they spooked the passengers, but it carried on and continued east into Pasadena. There was another brief stop, and Fox became so irritated by Pyne's frustration with Los Angeles traffic that Fox traded places with him. Back in the driver's seat, Fox continued following the limo east on I-210 until it inexplicably merged south onto I-605.

The travel made no sense, almost as if Hannah Stevens asked the driver to purposely drive an incoherent path to their destination. Actually, when Fox thought of it like that, the travel path made sense. They eventually turned again heading southeast into Orange County, passing through Anaheim. Pyne fell asleep as they drove through the O.C., and the late hours of nighttime began to catch up to Fox as she struggled to keep her eyes on the limousine while also maintaining a safe tail distance. Somehow, among the travels through the cities and neighborhoods, they found themselves driving alongside the coast. Stevens' limo continued on I-5 into San Clemente. Finally, once they were through the city, the limo slowed and found the nearest exit. They had been on the road for a little more than two hours since the auto shop in the San Fernando Valley.

Pyne woke up when he heard the car slowing down to exit off the interstate. Fox wondered how far back she could keep her car while also keeping her eyes on the limo. There was sparse traffic at this time of night and this far south of LA. She kept her eyes on the limo's tail lights as it rounded off the exit and headed toward the beaches. Fox slowed down to a snail's crawl, and she hoped that the driver who had been given the task of delivering Hannah Stevens wasn't worried about being followed.

"Are you awake, A.C.?"

"I'm here, Jett."

"Standby to call the authorities. Pyne and I have to tidy the place up first. Also, after you call the police, start packing up your mobile armory. It won't be safe for us to stay at our hotel anymore after tonight."

Fox knew that if they were successful stopping delivery of these diamonds, then that might just be enough to push Blaze over the edge and risk the scandal. She could see Blaze saying, "enough is enough", and killing them before the race.

She parked the car a half mile down the road from where she saw the limo stop near the beach. Fox reached into the seat and grabbed two gas masks.

"Just in case things get a bit smokey."

Already armed with grenades, a knife, and her Beretta, Fox got out of the car, followed closely by Pyne. They hopped the barricade from the road down onto the sand and jogged until they saw Hannah Stevens and three armed bodyguards walking ahead of them toward the ocean. Fox and Pyne crouched low and allowed them to get some distance before they crept forward.

The waves crashed against the sand, and the smell of sea salt filled the air around Fox. They slunk through the soft soil under their feet until they came to a set of cliffs that wrapped around the interstate. Hannah Stevens and the bodyguards stopped at the cliffs and stayed put at a safe spot where they could watch the nighttime waves hitting the rocks and washing ashore. Fox and Pyne said nothing. They simply watched, both as professional as ever. This was the most "no nonsense" they had been since they met each other, and Fox gained an amazing respect for Harry Pyne. Through all the sarcasm and the teasing, when it was time to focus, he was a reliable companion.

Stevens and the bodyguards watched the ocean. They were completely still, as if they expected the armies of Atlantis to emerge from the sea at any moment. Fox looked up and down the coastline. Were they waiting for a boat? She got the answer to her question a second later. Off in the distance, coming up from the south and slicing through the currents, Fox saw the dark shape of an enormous black swan that glowed under the moonlight. The shape formed more realistically the closer it drew as the black swan transformed into a stylish black yacht. Fox got out her phone and recorded the watercraft making its way up the coast until it came to a pronounced stop just a few hundred yards offshore.

"We need the Coast Guard, too, A.C." Fox worried her voice was lost among the waves splashing on the rocks and sand as she spoke softly. But, A.C. acknowledged the request.

"Making the call now. Coast Guard and local police should be there in twenty minutes. I'll send you the address of our new hotel when I'm checked in."

A speedboat launched from the yacht's stern. A spotlight tore through the darkness and nearly blinded Fox as she staggered backward. How exposed were they? Did they need to make their assault now?

She and Pyne glanced at each other and put the gas masks over their faces. Fox pulled a grenade from her belt and heaved it at the group of four standing in front of them. It landed at their feet, rolled through the sand, and came to a stop just in front of them. Their bodies went taut as all four of them looked down at the ball at their feet. Before they looked back to see who threw it, the grenade exploded.

Whether it was the sudden pop or the shriek from Hannah Stevens, the speedboat came to a halt halfway between the shore and the yacht, shining the light on the smokey haze created by the grenade. Fox could only imagine the thoughts swirling through the mind of the boat driver, but she had to set that aside as she and Pyne sprinted into the cloud and got to work detaining Stevens and the bodyguards. The four of them coughed excessively as they choked on the smoke and stumbled around the beach in search of fresh air. This made it easy for Fox and Pyne. They attacked the bodyguards first, divorcing them from their weapons and binding them with zip ties. The ocean breeze pushed away the smoke faster than they would have liked, but Fox and Pyne worked with precision. Once they dropped the tied bodyguards onto the sand, they grabbed Hannah Stevens, still holding the briefcase with the diamonds.

That's when the figures on the speedboat made their move. The smoke had mostly vanished by this point, and Fox heard the unmistakable sound of automatic weapon fire exploding behind them. She and Pyne instinctively dropped to the ground, shoving the beleaguered Stevens into the sand when they did. Sand volcanoes erupted all around them.

Fox fought against the fear building up inside of her, just as she was taught. There was nothing that could prepare anyone for the sheer terror that comes with gunfire, but Fox knew that the body's natural instinct in that moment was to panic. The ability to harness that panic into action was what separated the field agents from the desk agents. Fox released her hold from Hannah Stevens and rolled onto her back with the Beretta at the ready. She fired five shots from the nine millimeter pistol in the direction of the moving speedboat, an impossible shot to hit. But, it bought Pyne the time he needed to drag Stevens farther up the beach until they were out of range of the speedboat's weapons. Fox jumped to her feet and sprinted, kicking sand in every direction.

The people on the speedboat shouted inaudibly, and to Fox's surprise, the boat turned away from the shore and hurtled back in the direction of the yacht. Good, have fun trying to outrun the Coast Guard, Fox thought. The person in charge on the yacht must have sent the message to the speedboat to return. They were on a time crunch, too, and it was clear they weren't getting their diamonds tonight.

Pyne secured bindings around Stevens' wrists and ankles just like they had done to the bodyguards. Stevens watched the two masked figures standing above her, and she scowled.

"Whoever you are, you're going to pay for this."

Pyne opened the diamond case and set it next to Stevens.

"Say cheese," Fox said. She held up her phone and turned on the flashlight. Stevens cowered back when the light hit her face. Fox snapped the picture.

CHAPTER 29

A.C. chose the perfect low-profile motel in Pasadena for the team to squat until race day. It was shabby and dirty, the exact kind of place no one rich would ever think to look. Fox turned on the television as soon as she woke up, and the arrests from the previous night were all over the local news.

"Anonymous citizens halted a diamond smuggling operation in progress, as nineteen people, including Los Angeles area banker Hannah Stevens, were arrested last night. Members of the United States Coast Guard and San Clemente Police Department both received anonymous tips about the illegal diamonds, and they collaborated to make arrests on the beaches just outside San Clemente and at sea. Members of the Coast Guard ran down a yacht involved with the operation…"

A.C. interrupted the TV news with her own news, "Blaze's phone is blowing up. She's gotten dozens of angry phone calls, emails, and text messages about a *catastrophe* last night, and her only response is to call her office line. She's going old school, trying to destroy the digital trail. I'm running those other numbers as we speak, and so far, the ones I've gotten back don't belong to specific people, but rather corporations."

Fox knew what that meant. They were all people that were much more important than a "low-life" banker like Hannah Stevens. Fox and Pyne took down the small fish last night, but that was really all she wanted to do. As she said, last night was about rattling the cage. Fox wanted to send a message that Blaze shouldn't get too comfortable. Still, she wondered what consequences the beach stunt might have. Should she withdraw from the race? That was the easiest way for Blaze to kill Fox. Force a wreck on the course and chalk it up to an unfortunate accident.

As if fate could read her mind, Fox's phone buzzed. It was Chairwoman Solace. Fox swiped the green button and pressed the microphone icon.

"Hello, ma'am. You're on speaker phone with A.C. and me."

"Agent Fox, I read the report you submitted last night. Thank you for telling me about the arrest before I saw it on the news."

"Are you upset?"

"No, nothing like that. It's not exactly what I would have done, but I trust you."

"What would you have done?"

"It's difficult to say. Nobody's life was in danger if you had let them take the diamonds, so I might have let them make the delivery and used that information later on. I'm worried you might have lost any leverage you had. But, you sent a message last night, and the enemy is scrambling. That can be a good thing, too."

A.C. spoke. "Uh oh."

"That's not what I want to hear," Solace said.

"What is it?"

"Blaze figured out we cloned her phone. She just destroyed it."

Fox sighed. "Well, that answers the question I've been debating all morning. It looks like we'll have to compete in this race after all if we want another chance to get close to Blaze."

"Yes, well, it was a nice effort to solve the case before the race, but the arrests you made last night were at the end of the pipeline. Who knows how many powerful people are involved in this? We need solid evidence at the beginning of the pipeline before we go to the authorities."

"Understood, ma'am. We'll find out where they're getting the diamonds."

"I know you will. Now, onto the race itself. Our shell company just got the call that we qualified in the top forty. And they just posted the field of forty on Sporting Times Network."

Fox flipped the channel, and Rhiannon Misrasi came on the screen. She was giving a report on the field of forty.

Solace continued, "I just want to say you've both done an excellent job with this assignment. I'm especially proud of you, A.C. You just might have what it takes to be a field agent."

"Thank you, ma'am." A.C. was polite, but her face showed irritation. Fox could tell she wished she was back in the laboratory.

"Agent Fox, do whatever it takes to get another face-to-face meeting with Mickey Blaze, even if you have to win the race to get it."

"Understood, ma'am."

They hung up as Fox watched Rhiannon give the sports report. Fox's instincts told her that Rhiannon knew more than she let on, but what side was she on? Was she in on the smuggling ring, or did she suspect something was amiss with Blaze? It was too dangerous to find out right now, and she might very well put Rhiannon in harm's way if she tried to rope her into things this late in the game, but after the dust settled on this case, maybe Rhiannon was an ally she could call on in the future.

"I met her at the luncheon." Fox motioned toward the television.

A.C. watched for a second. "Was she nice?"

"She was the only one there who wasn't plastic."

They listened to Rhiannon's report. "... all four members of Mickey Blaze's racing team, including Mickey Blaze herself, qualified in the top forty. The other three members are rising star Theseus Kastellanos, Bill Curraway, and Timothy Charles. Depending on Blaze's strategy, the rest of the field should have its hands full, as it seems likely Kastellanos, Curraway, and Charles might do whatever it takes to help Blaze cross the finish line in first place on Sunday."

Fox's ears perked when Rhiannon said this. Was the reporter giving her a warning? It was normal for an on-screen reporter to editorialize, but given everything that had happened during the last three days, Fox couldn't help but wonder if Rhiannon was sending a signal to the newcomer she met at the networking event. In any case, Fox smiled at the thought that Blaze once again tipped the scales in her favor. It was the craps game, but this time instead of loaded dice she loaded the racing field.

The team had two full days to kill until the race, and they couldn't afford an appearance at the Palisades. It was no fun, but the team spent the next two days cooped up in their dingy motel. They kept the recreation to a minimum, but they visited the beach, walked the Hollywood Walk of Fame, ate taquitos at Olvera Street, and did various other Southern California tourist traps. The three of them enjoyed themselves as they acted like tourists, and Fox even noticed Pyne and A.C. grow close together in those two days. A hint of jealousy hit her, and Fox hated herself for feeling that way. She wondered if it might be best to distance herself from the two of them after the mission ended, not only because she needed time to get over whatever crush she had on Harry Pyne, but also to give A.C. and Pyne a chance to see if their feelings were real. Maybe Chairwoman

Solace had another case outside the country where Fox could work.

That's not to say Fox didn't play her role as the wing woman exceptionally. She gave them as much alone time as she could and lost herself at the gym with rigorous military-level exercises that caught the gaze of more than one personal trainer. They had nothing to teach her, and they couldn't understand why this stranger put her body through this sort of physical torture. Drenched in sweat and sore, Fox smiled at them at the end of each workout before she hit the showers.

Sunday morning arrived. The three of them met with the pit crew, and their convoy set off for Santa Monica Pier and the insane hundred mile street race that would decide everything.

CHAPTER 30

The logistics of the Palisades street race took careful planning and a lot of time to solve. Los Angeles County spent an exorbitant amount of money, thanks in part to a generous fee paid by Mickey Blaze, to close off a twenty-mile section of California State Route 1 for the Open Circuit Challenge. To shut down the Pacific Coast Highway from Santa Monica Pier to Malibu was an unpopular decision among locals, but Los Angeles County sold the race to the public like it was the Super Bowl. As Fox sat in the pit area next to her car listening to the blaring loud music and thousands of cheering spectators out on the beach with falcons flying in her stomach, she knew that this event was as advertised.

Pyne pulled up a chair and sat down next to her. He was dressed in a light-colored polo and slacks. The mid-morning rays reflected off his sunglasses. A small curl of brown hair came down over his forehead.

"Lighten up, Fox. You're bringing down the team."

Fox was annoyed but also relieved that he teased her. "It's not too late for you to drive instead of me."

Pyne laughed. "Maybe the next one."

Fox considered that. "Can I ask you a question?"

"Of course."

"Why didn't you just do this all on your own? You already went rogue. In for a penny, in for a pound, you know?"

"There are several reasons, but I think the biggest one is that my supervisors were right about one thing: I'm too close to the case. Sharon deserved an unbiased investigator to bring her justice."

"What are some of the other reasons? If you don't mind me asking."

"I needed Solace's resources. I had the financing by dipping into my inheritance and, of course, being the Service's best card sharp through the years, but I wouldn't have spent the money properly. Your boss knew exactly how to budget the mission." He paused for a second and then started again. "Another reason is that, frankly, I needed an out in case the mission was a failure. It's not to say I don't have confidence in you, but because I went rogue, I needed one foot out the door. I hope you understand that."

"I understand. Don't worry."

"I knew you would." Pyne stood up from the chair. "I'll see you after the race. Try not to die out there."

A.C. entered the pit garage a moment later with a tablet in hand. She sat down in the chair that Pyne left behind. "I hate that we have to get under Mickey Blaze's skin one last time. We have solid evidence. There's no reason we should go through with this race."

Fox had been back and forth on this several times. "Normally I'd agree, but Blaze has too many powerful allies. Everything we have would just disappear. Our only choice is to keep humiliating her until she has no one to turn to except us." Fox studied her friend's face. "I know this is more than you signed up for, and I promise that after today I'll make sure Solace calls you back to the home office."

A.C. nodded and stood from the chair. She patted Fox on the shoulder and said, "Be ready in thirty minutes." She walked a few paces and stopped. She said, "Before I forget to tell you, there are a few items in your middle console that might come in handy, just in case."

Pre-race preparations ended as Fox loaded into the car and drove it from the pit area to the starting line and shut off the engine. Thanks to her qualifying time, she was in the twenty-second position. As she pulled her car to her starting zone, she looked over to see one of the brand-new Blaze race cars next to her. She looked over to see the hazel eyes and tanned face of Theseus Kastellanos. He snarled at Fox and closed the visor on his helmet. Up ahead, Fox saw Mickey Blaze's car in the third position. It was black with red trim, and Fox noticed the artistic marriage of modern design with inspiration from the 1953 Jaguar C-Type as Blaze had promised.

Fox watched the beachside and saw the spectators. Her nervousness was at an all-time high as the crowd reached a fever pitch ahead of the race starting. The announcer over the PA was deafening as he hyped up the crowd and announced that the officials would wave the green flag in two minutes. That's all the time Fox had left to calm her nerves. She let the moment get to her, and she had to remind herself that this was just a part of the mission. Don't focus on the danger, she thought. Don't focus on the crowd. Don't focus on anything except Mickey Blaze and putting on the show of a lifetime for her. I have to make her angrier than I did in Morocco.

A.C. came alive in Fox's helmet. "OK, three laps. Up to Malibu and back three times. Each lap is about thirty-four miles. Race should last between fifty minutes and an hour, depending on how fast the leaders carry the pack."

This was information that Fox already knew, but clearly A.C. was repeating the race details for herself more than Fox. The PA announcer shrieked into the microphone again, and the crowd let out an anticipatory cheer. And then, Fox heard the six words that signaled the point of no return.

"Ladies and gentlemen, start your engines!"

Fox turned the key and the Takahashi 72 roared to life. Hers was just one voice among the cacophony of American muscle cars and European sports cars that sang the ebullient melody that reverberated off the pavement. Fox kept her eyes on the tower above the street. A few seconds felt like a millennium as she waited for the signal, but it arrived. The green fabric appeared and whipped to and fro in the air, and all at once the line of athletic automobiles squealed and jolted forward.

The opening four miles of the Palisades street race was a straight-forward sprint from Santa Monica Pier along the beach until the road began to wind toward the west. As expected, Fox had virtually no room to make pass attempts during this stretch as the cars held identical speeds. She made subtle corrections with the wheel to maintain her course and follow the driver in front of her. Up ahead she could see the leaders picking up speed, and that increase worked its way toward the back as everyone gradually accelerated to match. Fox recognized the car at the front belonging to Luca Monreal, the driver with whom she kissed at Mickey Blaze's party. Blaze moved ahead of the driver in second position and now pulled even with Luca.

The ocean and beach shops whizzed out of view as quickly as they came into it. Fox checked the speedometer to see that they passed 90 mph and still pushed ahead. However, the driver in front of her was the epitome of defensive driving, racing not to lose rather than to win. Fox couldn't afford to stay in this position. She glanced to the side for the briefest of moments to see that Theseus Kastellanos was still right next to her.

A.C. spoke into the headset. "You're coming up on the first turn. You have maybe one minute to try and pass someone if you'd like to try it."

"On it."

Fox performed the maneuver, sidling up next to Theseus so that their cars were almost touching. Fox could imagine the disgusted look he must be giving her as she shifted and pulled ahead. The defensive driver's car slowly disappeared from her peripheral vision. Fox gazed at the spot and slipped in ahead. The front half of the pack began to create a small gap between itself and the stragglers. Fox accelerated and moved in with that pack. Another car came up in her peripheral vision. She looked and saw Theseus made the same move.

"Good job. First turn coming up in half a mile."

The initial veer west was gradual and allowed the drivers to maintain their speed as they used the momentum to carry them round toward the Pacific Palisades Beach on the coastline and the Palisades racetrack inland. Fox finished her turn and stared ahead at the westward blue skies, the mid-morning sun on top of them, and the dangerous cliffs that lie ahead on winding roads into Malibu.

Fox understood why A.C. pushed for the 72 last month as soon as the roads began their switchback motions around the cliffs. The car handled every movement with ease and hid Fox's shortage of racing experience. Meanwhile, the expensive, high-velocity sports cars fell back to Fox's position. The downside was that she had very little room to make any passing attempts, and she quickly learned how crucial it was to score a sufficient qualifying time during race week.

After a few miles of hard-braking and drifting, followed by quick bursts into football-field-length straightaways, Theseus cut around and zipped through an opening to pass ahead of two cars in front of him. Fox wondered if he and his friends had a trap set for her up ahead. It was likely that he was luring her to follow him, but she took the bait anyway and made her move. If it was a trap, then she was ready to counter it.

This was the most difficult racing maneuver that Fox had attempted in her short stint driving, but every action from here on out would be more dangerous than the last. The opponents in front of her went wide on a turn and attempted to drift back into position. Fox jerked the steering wheel the other way and went under them. She shifted and accelerated, zipping by four drivers ahead of her. She didn't finish it clean, however. A hard thud followed by the unmistakable crunch of metal snapped her to the side. Fox kept the car's balance and accelerated ahead. She moved into position ahead of those four cars to complete the action and catch up to the Theseus.

"I saw the sparks on that one," A.C. commented. "Street camera had a great view of it."

Fox heard low muttering in her headset.

A.C. then said, "Harry says nice move."

The pack stayed fairly the same for the remaining stretch of road to Malibu. The drivers zoomed past Malibu Pier that jutted out from the beach into the ocean. They then climbed slightly in elevation and moved inland away from the beaches, driving past Pepperdine University and then back toward the coastline through a row of seafood restaurants and shops that were ultra-protected by the barricades surrounding the street race course. Then, multiple signs appeared above the street warning that the drivers were approaching the loop back to Santa Monica Pier.

"Is this just like how we practiced in Rochester?" Fox asked.

"You got it. Hard brakes and a smooth burst on the other side to slingshot the car through the turn."

It was one thing to perfect the technique on a practice course with no other vehicles on the road. This was something else altogether. Fox watched the leaders increase in size exponentially in her windshield, and she realized she was coming in too hot. The turn looked awkward compared to the perfectly symmetrical racetrack in upstate New York, but there was no time to doubt herself. Fox hit the brakes just as she practiced and wheeled around, feeling the tires underneath her peel away on the pavement. The cliff at this point of the highway was at its highest point, and Fox could practically look out her window down into the sea with the waves slapping against the jagged rocks. She continued the turn and noticed Theseus had matched her as the two were locked in a bit of a drift dance. Fox found her marks, shifted, and hit the gas out of the turn. The 72 sprang forward with the momentum, and Fox was back on a straight path, this time headed east with the ocean and westward track to her right-hand side.

This game of passing and falling behind continued with only some movement for the remainder of the first lap as the cars returned to Santa Monica Pier. Fox and Theseus challenged each other. Occasional glances to each other's windows were met with increases in speed and passing attempts until finally the two of them had moved up into the top twelve. That's when the madness started.

Fox curiously watched Theseus' movements. They never wavered from hers. Was this the trap she suspected?

"What is he waiting for?"

"I might know," A.C. said. "You have two Blaze cars on your rear."

Fox peered at her driver's side mirror and saw one. She looked to the passenger side mirror and saw the other. Theseus glanced at his two driving comrades, and he motioned directions. Fox saw the signs that signaled the turn back toward the starting line. More spread out now than they were in Malibu, each driver made fluid turns as they raced past the screaming spectators at Santa Monica Pier and onto the beginning of the second lap. Fox saw the three Blaze vehicles attempting their formation again.

Rhiannon Misrasi's warning over the television became crystal clear. Fox shifted and pushed the 72 to its limits. The RPM needle twitched in the red zone, and Fox soared ahead.

CHAPTER 31

The three-headed Blaze monster of Theseus Kastellanos, Bill Curraway, and Timothy Charles was hardly fazed by the burst of speed. All three drivers' muscle cars exploded from their original positions. They whirled around opponents, and they moved into the top ten positions with Fox just as the road veered west toward Malibu. Fox could practically smell the exhaust coming from the leaders now. Luca Monreal maintained his small lead ahead of Mickey Blaze. Fox imagined the television broadcast going bananas for that potential photo finish.

They lined up for a standard team passing maneuver. Curraway brought his car directly behind Fox as Kastellanos came up on the driver's side. Kastellanos forced Fox into the farthest right as he accelerated forward. Charles followed him closely to keep Fox on the right-hand side of the road. Meanwhile, Curraway matched Fox's movements to thwart any potential escape routes, and Kastellanos accelerated ahead and slid his car over to create the box.

Blaze's racers trapped Fox at the front, rear, and driver's sides, and the barricade trapped Fox on the passenger side. What was the end game here? Did Blaze really think Fox was that much of a threat on the racecourse? Was this some kind of punishment for halting the diamond payoff? Either way, Blaze's team had played its card, and sticking to the cover didn't matter anymore.

"A.C., it's time for you and Pyne to get out of here. Things are about to get messy. I'll catch up with you in a few hours."

"Are you sure?"

"Yes, go!"

Fox heard A.C. say something to Pyne away from the microphone. She came into Fox's ear and said, "OK, we're on our way out. Stay safe."

The winding cliffside roads appeared at once, and Fox was done being careful around them. She weaved and clipped Timothy Charles more than once, and she nudged at Kastellanos' bumper when the road straightened. Fox looked over at Charles on her left-hand side, and the driver looked at her. He steadied his car with one hand and reached down for something at his dashboard. There was no mistaking the next motion. Fox had seen it before, the flick of the wrist and the instant flash. Instinct took over in that moment as she ducked while keeping her hands firm in place on the wheel. The high pitch of a ricochet jutted against her window frame followed by a spark.

Fox smiled underneath her helmet. "It's about time."

She tapped the brakes for a brief drop in speed, falling backward and colliding into Curraway's car at the rear. This jolt of momentum surged her forward as she accelerated and rammed into the backside of Kastellanos' car. In the rearview mirror, Fox briefly saw Curraway lose control and break formation. Kastellanos, on the other hand, corrected himself and kept his position. The opening was miniscule, likely leading to some damage to the vehicles around her, but the rules had been thrown out the window. She just needed another push from Curraway. She waited until the driver got himself back into the box formation, and Fox repeated her first motion. Curraway hit her car much harder this time and he spun out of control toward the middle of the pack. Fox accelerated tenfold into the back of Kastellanos. This time, Kastellanos couldn't keep the grip as his car spun. Fox expertly dodged the spinning car and saw her brief window of opportunity. She zoomed through that new lane she created and watched the chaos erupt behind her.

Kastellanos collided with Charles, and the two of them then created a logjam. The mid-position racers slowed and looked for paths around the stopped cars. But just as Fox began to celebrate to herself that she might catch the leaders and beat Mickey Blaze at her own game, the Blaze muscle cars emerged from the pack. Scraped and dented more than they were before, Blaze's drivers looked all the more menacing than they did prior, like monsters in a dungeon.

Fox had pushed the Takahashi 72 to its limit already. Without A.C. in her ear to guide her, there was no way to know how much more the 72 could take at maximum RPM. She eased off the throttle as she wound her way around more cliffs until she came to the point on the track where the highway veered away from the beaches and passed the university and tourism-trap restaurants in Malibu. The Blaze racers gained on her. She knew the next confrontation was inevitable. The three of them would try to kill her again, and there would be no showmanship of a formation this time. They would get it done swiftly, and there would be a messy cleanup required.

She lost track of which one was which, but based on the damage of each vehicle, she guessed that it was Curraway coming up from behind just as he did the first time. One of the cars moved in close to Curraway, and an arm appeared in the windowsill. Fox recognized the slender frame anywhere. It was Theseus Kastellanos. He brandished a pistol, identical to the one Charles just shot at Fox. In fact, Fox checked the other side-view mirror and saw that Charles used Curraway's cover as a disguise, as well. He brandished the same pistol, aiming it from the driver's side toward the passenger window at an angle so he targeted the 72. So, this was how they would finish the job, Fox thought. Multiple gunshots light up the interior of the car. They wait until my car loses control as confirmation that I'd been hit. Wonderful.

The beaches vanished and were replaced with city driving. Pepperdine University came into view just as Kastellanos and Charles pulled the triggers on their pistols. The ricochets off the 72's exterior sounded like a war zone. Fox had no choice but to push the 72 to its limits yet again, completely unsure of whether the car could hold up under the pressure. She merged into the lane in front of Kastellanos, shifted, and gassed with all her might as the little budget race car scampered toward the leaders. Fox threw caution to the wind as she drifted corners like a maniac, scorching the tires and nearly colliding with the barricades on either side. She zipped past the university and into the brief canyon that spat her out onto the coastline once again. She saw the figures of the leaders up ahead as they slowed down to twist through the beach streets. Fox continued her pace, well aware that one wrong move could end with her crashing like a great ball of fire into a seafood restaurant. Her aggressors inched closer from behind. When would their bullets fly again?

The 72 screamed at her. It rattled against the RPM pressure that Fox had applied. She pleaded with the car to hang in there just a bit longer. It was sufficient evidence that Fox never stood a chance at winning this race. Sobeit. It was time to throw away Juliana Ferreira completely and let Jett Fox do her job.

Fox let off the gas to fall back. She attempted to break the formation and get the drivers distracted from the road. They climbed toward the highest cliff, and it was only a matter of moments until they'd have to hard brake and turn back to Santa Monica. If Fox could force them onto the service road before that point, then she was confident these three drivers wouldn't give her any trouble for the rest of the race.

She opened the middle console to find the "just in case" items that A.C. left behind for her. She looked in and saw the secret items from her handbag: the throwing knife, smoke grenades, and Beretta. She eyed the pistol and shook her head. That would be the last resort. Still, there was a voice inside her that beckoned her to use it first. How many times could Blaze and her goons try to kill her before she'd had enough? Did this meet the criteria that Fox required before she allowed herself to use lethal force? And even if it did, was it worth the sleepless nights to kill again? Fox shook off the thought as Charles and Kastellanos drove up from the sides with Curraway at the rear. She opted for the throwing knife. She saw the front tire of Charles' car in her sideview mirror.

Traveling at more than 100 mph on a dangerous beach cliff while also trying to keep her focus on the three race cars around her, Fox doubted her ability to cause any serious damage with a throwing knife aimed at the tire. She waited for the precise moment, keeping her eyes on the road in front of her while also watching Charles' car creep up in her peripherals. Kastellanos came up from the other end, and the trick here was to attack Charles before Charles attacked her while also avoiding the gunfire of Theseus on the other side.

Fox struck first as planned. She snapped her wrist and flung the throwing knife at the tire of Timothy Charles' car. The pop was unmistakable. The knife collided with the rubber and clambered into the spoke. The hubcap and wheel gobbled the knife, and there was a definitive explosion of air. The driver lost control. It was at that moment that Fox ducked. Theseus fired his gun from the other side, and Fox's quick movement narrowly protected her. Charles' car collided with the 72 and then ricocheted into the barricade before stopping at once. Fox darted from the middle lane into the spot previously occupied by Charles. She eased off the gas again as Curraway pulled ahead. He attempted to slow as well to keep Fox in his windshield, but she slipped back into the middle position so that both Theseus and Curraway were in front of her.

The two Blaze drivers accelerated and parted toward either barricade. Fox sensed they were luring her into the middle section again. She didn't take the bait. Instead, she matched their speeds and veered into Curraway's lane. She split them up, just as she planned. However, Theseus Kastellanos crossed from his side and pulled up behind Fox. They had her in another box, but this time there wasn't a third driver to keep her in. Just what she wanted! Fox maximized the RPMs again and slipped away from the new box. But, she realized why Theseus moved behind her. They arrived at the hard-brake turn!

Fox slammed on her brakes with a horrendous squeal. She drifted the 72 less than graciously, but her recovery was impeccable. The car jolted out of the turn for the return trip to Santa Monica. She officially completed half of the race and did not die.

Concentration on the course abruptly ended as Theseus Kastellanos and Bill Curraway continued their attempts to kill Jett Fox. They operated across the multiple-lane highway to set up a new trap. Fox gathered herself and saw an opening where she could slip to one side of Curraway with Theseus on the other side of him. She wasted no time in driving the 72 into that position. She glanced over to the two drivers. They looked at each other, and Fox imagined the panicked expression underneath their two helmets as they scrambled to change tactics. Fox grinned to herself and snatched a smoke grenade from the middle console. She triggered it and tossed it into Curraway's car.

The flash and pop may have been enough to end Curraway's day, but the smoke that followed led the race car driver into an all-out twist and turn. Curraway slammed the front of his car into the barricade and circled like a fidget spinner until coming to a complete stop.

Two down and one to go. The last one was the man who had become her sub-adversary since meeting Mickey Blaze. Fox picked up speed as she crept up alongside his vehicle. How should she play this? Theseus Kastellanos tried to kill her in her sleep. He threatened her the next day when he discovered she wasn't dead. And it all started with Fox outsmarting him in Casablanca by stealing the loaded dice and humiliating Mickey Blaze. There was only one man who wanted Jett Fox dead just as much as Blaze did. It was Theseus Kastellanos. The next confrontation could end only one way. Fox exhaled slowly as she kept her focus on the racecourse. She slipped open the middle console and gripped the Beretta.

CHAPTER 32

The two adversaries kept their distance from each other for the time being. They watched the stragglers coming up the track from the other side. The stragglers were out of the running for a top ten finish, and they were fighting over the scrap prize money. Jett Fox and Theseus Kastellanos, on the other hand, were looking at top ten finishes if results stayed as they were. They drove like it for several miles. Fox needed respite from the stretch that saw Bill Curraway and Timothy Charles make sudden exits from the race, and she guessed that Theseus needed the same. He just watched Fox eliminate two of his comrades from the chess board, and she didn't have to kill either of them. One could only imagine what she had in store for the man that released a viper into her hotel room as she slept. Of course, this was all speculation on Fox's part. For all she knew, Theseus had another trick or two up his sleeve, but this section of the racecourse wasn't the appropriate place to unleash those tricks.

Fox placed the pistol in an easy-to-reach position so that she was ready to use it, if necessary. The two competitors came upon the southbound bend toward

Santa Monica Pier, and Fox slowly increased her speed. The high density of spectators on this portion of the track provided some form of relief to Fox. She could outpace Theseus on this beach stretch and make one last run at the leaders. She might even distract Mickey Blaze just enough to cost her the race. Fox accepted that she had no chance of winning, but the next best thing was to cost the hometown hero a victory in her glorious return to the sport.

It was settled. Fox forced the 72 forward. She rocketed ahead of Theseus, and she saw that he watched her closely. He propelled his own car to keep pace. They bolted south on the Pacific Coast Highway with the spectators coming to life. Fox felt an unusual excitement coming from her window as she listened to the crowd erupt. She saw the leaders coming back up the northbound track. Luca Monreal and Mickey Blaze were neck and neck. So, at the start of the final lap, the two favorites to win the race led the pack, and the crowd anticipated a thrilling finish.

Fox reached the end of the straightaway and found her mark for the hard brake. She looped the turn and shifted with such ease that it was a shame A.C. wasn't on the other end of her headset anymore for Fox to brag about it. She pressed her foot onto the pedal gradually and watched the RPM needle. The 72 could only take so much more.

"OK, girl, whatever you have left, it's time to use it," Fox said to the car that she had grown to love over the past few weeks.

Jetting northbound along the beach, Fox spotted the leaders in the distance. They were far ahead but catching them wasn't out of the question. However, she knew the Takahashi 72 might die in the process. She checked the rearview mirror. Theseus was right behind her. He had the superior car, and it wouldn't take much for him to pull even with her. Whatever he had planned, he was saving it for later.

Fox gained considerable ground on the leaders as she approached the westbound bend toward Malibu. The slingshot effect that she experienced in the first two laps carried her forward again as she shot ahead. The 72 rattled like a cage against the pressure of the RPMs. The road began to wind to and fro around the cliffs. No slowing down, Fox thought. She drifted around the corners like a maniac. The tires screeched in agony with each turn. Even Theseus fell back at the turns, unwilling to face the dangerous cliffs the same way.

The car in sixth position was in plain view now. Fox could actually attempt a pass on a world-class racer! Fox threw out everything Harry Pyne and A.C. had taught her about race etiquette. She no longer cared. She crept behind the European sports car and waited for it to hard brake on the next beach cliff. The driver followed the racing textbook and took the inside lane with a hard brake that pulled the car to the outside barricade. Fox took this as an opportunity to pass multiple cars at once. She accelerated into the turn rather than braking. She zipped through the cliffside at an incredible pace, passing the sixth and fifth drivers and clipping the front side of the fourth-place driver before pulling ahead of them. Whoever was driving the fourth-place car was likely livid about Fox's antics, but she cared little about that now. This was the first and last race of her career. And in shocking fashion, she and her Takahashi 72 were now in fourth place.

Then, more surprises followed as Theseus Kastellanos matched Fox's dangerous maneuver stride for stride. He bumped sides with the driver that was formerly in sixth place and then burst ahead of the same three cars that Fox passed. His Blaze car roared behind her and gained ground at a rapid rate. He was ready to execute his final plan for taking Fox out of the race.

Fox noticed the three drivers in front of her and that she wasn't gaining enough ground to catch Blaze. Barring some miraculous driving by the rest of the field, they would finish in the top three. It was no use to continue chasing Blaze, and Fox turned her attention to Theseus. It became clear what this confrontation with Blaze's henchman represented. If Fox survived whatever happened next, that was her ticket to a final meeting with Blaze and a chance to arrest her.

Theseus pulled even with Fox and matched her speed. Fox wasted no time in kicking off the next batch of fireworks. She jerked her wheel and whacked her car against his. Theseus gifted her with the same slam. He hit her much harder, and the 72 began to rattle worse than it had before. Theseus lifted his pistol with Fox briefly dazed by the collision. She noticed the gun just in time and ducked to the side. Bullets pinged off the car. Fox snapped up and aimed the Beretta at Theseus. She pulled the trigger three times, but Theseus' reflexes rivaled Fox's reflexes. He got himself out of the line of fire from her shots. They went through another round of this. Fox kept track of the ammunition in her head. She had four shots left in the Beretta.

They both jerked the wheels of their cars at the same time and collided with each other again. That was a big one, and Fox felt the Takahashi 72 tearing at the seams. The car rattled, and she saw smoke coming from underneath the hood. It was only a matter of time before it gave out. Bail from the race, now! Fox thought. Next service road. Get out while you still can. Live to fight another day!

It was too late. She lost control of the car while battling Theseus. The man with the lizard frame took three more shots at her with his gun. Two of them ricocheted off the car. The third one hit the hood, which flew open in and blocked Fox's view through the windshield. Out of sheer desperation, Fox aimed the Beretta out the window and saw Theseus' front tire. She pulled the trigger, and then everything became distorted in a rolling motion. The windshield shattered, the hood ripped away, and Fox watched the world spin in front of her like an astronaut floating through space. She couldn't pinpoint anything in the chaos. The images passed her far too rapidly.

After what seemed like a lifetime, the world stopped spinning. Fox stared out the gaping hole in the car that used to be her windshield. Steam floated through the air from her own engine. She noticed Theseus' car was in front of her. Black smoke and flames rose from his vehicle. Was he still inside? Was he dead? Fox felt a surge of adrenaline. She should save him, even though they both tried to kill each other. The smoke and flames would be the signal for the rescue team. Any minute now, the wreck would be on national television, if it wasn't already. It took a full minute for it to register with Fox exactly what happened, but she recalled the wreck. The two of them flipped their vehicles end over end, crashing through the barricade. Theseus had obviously taken the worst of it judging by the state of his vehicle. Fox realized she was lucky to be alive and not toppled over a cliff. The alarms went off in her head. Over a cliff!

There was a scrape at the undercarriage, and the car skipped backwards a beat. Fox panicked inwardly. She maintained control on the outside as she peered out the window. She saw the slope. The Takahashi 72 hung to the edge of the cliff ever so slightly. She heard the waves crashing against the rocks down below. She guessed that it was a fifty-foot drop to the ocean. She carefully moved her foot over the brake and pressed down.

Cliffside escapes, Fox thought, what did she know? She already did the first part. She held the brake in place. Next step was to secure the emergency brake. Please don't be fried from all the drifting during the race, Fox pleaded with the emergency brake. She cranked the handbrake, and it held in place firmly. She slowly let off the foot brake, and the handbrake still kept the car in place. She sighed. She raced through the steps in her head. Next, she needed to shift the center of gravity. Fox removed her racing helmet. It was the first time she noticed how much she was sweating, as droplets trinkled from her scalp down her neck. Her forehead was soaked. She gently placed the helmet outside the shattered windshield onto the uncovered engine. She then leaned forward and gently pressed the button to unlock her safety harnesses. The car held strong. Finally, she planned her escape from the car. It was too dangerous to climb through the shattered windshield onto the searing hot engine. Her best bet was to climb out her driver's side window onto the patch of dirt right next to her.

Fox saw the Beretta on the passenger side floor. Did she dare to reach for it? She sighed. It was best not to risk it with the car hanging to the cliff. The car jolted backward again as Fox remained absolutely still. The 72 was losing its grip, and Fox had to get out. She left the gun behind. She climbed out of the driver's side window torso first and saw two helicopters approaching from the direction of Santa Monica Pier. One appeared to be a medical chopper, and the other had the Sporting Times Network logo plastered onto the side of it. Fox wedged her legs through the window, and the car jolted again. Fox clasped the roof. The car wasn't stopping. Fox swore aloud, something she rarely did. She planted her feet and jumped without thinking. The 72 fell backward completely as Fox sailed into the air. She reached for the cliffside in a desperate heave with her long wingspan. Her fingers latched onto a rock and gripped. Her body rammed against the cliffside. She felt the pain lurch through her, but she steadied herself. She hung on. The crash of metal against rock echoed up the wall, which was followed by a heavy splash into the ocean.

Fox found her footing and climbed. All those hours in the gym paid off for this very specific moment, apparently. Had she trained her body any less rigorously, she would likely be in the Pacific Ocean right now with the Takahashi 72. She pulled herself up over the side and rolled into the dirt. She peered briefly back over the cliff at the car in the ocean below.

"Sayonara, 72," she said.

Fox got to her feet and looked in the direction of the inferno. But not only did she see the flaming car, she also saw a man standing in front of it, gun drawn and helmet off. It was Theseus Kastellanos. He was seemingly unscathed from the wreck. Rage filled the bloodshot hazel eyes as he aimed the gun at Fox.

Suddenly, she *really* wished she grabbed the Beretta from the car.

"Put the gun down, Theseus," Fox said. She motioned toward the sky. "News helicopter."

"Imagine how little that means to me. Going to jail for Mickey Blaze is part of my job. She'll have me out and with a new identity in six months." Theseus smirked in a way that made Fox extra uncomfortable. "Do you really think my name is Theseus Kastellanos? It's just another alias in a long line of them. An alias like your own, *Juliana Ferreira*. Both of our names die today."

"Suit yourself."

Fox anticipated the gunshot with perfect precision as she rolled forward onto the ground. Theseus fired the gun, and the bullet sailed off somewhere into the sea. Fox leapt from the dirt and barreled toward Theseus just as the assassin whirled the gun back in her direction. He never got the shot off. Fox tackled him to the ground, and Theseus lost his handle on the gun. It skittered away. He responded with a vicious elbow to her skull. Fox's vision blurred momentarily as Theseus shoved her away and got up to his knees. He scrambled toward the gun, but Fox grabbed a hold of his shoe. She brought him back down. Theseus turned with a kick, and Fox blocked just in time. However, Theseus struck with such force that Fox's forearm collapsed upon the blow.

Fox rolled away and got back to her feet. Theseus did the same. The gun was behind him, well out of Fox's distance to reach it, but she also knew that Theseus couldn't afford the opening it would give to Fox if he tried to reach for it. This fight would be settled with hand-to-hand combat.

Theseus lunged first with his fists, but Fox assumed a textbook defensive stance and parried the strikes. She retaliated with kicks to his legs, attempting to break down the assassin's base. They carried this back and forth for a short time, and Fox became aware of the strategy. Theseus had backed her toward the cliff edge. Running out of room, Fox darted forward with a feint. Theseus took the bait and guarded the high area. Fox connected with a blow to his gut. This opened him up, and Fox kept up the pressure with two clubbing blows to his face. Blood gushed from Theseus' mouth as Fox made the second hit. He staggered backward and defended. Fox turned to her strengths: her legs. She whipped up high with her right leg toward Theseus' head. He blocked and countered with a fist to her face. She blocked and turned with a back kick at his chest. He got his guard up in time with a block as the two found themselves fighting near the edge of the cliff.

Fox had shifted the fight so that the sea was to their sides instead of at her back. The two helicopters got closer. No doubt they could see the inferno at Theseus' car and would soon see the two undercover agents trying to kill each other.

Theseus attacked from the side as he attempted to push her back in the direction of the cliff. Fox kept her footing and ducked the attack. She countered with a strike to the gut and follow-up punch to the face. Theseus staggered. Now was her chance to end this. Fox followed with more pressure and kept the assassin backpedaling. She struck at the weak points in his legs. She heard his knee pop as she connected with a stabbing kick. Theseus shrieked. Fox whirled for another back kick. This one struck the side of his head with a wet crunch. More blood gushed as Theseus toppled to the cliff's edge. Fox hesitated.

"Surrender, Theseus. It's over."

Bloodied and bruised, Theseus stared at Fox with death in his eyes. He leapt at her one last time, howling like a demon from hell. Fox reacted instinctively with a lunging kick to Theseus' chest. The assassin whipped backwards. Fox reached out to catch him, but it was too late. Theseus toppled over the cliff. Fox watched the body skid against the rocks and slam into the water. It was a survivable fall of fifty feet if he hadn't smacked against the rocks and if the water were still like a lake. But the beating waves punished the motionless body with a merciless crash into the cliffside over and over again. Theseus was dead.

Fox felt the effects of the last twenty minutes catching up to her. Her body was sore from the car wreck, even if she didn't initially feel any damage. The strikes she took from Theseus ached. She touched her head where Theseus elbowed her. There was a small trickle of blood. She lay back on the dirt and waited for the helicopters.

Wait, bad idea, Fox thought. She needed to escape the scene. Fox stumbled onto all fours and looked for a place to hide. But it was no use. The medical chopper arrived and landed thirty yards from the inferno. Three men disembarked the chopper with a stretcher and other medical equipment and ran toward the flaming car. Another group rushed to Fox with a stretcher of its own. She stood up, and one of the medical personnel spoke.

"Try not to walk, Miss Ferreira. Here, on the stretcher."

"I don't need a stretcher. I'm fine."

"Where's your car?"

Fox pointed at the ocean. They looked at the cliff's edge, and then they looked at the inferno as the men used fire extinguishers.

"Come with us."

Fox didn't want to, but it would be far worse to escape with the news chopper in the air than it was to go with the medical crew. She'd need to figure out an escape at the hospital and then pick her moment. Maybe Pyne and A.C. were thinking of a plan at the very moment to spring her out. Mickey Blaze would go to ground after this catastrophe of a day. There was nothing she could give the press yet that would truly put an end to this. Going with the medical crew was the more dangerous option, but it was the only option that gave her a shot to catch Blaze before she disappeared forever.

"His body isn't in here!" The man that shouted referred to Theseus Kastellanos as he and the others tamed the fire. They turned to Fox.

"Did you see where he went?"

Fox shook her head and did her best to play up her injuries. "Sorry."

The medical crew escorted Fox to the helicopter. The door shut and the helicopter lifted into the air.

"Here, take this."

Fox turned to the man who spoke to her, but before she could protest, the man forced a wet towel over her mouth and nose. Fox struggled for a moment as she breathed in the innocuous substance that was on the towel. Her vision went dark.

CHAPTER 33

Vision blurry and head throbbing, Fox's senses returned to her. She woke up from whatever had happened on that helicopter. She remembered the man placing the wet towel over her face. What was that? Chloroform? Most likely. Her vision straightened and she noticed she was in a medium-sized room, no larger than her apartment's living room and kitchen put together. There was almost nothing in the room except for a television in the corner and a steel chair a few paces in front of her. She tried to move, but something restrained her. She looked to see her arms chained above her head to the ceiling. Her feet were secured to the ground with chains around her ankles. She rattled the restraints. She had very little movement. She also noticed that she was stripped down to minimal clothing, wearing only the black track pants and white tank top that she wore underneath the racing jumpsuit.

The door opened at the far end. Mickey Blaze stepped inside. Of course, Fox thought. Even the medical team was on her payroll. They drugged her and brought her to Blaze after the race. On one hand, Fox was a little scared. On the other hand, this was finally the one-on-one meeting Fox had been hoping to get with Blaze all this time. She had only hoped Blaze was the one chained up, and not the other way around.

Blaze sat in the chair. She was dressed in a white business suit with a black shirt underneath the jacket. She crossed one leg over the other casually and sat back, staring daggers at Fox. The two remained silent. Fox was the guest, and she had no intention of speaking first. The two women simply stared at each other in awkward silence. Finally, Blaze was the one who spoke first.

"I really wish you hadn't killed poor Theseus," Blaze said.

"At least he made a splash before it was over."

Blaze's expression sharpened. She did *not* appreciate the pun. She rose from the chair and moved to Fox. She clasped her by the shoulders and drove her knee into Fox's gut. She groaned. Unable to protect herself, the stiff knee sent shockwaves through her. It connected harder than any strike she received from Theseus earlier. Blaze returned to the chair and sat down.

"We have a lot to talk about, Miss Fox, so let's move along," Blaze said. "First, you'll be happy to know that *Juliana Ferreira* was taken to a local medical facility following the car wreck. She'll be fine, but she has some serious legal troubles ahead of her once the cops track her down."

Fox still reeled from the knee strike, but she let out a labored chuckle. "Let me guess. The police found Theseus washed up on the rocks."

Blaze said nothing. She turned to the television in the corner and clicked the remote. It flashed onto the Sporting Times Network and a recap of the Open Circuit Challenge. "Turmoil at the Palisades" was the headline on the screen. The broadcasters discussed the death of Theseus Kastellanos, the high number of wrecks on the track, and whether Mickey Blaze's reputation was ruined following this race despite her incredible second-place finish in her first race since coming out of injury retirement. Fox heard the result and used that as another dig she could make at Blaze.

"Ouch, second place? Luca Monreal finished the job, did he?"

Blaze exploded from the chair again and struck with a clubbing punch to the other side of Fox's gut. Fox grunted again. That punch hurt almost as much as the knee strike. Sweat formed at her brow, she spat blood onto the concrete floor. Fox was in incredible physical shape, but even the most chiseled soldier could only handle so much strain from unprotected body strikes like this. Blaze went back to her chair and shut off the television.

"Who sent you?" Blaze asked. "Who do you work for?"

Fox struggled through her words. "You… wouldn't be… lieve me if I… told you."

"I'm sure I have an idea," Blaze said as she crossed her leg casually over the other again. "You're a freelancer hired by MI6. One of their agents turned up dead in Morocco, and they suspected that I killed the agent. They sent you to investigate me, and they hoped that by sending an American it would throw me off. It worked to some degree. That is, until you showed up in California this week. How am I doing?"

"Close enough."

"There's a problem with my story," Blaze said. "I own MI6. I told them to drop this investigation, and it seemed I was getting my way. So no, I don't think you're working for them. No, you're working for someone else. A rogue agent, perhaps? Yes, that's it. A rogue agent named Harry Pyne."

Fox's heart sank. Blaze noticed the concern cross Fox's face.

"Don't bother hiding it, Jett. I captured your friends before I captured you. How fun it was for me to go fishing and catch an MI6 agent and his little engineer girlfriend. Of course, I recognized him immediately. He was your partner in the craps game. Very clever. I'm guessing the agent that died in Morocco was his friend? He went rogue and hired you to look into me, yes? Anyway, a quick check-in with my MI6 contacts got me his whole dossier. The engineer girlfriend was a little harder to pinpoint, but that's because I was looking in the wrong places. Once I checked social media, I learned all about *her*. Social media made it a lot harder to be a spy, wouldn't you agree?" Blaze sighed. "The three of you have caused me a lot of problems this week, and I'll make sure you get a nice receipt for your efforts."

"Where are they?"

"You'll see them in a minute," Blaze said. "I wanted to talk to you alone. I want to know everything you know about my operation."

It seemed pointless to carry on the charade. Blaze was going to kill her no matter what. But, she had one question on her mind that she wanted answered before she cooperated.

"Tell me something, first," Fox said. "Did you kill Sharon Graham?"

Blaze remained silent for a moment and simply stared at Fox. Was she having an inner monologue struggle just like Fox?

"Yes, I did," Blaze said. "But grow up and stop looking at it as murder, Jett. Sharon Graham is a casualty of war."

"Whatever helps you sleep at night. The way I see it, you had the motive to kill her, the means to do it, and the opportunity presented itself in Casablanca. That's murder."

"And what would you call your stunt at the Palisades today? You had the motive to kill Theseus after everything he did, you had the means to do it with your abilities as a trained operative, and the opportunity presented itself after your fantastic car crash."

Fox refused to dignify that claim with a response. She knew the kill was self-defense. There was no point arguing its validity to Blaze. Although, the regret of taking another's life was difficult to bear, and Blaze made an interesting point about Fox's rivalry with Theseus. The guilt was there, buried underneath Fox's loyalty to justice for Sharon Graham. She would eventually have to face herself in the mirror about killing Theseus just as she did the first time she killed. Perhaps there was some comfort in how Fox felt in that moment. She felt remorse despite the kill being justified.

Blaze changed the subject. "I'll ask you again. What do you know about my operation?"

Fox considered. "Can I get a glass of water?"

Blaze burst from the chair a third time. She wound her arm and followed through with a stiff punch across Fox's jaw. The taste of blood filled Fox's mouth once again. She spat.

"It seems like you already know everything," Fox said. "Why do you need to talk to me?"

Blaze paced back and forth. "Covering my bases, I guess. And maybe I'm intrigued by you. How can a private citizen with no military or government training have such a wide range of skills and resources? Your boss must be remarkable and someone I should get to know. I suspected you were the one sent to investigate me, but you handled yourself with such finesse that I was only ninety percent sure. I poked and prodded.

Theseus thought of a more direct approach with the rattlesnake. A bit barbaric for my taste, but I was curious if you could get out of that one. The craps game in Casablanca, racing at the Palisades… you are quite the accomplished lady. Jane Austen would be impressed."

Fox stifled a laugh. She was in a lot of pain. "Like I said, you already have me figured out. Why this little meeting?"

"You tell me," Blaze said. "You've gone to great lengths to embarrass me. Isn't this little meeting what *you* wanted?"

"You got me there."

"So speak."

"I don't know anything else. I stopped the diamond drop, but that was pure luck. I don't know where your diamonds come from, and I don't know who's receiving them." Fox paused and laughed. "Well, except for the idiots on the yacht."

Blaze punched Fox in the gut three more times. The air left Fox's lungs as she gasped desperately. It took several minutes for Fox to regain her facilities. She wondered about internal injuries, but hopefully her rock-solid body could hold up under pressure a little while longer. However, she knew that couldn't take too many more of those.

Blaze clutched Fox by the jaw. Fox resisted.

"Keep joking around and I'll keep hurting you."

Blaze released her with a shove. The chains rattled. Fox waited until she had got the air back into her lungs before she spoke.

"I don't know anything else, and that's the truth," Fox said. "I'd be happy to guess what you're doing, if you'd prefer."

Blaze sat down and pulled the chair closer to Fox. "OK then. Let's hear it."

"You're connected at the top level of multiple governments," Fox said. "That much is clear. You'd have to be to call off the investigation of a murdered MI6 agent. They consider killing their agents an act of war. However, you're not the shot caller of your organization. You're middle management. This crime syndicate to which you belong needs financing in any form. They use your racing team to get that financing. You smuggle a little bit of everything. Right now, it happens to be diamonds, but it's not your exclusive export. Maybe it's drugs. Maybe it's counterfeit cash. It doesn't matter what it is. You go around the world to these different racetracks, and that gives you the access you need to move your exports. Right now, I'm guessing you have a diamond mine somewhere nearby, and the plan was to move as many of the diamonds as possible to your syndicate's allies. However, you didn't count on Sharon Graham. She threw a wrench in the plans. And you especially didn't count on Harry Pyne going rogue and hiring me. Now, you're scrambling.

Your superiors are angry, and you're running out of time to fix all of this."

One side of Blaze's mouth turned upward for a half smile. "I'm impressed. You really don't disappoint, Jett Fox. It's a shame I didn't discover you sooner. Someone with your aptitude would make an amazing partner." Blaze's eyebrows went up. "I *do* have a job opening thanks to you. What do you say? Join me?"

"International crime isn't really my thing."

"Isn't it, though? Think about it. You've committed more than a few crimes in your efforts to keep tabs on me. You're harboring a rogue British agent. You violated my privacy when you cloned my phone. You carried concealed weapons without a concealed weapons permit. You fabricated a social security number to enter my race. You practiced vigilante justice when you made those arrests at the beach. And, of course, you killed Theseus Kastellanos."

Was she right? Had Fox crossed the line in her efforts to get Blaze's attention? Melancholy settled over her. She didn't believe she had done anything wrong, but that didn't mean she hadn't. What a twist that would be! This whole time Fox thought she was the hero. But what if she was actually the villain?

Fox shook off the thought. She was the one chained up in some windowless room and getting beaten to a pulp by Mickey Blaze. Screw her and her mind games, Fox thought. This interrogation was over. Fox thought only about her friends and how to rescue them. But first, she had to rescue herself. Easier said than done. She made one last plea to Blaze's conscience.

"Blaze, turn yourself in," Fox said. "We both know you're not the one giving the orders. Someone forced you to kill Sharon Graham, yes? Turn yourself in, and I'll vouch for you. I'll convince the feds to give you a lighter sentence. Testify against your superiors."

Blaze shook her head. "It's too late for that. If you have nothing useful to give to me, then it's time for me to kill you and your friends."

That was that. Fox sighed. An improbable escape attempt was the only card she had left to play. Blaze went to great lengths to keep Fox from performing any heroic feats. If she could somehow get one hand free from the cuffs, then maybe she could work her magic with a piece of broken metal. Or maybe she could get Blaze to voluntarily remove her from the shackles. That one seemed unlikely.

"When I asked for a glass of water a minute ago, I was serious," Fox said. "Either let's get on with my execution or get me something to drink."

Blaze laughed. "That eager to die?"

"I'd prefer the glass of water."

"I could kill you with that, too."

"I don't doubt it."

Blaze considered. "I'll be right back."

She went out and closed the door. That actually worked? Fox was incredulous, but she got to work on her restraints.

CHAPTER 34

Cuffed by her wrists and ankles, Fox had limited options. She knew one surefire way to get her hands free, but after all the punishment her body took that day, she wondered if she had the fortitude to do it. She glanced at her thumb and cringed. Her body was rejecting the idea before she even spoke it into fruition. It's just one little bone, she thought. Pop it out of place, slip the cuff off your wrist, and then pop it back in.

Fox was running out of time. Blaze would be back any minute. She took three deep breaths and then pressed her fingers over the top of her thumb.

"This is going to suck," Fox said as she squeezed her eyes closed.

The pain roared across her nerves, and Fox stifled a moan. She was amazed that one tiny pop of the joint could cause her so much pain. Contorted, she slipped the thumb area of her hand down through the steel cuff, followed by the rest of her hand. The cuff went limp as her arm dropped below her head. Fox swirled her fingers around her thumb again and guided the joint back into its place. Putting the thumb back into the right spot was a lot more difficult than breaking it, and the slightest movement sent more pain through her. She cursed her nerves for working so well and wished she had a martini or two to dull the pain. The thumb finally jerked and popped into place, and relief flooded over her. She breathed hard, wiped the sweat from her brow, and then moved her arm and hand around to get the circulation flowing back into them. There was a dull ache in her thumb that she knew would hurt even more tomorrow.

She turned to the chair. Thank goodness Blaze moved it closer, she thought. She reached for it. It was still a bit far away. Her fingers grazed the seat. She sighed and then focused. She extended her arm as far as she could and created pincers with her index and middle fingers. She clamped onto the edge of the seat with her finger pincer and gently tugged until she felt like she had a solid grip on the chair. Although she had almost no way to move while strapped to the chains, the plus side was that the restraints gave her great balance. She dragged the chair, and the metal legs scraped along the concrete. Fox hoped no one on the other side heard that, but she refused to waste time worrying too much about it. She gripped the chair and turned it over end on end to see if there was anything she could use from it. The screws holding the legs to the seat. They weren't ideal, but it was the best option she had.

Using just one hand she worked against the screws with her fingers. They were practically welded against the seat. Fox would have to force harder. She twisted.

The skin on her fingers pinched, and she felt blood drip from the pinch wounds. She ignored the pain. She had no choice but to ignore the pain! She pressed and twisted, letting out a low grunt against the pressure. There was movement! Fox twisted and the screw came loose.

She eyed the piece of metal. It was short, but at least it was thin. She stabbed it into the keyhole of her other handcuff. Ideally, she needed a piece of metal that was thinner and longer than the screw she got from the chair, like a hairpin or a common nail from the hardware store, but this particular screw was thinner than she expected. She could work with this. She concentrated on the prongs. There was movement outside the room. Had Blaze returned with the glass of water? It didn't matter. She was in it now. No turning back. She turned the screw, and the handcuff clicked! Her arm dropped to her side, and she worked the circulation back into her joints as she stared at the ankle shackles.

The cuffs holding her ankles were the same as the ones at her wrist. She placed the screw into one cuff and began working it around to try and find the sweet spot. Her legs ached as she bent down to the lock. There was more commotion outside the room. Fox had made too much noise as the door opened. A security guard stepped into the room and observed the escape attempt. His eyes went wide, and he raised his gun. Fox reacted right away as she grabbed the chair. She picked it up off the ground and heaved it at the security guard before he could pull the trigger.

The scrap heap distracted him as he moved his hands up to block the chair from hitting him. The collision was enough to knock the gun loose. It clambered across the concrete as Fox leapt forward. The ankle restraints pulled her down, but her long wingspan was enough. She reached for the gun as she hit the floor and snatched it. The security guard moved to attack her, but he saw that Fox had the gun pointed at him.

"You have keys for the ankle chains?" Fox asked.

He nodded.

"Good. Unlock me and then lock yourself in." The guard hesitated. Fox raised her voice. "Do it now!"

The guard moved to her feet and unlocked the restraints. Fox kept the gun aimed at him as he hesitantly snapped the handcuffs over his wrists. She patted him down to see if he had anything else valuable besides the gun and the keys. Nothing. Satisfied that the guard wasn't going anywhere, Fox snatched his keys away and moved to the door. She opened it just a crack and looked down the barren hallway. It was a small hallway with two other doors. There was also a set of stairs that went upward. She didn't know for sure, but her friends were probably in either of the other two rooms in this dungeon.

Fox stepped into the hallway and closed the door behind her. She held the gun at the ready. She stepped up to the next closest door and listened. There was no noise. She opened it slowly and peered inside. Inside the room, a startled A.C. jolted up from where she was handcuffed and watched the door. Fox hurriedly stepped in and closed it. A.C. looked physically unharmed. She wore the same clothes that she had on at the racetrack earlier in the day. Blaze probably knew that she wasn't a regular field agent and kept her locked away as an insurance policy in case Fox wouldn't play ball. Had their interrogation gone on any longer, Blaze might have dragged A.C. into the room and threatened to kill her if Fox didn't talk.

"Jett!"

Fox motioned for A.C. to quiet down. "Are you hurt?"

A.C. shook her head. She shivered out of fear. Fox crossed the room with the keys and unlocked her cuffs. A.C. collapsed into her friend with a desperate hug. Fox held her and felt A.C. shaking uncontrollably in her arms.

"Can we go home now?" There was no amusement in her voice. A.C. was serious and more scared than Fox had ever seen her.

"Let's go," Fox said. "Do you know if they're keeping Pyne in the other room?"

"I… I think so. They put us down here after they kidnapped us at the race. They shot Harry in both legs! He was bleeding a lot in the van, and he couldn't walk. They dragged him around like a piece of furniture." The word *furniture* cut from her mouth with anger.

That made things complicated. If Pyne couldn't walk, the window to escape was smaller. Fox believed she could do it, but everything had to go right.

"Stay close to me. Come on."

There was no one in the hallway, and she began to wonder if Blaze forgot about her. Not likely. She probably wanted Fox to wait as long as possible before getting a drink of water. The bitch.

Well, I couldn't wait forever, Fox thought. She and A.C. went into the hallway, passing the stairwell that led up, and moved to the final room. Fox peered inside. She saw a limp body dangling from the chains, and her heart sank. There was no one else in the room.

Fox charged inside and went straight to the body. It was Pyne, and he was in bad shape. A.C. gasped. Fox turned to her and signaled to her again that she had to stay quiet. Fox went to Pyne and checked for a pulse. He was alive, but he looked dead. He was unconscious.

"He's alive," Fox said softly to A.C.

Pyne had been stripped of all his clothing, and he had been beaten worse than any of them. He was bruised and bloodied from head to toe and drenched in sweat. The gunshot wounds on his legs had, thankfully, clotted, but the severe swelling and coloration suggested to Fox that his legs were broken. They needed a miracle to get him out of the dungeon, and Fox didn't think she had too many of those left in the bank.

Fox clapped gently on the cheek a few times. "Pyne. Pyne, wake up. Pyne."

The Englishman stirred. He sucked in a deep breath. His vision darted over the room in a panic. His breathing was labored and heavy. Fox tried to calm him.

"Hey, hey, it's us. It's us."

Pyne's breathing slowed as he recognized Fox and A.C. "Fox?" His recognition was a question. He turned to A.C. "Alice." That one was not a question, and a smile formed on his face. He looked back and forth between the two of them. "Well, what are you waiting for? Get me down from here."

Fox unlocked the chains. A.C. and Fox caught Pyne as he stumbled from the chains into their arms. Fox helped Pyne to a chair as A.C. found Pyne's clothes in a corner of the room. They helped him put them on. He couldn't move his legs at all. Just gently guiding his legs through the pants gave him excruciating pain. It took several minutes, but he was dressed. Dark stains showed on the parts of his clothes where the blood hadn't quite dried on his body.

There was a creaking sound coming from the hallway. It sounded like a door opening. That was followed by footsteps coming down the stairs. Not just one set. Multiple sets of footsteps, at least four people. The first set reached the bottom of the stairs. The sound went away from the room toward Fox's room at the other side of the hallway. A plan formulated in Fox's head. She had little time to execute it, and it relied on A.C. pulling herself together.

"Pyne, how much do you weigh? 210? 215?"

"Thereabouts," he said.

Fox nodded. "You're going to hate this."

She gathered him up by the wrist and swept an arm between his legs, scooping him over her shoulders. She balanced the Englishman and stood up with him in a perfect fireman's carry. He groaned, and Fox snapped at him to shut up. She initially struggled with him over her shoulders. He was heavier than she guessed, but not by much. She readjusted and was just fine.

"You're closer to 225, aren't you?" said Fox, doing her best to lighten the mood of this impossible situation.

Pyne must have sensed what Fox was trying to do, and he played along. "It's all the avocado I've eaten on this trip."

Fox turned to the armory chief with pleading in her eyes.

"A.C." Fox said. "Take the gun. You're a crack shot. I've seen it. You're going to have to lead us out of here."

A.C. froze for a moment. There was a shout at the other side of the hallway. Blaze and her goons must have discovered their fellow teammate chained in Fox's place. The door to the middle room burst open, followed by more shouting. Blaze's villains would be on top of them in mere seconds.

"Please, A.C. We need you right now."

A look of determination crossed her face. She understood the situation. Fox saw the fear leave her, replaced by pure rage, as the armory chief readied the gun.

CHAPTER 35

Chairwoman Solace once told Fox that the mark of a good leader was knowing when to help your teammates rise to the occasion. Fox had also heard that from her college volleyball coach and her grandfather. Only someone truly foolish would attempt to take on the world by herself. Fox believed in this, and she believed in A.C. as the two of them charged to the door in a desperate attempt to fight their way out of Mickey Blaze's dungeon.

In truth, Fox knew that this daring escape was dangerous on so many levels and not necessarily the smart decision. She could have taken her chances with Blaze getting all of her friends into the same room and then somehow figuring out a way to convince Blaze to remove her restraints. However, that option seemed unlikely. They were marked for death before Blaze ever threw them in the dungeon. So, Fox opted for the frantic prison break instead.

This tactic required quick decisions and no looking back. To charge through uncharted enemy territory with no tactical support was a borderline suicide mission. But, it was doable with flawless communication, using cover wherever possible, and not being afraid to improvise. Fox also knew that it was critical to not second guess her teammates as they performed their own tasks. In this situation, let A.C. get the job done her way.

A.C. burst through the door and fired off two blind shots. The first one splintered the door frame leading to the middle room. The second clipped the shoulder of an enemy operative. Fox got her first look at the obstacles that stood in their way. There were two men standing outside the door, one of whom was the man that A.C. hit with her second shot. The door at the far room was open, and Fox saw a man trying to free the guard from the shackles. A fourth guard bear-hugged Mickey Blaze and moved her into cover behind the wall.

A.C. darted ahead in a perfect shooting stance and got off two more shots. She hit the two guards in the hallway, one in the arm and the other in the leg, and they both dropped to the floor wailing in pain. The one she shot in the leg was the same one she hit in the arm with her initial shots. A.C. positioned herself in front of the staircase as Fox sprinted with Pyne on her shoulders. A.C. fired one shot down the hall toward the two men in the far room, and then she fired another shot toward Blaze and the guard in the middle room.

These were cover shots, not intended to do any actual harm, but they gave Fox the time she needed to run up the stairs without returning fire hitting her in the back. The climb up the stairs was a solid test of Fox's physical abilities. Her legs pressed upward with each step under the strain of carrying Pyne. She reached the top of the stairs just as A.C. fired off two more cover shots for herself. A.C. turned and ran up the stairs. Fox moved to open the door, but it flung open on its own.

Another member of Blaze's private security team stood in the door frame. His eyes went wide when he saw Fox standing in front of him. He whirled his gun into position, but Fox beat him to the spot. She rounded a kick to his hand and knocked the gun away. It clattered to the floor. Fox followed with another kick to the man's head. He crumpled to the floor unconscious.

Fox hurried through the door into a hallway that was a monarch's palace by comparison to the dungeon. Fox studied the architecture and the colors. She noticed the art, the relics, and the granite walls. It all seemed familiar. In fact, she knew exactly why it looked familiar. She had been in this place before. This wasn't some remote location where Blaze took her enemies to torture. They were inside Mickey Blaze's home.

"Where are we?" A.C. asked.

"Blaze's mansion. We're in Calabasas."

"You can get us out of here, right?"

Fox heard the security team in the dungeon bound up the stairs. She turned a corner through a door and found herself in an elaborate dining hall. There was no one inside this room. A.C. softly shut the door behind them.

"I think so," Fox finally responded to the question. "This place is like a maze. From what I remember, there are six different tunnels that lead back to the main foyer."

"So just keep going and we'll eventually find our way out?"

"Right." Fox turned to A.C. and the gun. "How much ammo do you have left?"

"Two shots."

Pyne grunted. "Maybe you should leave me here."

"What?" Fox turned to him on her shoulder. "We're getting you out of here."

"I'm in a lot of pain," he said. "Just leave me."

A.C. answered him a little too loudly. "Blaze will kill you!"

"I can talk her out of it. Promise to hush. Tell her it's too much trouble to kill a second MI6 agent in as many months. Whatever I need to say."

Fox pulled up a chair from the dining room table and gently helped Pyne into it. He seemed intensely relieved to be off Fox's back and sitting down. He motioned toward his shoe.

"My tracking device," he said. "Let me stay, and you can use me as a homing beacon."

A half smile formed on Fox's face. She knew he was right. It was a risk, and if Blaze discovered the tracking device, she'd kill Pyne on the spot. However, if Pyne could sweet talk his way into staying alive, then maybe he could lead them right to Blaze's diamond mine.

"You think she's going for the diamonds," Fox said.

Pyne nodded. "She's on her last leg. You've beaten her. She'll go to the diamonds and take whatever she can and disappear. Let me stay and see if I can convince her that I'm more useful to her alive than dead. I might even talk her into giving me a nice black-market doctor to fix my legs."

Fox thought about her short time knowing Harry Pyne. When she first met him, he annoyed her to the point where she delightfully slapped him across the face, and then he somehow became one of her closest friends. How in the world did he do it? If there was anyone who could talk Blaze into keeping him alive, it would be Pyne.

"OK," Fox said. She bent down and removed Pyne's shoe. She took the microchip out of it and handed it to him. "Swallow it. We can't take a chance of her finding the chip on you."

"Are you sure?" Pyne asked. "It only gives you a few hours to track me."

"I think I know where she has the diamonds," Fox said. "We just need to see which way she's taking you, and then we can meet you there."

"And where's that?"

Fox clapped him on the arm. "I have to leave you with *some* plausible deniability, don't I?"

"I suppose you do."

Pyne stuck the microchip in his mouth. He grimaced as he gulped. He let out a beleaguered "yuck" after successfully getting the chip down.

A.C. placed her hand over his. He smiled at her.

"Just stay alive, yes?"

He didn't say anything else. He pulled A.C. in gently and then kissed her passionately. His hands went to her hair, while she caressed his jaw with one hand and clutched his chest with the other. Fox turned away to give their moment of intimacy some form of privacy. She smiled the whole time. She was quite happy for her friend because Harry Pyne was hot as hell. She heard their lips part with one last smooch and she turned back to them.

Fox gave Pyne a stern nod. "Good luck, Pyne."

He nodded back at Fox. A.C. handed the gun to her. The two of them broke away toward the foyer door, leaving Pyne to fend for himself. A wave of guilt swept over Fox, but she knew she had to trust Pyne's instincts. He gave Fox and A.C. a better chance to escape, a punt on fourth down to live and fight another day. She could live with that, and she trusted her friend to keep himself alive long enough for a rescue at a later date.

Fox peered through the doorway and recognized the hall from her first night at the mansion. She heard shouting all through the quasi-palace. The voices seemed far enough away that she and A.C. could make a run for it. She led her friend into the hall in the direction of the front door. They rounded a corner and came upon a familiar man standing in the grand foyer just ahead of the staircase. It was the valet that greeted the guests at the party. He turned around when he heard Fox and A.C. coming up from the hallway. His eyes went wide. He shouted that he found the intruders!

Fox retreated. A.C. followed closely behind her as instructed. Escape out the front door wasn't going to happen. They'd take their chances through the backyard.

They ran through the maze and came to a door. Fox didn't recognize this area. The valet had taken her through one of the other grand halls earlier in the week, and she hadn't come this way. She peeked into the room. It was the kitchen! Maybe she was closer to an escape route than she thought. Perhaps if she could find some sort of alternative employee entrance in the kitchen, she and A.C. could sneak out without drawing any attention.

Fox carefully pushed through the door, gun at the ready. No one was in the kitchen. The room was dimly lit with only half the lights turned on. Fox checked the corners for an ambush, but there was no one waiting to pounce. She ran to the window to see the dark backyard. The blue-green glow from the swimming pool was the only thing illuminated under the night sky. Fox scanned down the long football field and saw the vineyard. She then looked the other way and saw the stable. An idea formed.

"Have you ever ridden a horse bareback?"

"No," A.C. responded. "Why?"

"Me neither. I wonder if it's hard."

She rejected the idea even though she was the one who came up with it. Obviously riding a horse without a saddle was hard. Riding a horse *with* a saddle was hard on its own. What should they do instead?

Voices came up from the door behind them. Fox and A.C. moved through the kitchen toward the back corner. They pushed through another door and entered the butler's pantry. The lights were turned off. They looked around for a door, but they didn't find one. Dead end, Fox thought. She glanced around the dark room. The light coming through the door cracks went brighter. The security must have turned on the rest of the kitchen lights.

That provided just enough light for Fox to have a better look around the butler's pantry. She spotted a window up high. She tugged on A.C. and went to the shelves. Footsteps outside the door got closer to the pantry. Fox and A.C. remained completely still.

"They must have gone to the garage," a man's voice shouted from across the kitchen.

The footsteps closest to them moved away from the pantry. Fox and A.C. both exhaled. Fox climbed the shelves toward the window. She slid it open. It was a small opening, almost too small. Fox stretched her arms and made herself thin. She got her torso through the tiny window frame and then squeezed the rest of her hourglass body until she tumbled onto the bushes. Twigs scraped against her bare arms, and her hand with the broken thumb is what hit the ground first. Fox stifled a yelp. She got up and brushed herself off. A.C. looked out and mimicked Fox's form. Fox reached out and pulled her the rest of the way. She caught her upright so that A.C. didn't also tumble onto the ground.

"I have an idea," Fox whispered. "We don't have to ride the horses, but maybe they can still help us. Come on."

Satisfied that there were no security guards in the backyard, Fox ran across the lawn past the pool. A.C. fell behind slightly and breathed much harder than Fox as they ran. Fox slowed the pace to allow her friend to keep up. They reached the flamingo pond. The birds were still hanging out in the water. One of them flapped its wings madly when they passed, and Fox hoped no one inside the mansion noticed the movement. She didn't turn back to see. She just kept running toward the stable.

Fox threw open the stable doors. She saw the outlines of the two horses in the darkness. She approached them gently. Both had woken up upon Fox's intrusion and neighed in disapproval.

"*Ssh*, it's OK."

She got them both to settle down and then unlocked the palomino's stall. This was the stallion, Outlaw.

"Are you sure about this?" A.C. asked.

"Too late."

Fox beckoned him to come out of his stall. He obliged. Fox moved to the chestnut's stall. This was the mare, Scarlet. She unlocked this stall and beckoned her outside, too. The two horses pranced out of the stable and ran toward the corral. Fox turned to the mansion and aimed the gun at the kitchen window. She pulled the trigger for the loud *pop*. The flamingos scattered from the pond when they heard the sound.

Fox expected A.C. to argue about the tactic, but she remained silent. Fox pulled her into a hiding place inside Outlaw's stall. They climbed into the smelly straw bedding. Fox fought against her body's natural disgust of the situation. Rather than think too much about what came out of the horse while it roamed in this straw, Fox focused on the next part of her plan. However, she could tell A.C. was having a harder time with the prospect. She couldn't blame her. This was her first field assignment, and she was getting the full covert operative experience, including hiding in unsanitary places. They covered themselves in straw and lay flat on the ground. Finally, A.C. spoke.

"What now?"

"Hopefully the guards come this way and see the stable empty. They'll think we escaped on the horses, and then we double back to the mansion and get a car from the garage."

It happened just like Fox predicted. The guards ran to the stable. They were flustered and out of breath. Blaze wasn't with them, and Fox hoped that meant she was still inside discussing terms of Harry Pyne's surrender.

One of them said to the others, "Look! They're at the corral!"

All of them left together without inspecting the stable more thoroughly. Fox had banked on this. Under the stressful nature of the situation, she hoped that Blaze's security were prone to mistakes. She just exploited one.

Fox burst from the straw and tugged on A.C. to do the same. They ran back to the mansion. Fox saw the garage attached to the mansion. It was large enough to be a house on its own. There was a backdoor leading inside it. Fox opened it gently and looked inside. Dark. She went through and flicked on the light.

Rows of lights brought the garage to life. A.C. gasped. The room was filled with old sports cars, at least ten models from every automotive era. This wasn't a garage; it was a museum. There was only one car that Fox had her eyes on. She saw the 1953 Jaguar C-Type and licked her lips. One last humiliation for Blaze, Fox thought. She'd steal her favorite race car.

"Find the garage door opener," Fox said. "I'll get the car started."

A.C. ran to the wall and pressed a panel. There was a low hum and creak of metal as the door lifted from its stationary position. Fox hopped into the driver's seat of the C-Type, which was on the right-hand side. This is weird, Fox thought. She ignited the engine. A.C. ran to the car and got into the passenger seat.

The garage door lifted, and Fox saw the security guards running toward them. They were still a solid distance away. Fox shifted with her left hand and pressed down on the gas. The car jerked and idled.

"Whoops, everything's backwards. Give me a sec."

Her brain made the adjustment, and she accelerated out of the garage just as the security guards shot at the car. The bullets pinged off the metal. Fox had one shot left in the gun. She aimed in the direction of the guards and fired. The bullet hit none of them, but they bolted for cover after Fox fired.

A few more shots came from the guards, but nothing connected. Fox shifted, the tires screeched, and the Jaguar shot off like a rocket out of the garage and along the driveway. Fox drove the Jaguar off the property ground and onto the main road. She burst away, and the mansion disappeared in the rearview mirror.

They were on the road for several minutes in silence as they drove through town and arrived at an outdoor mall. As much as Fox wanted to keep the car, she knew they had to switch vehicles as quickly as possible. Fox pulled into the outdoor shopping center. She and A.C. got out of the car, but before they abandoned it, Fox had another gift for Blaze. She snatched the keys from the ignition and scraped the metal over the Jag's driver-side door. She scratched the word "Bitch" into the paint job. She threw the keys across the parking lot.

CHAPTER 36

It took all night to get back to the motel in Pasadena. Fox and A.C. arrived at their room just as the sun began to rise. The bodily pain that Fox sustained, from the car wreck in the race to the torture in Blaze's mansion, both self-inflicted and otherwise, all came crashing onto her at once. A shower and a fresh change of clothes helped, but Fox was beat up.

She covered her wounds as best as she could with concealer. Thankfully, A.C. had far fewer cuts and bruises, and a shower was all she needed to look back to her old self. But Fox knew she might never be her old self again after the night they just had. All agents received the same training, but some were meant for the field while others were meant for tactical support. Fox got to see firsthand that A.C. was tough, but did she have the mental fortitude to regularly do missions like these? Maybe. Only time would tell. At the very least, she hoped to have her confident and happy friend back sooner than later.

They packed up everything and left the motel in a taxi a little after breakfast time. Neither one of them thought about food. They just wanted to get on an airplane back to New York as soon as possible. They arrived at LAX and bought tickets for the first available flight to Newark Airport.

A.C. slept the entire flight. Fox sat in her chair and thought about the mission. Last night was a mess, Fox thought, but the mission itself was a success. She went out to California to confront Mickey Blaze and get a confession to Sharon Graham's murder. Now, she had what she needed to bring Blaze in. She just had to convince Blaze that it was the only move she had left. Find the diamond mine, confront Blaze again, rescue Harry Pyne, and have Blaze testify against her bosses. Simple enough, right?

The Manhattan skyline came into view as the plane descended toward the opposite side of the Hudson River. They touched down on the runway, and A.C. woke up from her nap. Since they were already in New Jersey, Fox thought it would be best to go back to her apartment and rest. They got their bags and hailed a cab. The driver dropped them off at Fox's apartment.

A.C. collapsed onto the couch and fell asleep again almost immediately. Fox dialed Chairwoman Solace. They connected to a secure line.

"Sorry to go dark as long as we did."

"What happened?" Solace asked.

Fox recounted the tale exactly as it happened. She asked if they could rest for a few hours before meeting her in the city for a debrief.

"That's fine. Call when you're on your way. Just be aware that we might have to get you back in the air tonight."

"Understood."

Fox slept for an hour. She woke up to the sound of A.C. raiding her refrigerator. She went out to the kitchen to see the armory chief looking inside and cringing at the options. Fox had been gone a week, and she probably needed to throw out some of the food, anyway.

"Do you have anything that's *not* super healthy?"

Fox opened the pantry and tossed a Pop-Tart to A.C. "All I have is strawberry flavor. The classic."

A.C. opened the metallic packet and gobbled the toaster pastry without toasting it. An odd choice, Fox thought.

"If we leave now, we should get to the office around six p.m.."

A.C. finished chewing and then responded. "I've been watching Pyne's tracker. They took off from LA while we were in baggage claim, and they're flying over rural Nevada right now."

Fox grinned. That confirmed her suspicions about the diamond mine's location. She just had to show Solace, and she could be on her way that night.

"Does that tell you where they're going?" A.C. asked.

"Yes," Fox said. "I think the diamond mine is somewhere in the Canadian Rockies. I'll tell you more when we meet with Solace. Let's head out in ten minutes."

They climbed into Fox's Japanese commuter car and made the journey through the Lincoln Tunnel to Manhattan. Traffic was especially raucous at that time as they sat in virtual silence and traveled at a snail's pace to the upper east side. Just as Fox predicted, they arrived at the bookstore around six p.m.. They walked in and saw Agent Stonecreek at the cash register.

Stonecreek, the woman who Fox claimed was her workplace rival, looked at them with relief as they walked through the door. She had brunette hair and brown eyes. She was dressed in a simple blouse and jeans. Considering how much volunteer time she had already contributed to the bookstore, Fox guessed that she was on the last leg of her minimum required time at the cash register. They all knew the rules of the bookstore. No one was allowed to talk about the spy firm when they were downstairs. They all shared a knowing look. It was the same respectful look they all shared when agents returned to the office after a grueling assignment. Stonecreek and Fox may have been work rivals, but at the end of the day they were colleagues and teammates. They didn't have to like each other; they just had to respect each other.

Fox and A.C. entered the elevator in the back of the bookstore. Fox swiped her card and pressed the key directly to Solace's office. The elevator opened into the waiting area. Eddie Muncey was gathering his bag looking like he was headed home for the day when Fox and A.C. arrived. He smiled at them.

"You missed one hell of a race on Sunday, Jett," Muncey said. "This woman Juliana Ferreira really caused some damage on the track."

Fox smiled conspiratorially. "I heard about it on the news. It's nice to see someone wreck the competition the way she did."

Muncey laughed and threw the strap to his bag over his head. "Good luck in there, you two. I'm guessing this isn't over yet."

Fox shook her head. Muncey nodded in understanding and gave them a casual wave goodbye.

Fox and A.C. entered Solace's office. She looked up from her computer and waved them over. They sat down across from her. They sat in silence for a brief moment. Solace sighed and looked at A.C.

"Are you OK?"

A.C. hesitated. She then said, "I will be."

Solace nodded. She turned to Fox. "What do you have?"

"Harry Pyne's tracker went dead on our drive over here," Fox said.

"He was flying over Idaho," A.C. added.

"We intercepted a report a few weeks ago about rumors of a diamond mine somewhere in the Canadian Rockies," Fox continued. "RCMP didn't investigate because the target area was too large, and the report was unsubstantiated. My theory is that Blaze's diamond smuggling operation is connected to this rumored diamond mine."

"The tracking path on Pyne's chip suggests that he was heading to Calgary," A.C. said. She showed the tablet to Solace. "It could be a coincidence, but it seems like the report was right."

"Mickey Blaze is illegally mining diamonds in Canada and distributing them to various criminal organizations," Fox finished.

Solace was careful. She didn't react too quickly to the information. She eventually nodded, seemingly pleased with the report.

"Then we should get you on a flight to Calgary right away, Agent Fox."

"Ma'am," A.C. started. "If possible, I'd like to accompany Jett to Calgary."

Fox smiled. She backed up her friend without hesitation. "I could use the help. This operation is two-pronged. We're not only arresting Mickey Blaze, but we're also rescuing Harry Pyne."

"I see," Solace said. She studied A.C. for a moment. "The last assignment didn't put you off from field work?"

"No, ma'am."

"Very well," Solace said. "Tell me about this intercepted report. Who filed it initially?"

Fox retrieved the old email on her tablet. "The report came from RCMP Inspector Cassandra Campbell. She's stationed at the Calgary field office."

"Then we know who to contact," Solace said. "You two get down to the armory and grab whatever you need for the mission. I'll make a call to my RCMP contact and see if we can set up a meeting with Inspector Campbell. We'll also need their permission to bring any weapons across the border." She turned to A.C. "That means we might have to trade one of your designs to them. Have you worked on anything the Canadians might be interested in?"

A.C. nodded. "The super snowmobile. We can assign it to Jett so the Canadians can see it in action."

The irony wasn't lost on Fox. They needed government approval to carry contraband into a foreign country, much like Mickey Blaze and her own operation. The difference was that Blaze hid her merchandise, used her contacts to do things in secret, stole valuable minerals that belonged to the Canadians, and threatened or killed anyone who tried to stop her. Solace, on the other hand, was going to outright tell the Canadians what her team was bringing, and the purpose was to help them retain what rightfully belonged to them. It was a fine line, but it was a line, nonetheless.

Fox and A.C. went underground to the armory and stood in front of the super snowmobile. A.C. inspected it as Fox climbed onto the driver's seat and gripped the handlebars, visualizing a run through the snow-capped Rocky Mountains.

"Everything looks good," A.C. said. "If you want to pick out a new gun, I'll run a diagnostic on the weapon system."

That was A.C.'s way of saying "get lost so I can work." She handed Fox the key to the gun rack. Fox wandered around the armory. It was sparse compared to work hours, but there were still a few grunts working at their computers and giving Fox polite nods as she paced around the laboratory. She reached the guns and studied each one, grabbing one or two and aiming them across the firing range to see if liked them. She picked up the Beretta 9 mm compact, her usual weapon of choice. She still liked it better than the others. She locked the gun back into the rack and wrote on a notecard, "Reserved for Jett Fox." She placed the notecard by the gun.

Fox picked out other possible essentials for the mission: winter clothing, binoculars, a long-range listening device, night-vision goggles, pepper spray, handcuffs, and other miscellaneous items. She'd been on plenty of missions where she didn't need all the items she brought with her, but it didn't hurt to be overprepared.

She returned to A.C. to check on the snowmobile diagnostic. A.C. stared at her computer screen and clicked the mouse a few times. She turned back to the snowmobile and continued tinkering with it.

"It doesn't have to be perfect," Fox said.

A.C. sighed. "It's like you don't know me at all." She went back to her computer. "So, what's the plan after we meet with the RCMP inspector?"

"Capture the villain, rescue the bachelor in a bind, and give the Canadians their diamonds back."

A.C. laughed. "That's not a plan, Jett. That's the goal."

Fox laughed, too. "We'll recon the mountains until we find the mine. Hopefully we can talk RCMP into taking us up in a helicopter. Once we find the mine, we'll land a few miles off, close enough to get there on the snowmobile, but far enough away to not alert Blaze's cavalry. And then we arrest Blaze. She'll either come with us to testify or she'll try to kill us one last time. Or both!"

A.C. pondered for a moment. "Wait, what is a bachelor in a bind? Is that Harry?" She paused. "Is a bachelor in a bind like a damsel in distress?"

Fox's mouth turned upward in a guilty smirk. "A damsel in distress, but, you know, for dudes. Bachelor in a bind!"

A.C. laughed, but there was a hint of sadness behind it. Fox chose not to say anything. There was nothing she could say to make A.C. feel better about Pyne as Blaze's prisoner. And to A.C.'s credit, she handled it wonderfully.

Fox's phone buzzed. It was a text from Solace to meet upstairs.

"You go ahead," A.C. said. "I'll make sure everything is ready for the trip."

It was dark outside by the time Fox got up to the presidential suite. The upper east side was illuminated by streetlights and taxi brake lights. It had been a weird day, and it was far from over. Fox operated on miniscule sleep, and her body felt it. Her thumb that she broke the night before ached the most, and the makeshift splint didn't stop the irritation. She sat across from Solace, who jumped right into the briefing. Fox both loved and hated that about her boss.

"You're meeting with Inspector Campbell at the RCMP Calgary office tomorrow morning at nine a.m. Your flight leaves from Newark in four hours. You'll have a little bit of time to catch your breath in Calgary before the meeting, but try to get some sleep on the flight. You look like hell, Agent Fox."

"Yes, ma'am."

"RCMP will be on the tarmac in Calgary to approve your equipment. They weren't thrilled about the idea, but they're excited to get their hands on the schematics for the armory's snowmobile. It seems like they're taking Inspector Campbell's diamond mine claim seriously after the bust you made in California. They want to cooperate, but they're a bit skittish. Be nice to them."

"Yes, ma'am."

"Any questions?"

"No, ma'am."

"Very well. You're excused. Flight itinerary is in your email. Good luck, Agent Fox."

CHAPTER 37

Nestled in the foothills of the Rockies, the orange glow of the sun reflected off the icy sheet covering the mountains in the west as the city came to life for the morning bustle. Small patches of snow sprinkled over the grass that had mostly thawed after resting all winter. The thin air and nonexistent wind chill made for a comfortable morning in Alberta's largest city as the commuter traffic moved along at a decent pace. Fox and A.C. sat in the backseat of the RCMP SUV, as it transported them from the airport to downtown Calgary. Fox watched a woman jogging dressed in colorful cold weather running gear as the SUV turned onto the Reconciliation Bridge and crossed the Bow River. The officer assigned to drive Fox and A.C. from the airport to the police department rattled on about Canada and the misconceptions. His name was Tyler Wilson. He had scruff on his face that looked like he hadn't shaved in about ten days.

"Everybody thinks they know everything about Canada," Wilson said. "They think we're crawling in snow up to our necks year-round, but that just isn't true.

Hell, they had to make snow for the Vancouver Olympics because it was too damn hot outside!"

Fox was amused. "Are you from Calgary originally?"

"Winnipeg, actually. I've been in Calgary about five years."

Fox took a shot in the dark that Wilson was a big hockey fan. "Who's your NHL team?"

"The Jets, of course! I try to get tickets any time they're in town to play the Flames. Are you a big hockey fan?"

"Not really, but I've been to a Devils game and an Islanders game," Fox said. "Both times were on first dates. The games were fun, but the guys were not."

Wilson laughed. "Yep, I made that mistake when I was younger. You do that, a first date is usually a last date. My wife puts up with hockey being on in the house all the time, but she definitely doesn't love it. She'll stay off my back about it as long as I take her for a nice date night every week."

The only sport, other than volleyball, that Fox enjoyed watching was football, and that was thanks to her grandfather. He took her to a Dolphins game a short time after she moved to Miami to live with him, and she developed a gigantic crush on Jason Taylor after the superstar defensive end waved at her from the sideline during the game. She asked her grandfather to buy Jason Taylor's poster before they left the stadium, and she put the poster up in her bedroom as soon as they got home.

As Fox became a private intelligence operative and developed the need to blend in, she understood that it was important to keep tabs on sports, even if it was just surface level knowledge. She learned early on that the quickest way for a person to endear herself to a group of people was to feign interest in local sports.

They continued driving through the city. Fox saw billboards promoting "The Greatest Outdoor Show on Earth." Fox wondered what that was, and so Wilson told them all about the Calgary Stampede, arguably the biggest rodeo in the entire world, and how the city got the nickname "Cowtown."

"It takes place every July," he said. "It's not for a few months, but the city is already promoting it. You should come back this summer and check it out."

Wilson drove the SUV up and around the skyscrapers until they came upon a modest office building, which featured the majestic crest of the Royal Canadian Mounted Police. They had arrived at their destination. Wilson brought the SUV around to the parking garage and escorted the two women into the building and into a large police bullpen where a few officers worked at their desks, dressed in white button-down shirts with shoulder epaulets that featured various patches to signify their ranks within RCMP. Wilson directed Fox and A.C. to have a seat in a waiting area near a glass-walled office. "Inspector Cassandra Campbell" was painted on the glass door.

A half hour passed. Campbell was late to the meeting. Wilson brought out two cups of coffee to Fox and A.C. She expected the coffee to taste terrible, like office coffee normally tastes, but this cup was excellent.

"Where did this coffee come from?" Fox asked. "It's delicious."

Wilson smiled. "Welcome to Cowtown, Miss Fox."

Another twenty minutes passed, and Fox felt impatient. However, she wasn't showing it like A.C. The armory chief was clearly upset to be sitting and waiting, and it occurred to Fox that A.C. had not been herself that morning. She wondered if it was a mistake to bring A.C. along for the mission. She's here to rescue Pyne, Fox thought, but what if she's too single minded? How might it affect the mission? Fox made a mental note that course correction might be necessary on her part to counter any mistakes made by her friend. Fox placed a hand on A.C.'s shoulder. The armory chief stopped fidgeting and looked at Fox.

"Relax," Fox said softly. "We'll be out searching the mountains in no time."

A.C. exhaled slowly and nodded. She sat back and tried to relax.

Finally, a woman entered the bullpen and walked briskly toward the glass office. She was short, only slightly taller than five feet. She had a stocky build, although she was in good physical shape, like a wrestler. She wore her brunette hair tightly pulled back into an unimpressive ponytail. She had brown eyes and a face full of freckles. The epaulets on her shoulders bore the crowned insignia of a Mountie inspector. She smiled when she saw Fox and A.C. waiting at her office.

"Jett Fox and Alice Cooper?" she asked.

They both stood from their chairs. Fox addressed her first.

"That's us." Fox extended her hand, and the woman graciously accepted with a firm handshake.

"So sorry to keep you two waiting. We had an overnight incident. I won't bore you with the details. I'm Inspector Cassandra Campbell. Please, come in."

Campbell led them into the office and sat down behind her desk. Fox and A.C. took the seats across from her. It reminded Fox of a briefing with Solace, except that Campbell's glass cube was much smaller than Solace's presidential suite.

"I understand you two have some information that I'll be happy to hear."

"I hope so," Fox said. "We came across your report last month about a diamond mine in the Rockies. We've been investigating a murder on our end, and our murderer just might be the person who illegally set up a mine in your borders."

"Investigating a murder?" Campbell looked confused. "Are you FBI? CIA? That part was a little unclear to me when I agreed to this meeting."

Fox elected to give full disclosure to Campbell. "We work for a private intelligence firm in New York. We were hired to investigate the murder of a British agent. I'll give you all the details if you'd like, but the short version is that our suspect has been smuggling diamonds all around the world, and we have actionable intelligence that suggests she's somewhere in Alberta right now, stealing diamonds from your mystery mine. You might have seen the news last week about a busted diamond handoff in California. That was us."

"No kidding? I heard about that. Everyone here heard about it. It got people talking again about the rumors."

"So do you have any information that might help us?" A.C. asked. It jolted Fox awake to hear her friend talk for the first time all morning.

"If you mean the location of the mine, no. People get spooked talking to cops." She sighed. "I tried to follow up on the mine, but no one would talk once I showed up. And so, I filed that report, just hoping that maybe someone with a little more power than I had might do something about it. The higher-ups were interested, but without a more focused search area, it was just too daunting for them to make a commitment. You're talking about a thousand-mile search area."

"Maybe we can talk to your sources," Fox said. "We can approach them as tourists and see if we can get them to drop information about the mine."

"That's not a bad idea," Campbell considered. "I'll have to think about it."

Fox and A.C. both cringed. Campbell noticed the hesitation.

"What's wrong?" she asked.

"Well, it's that we're in a bit of a time crunch," Fox said. "Our suspect is up against the wall, and she's cleaning out as much of the mine as she can before she disappears. My guess is she'll be in the wind in the next twenty-four hours."

"She also has a hostage," A.C. added.

Campbell sat back after receiving the two pieces of information. "I think you'd better start from the beginning. Let's hear it all."

Fox recounted the entire story to Campbell, starting with meeting Harry Pyne in Morocco all the way up until she and A.C. arrived in Alberta. Campbell raised her eyebrows and shook her head in disbelief.

"I guess we don't have much time to waste," Campbell said.

"So you'll help us?" Fox asked.

"Of course! You're helping me, too. I put out that report hoping somebody would help us. You're not exactly who I expected, but I'm not picky. Plus, you brought us that snowmobile. I want to check it out. Not that we really need another snowmobile. We already have plenty."

"Yes, but do yours have two machine guns and a heat-seeking rocket launcher?" A.C. seemed rather proud of herself.

"No, I can't say that they do."

The plan was coming together. Fox felt confident that they could reach Blaze in time and put a bow on this mission.

"We'll need a helicopter to patrol the mountains," Fox said. "Can you spare one?"

"All I have is one," Campbell said, "but yes, we can use it. It'll take me a few hours to get approval for all of this. Why don't the two of you relax for a bit while I run this up the chain of command? Go out and enjoy some Alberta hospitality."

Campbell clicked her speaker box. A man with a high squeaky voice answered. Campbell responded to him, "Send in Sergeant Wilson."

Wilson entered the room. "Yes, ma'am?"

"Get access to the facilities for Miss Fox and Miss Cooper. Allow them to freshen up from their flight. And then give them a little tour of the city. OK?"

"Yes, ma'am. Right away."

Wilson led Fox and A.C. out of the office and showed them to the locker room. He motioned toward it. "You can go on ahead. Your bags are already in there. I'll make sure no one comes in to disturb you. And then afterward, we'll take a drive around town."

"I'm sorry you're stuck babysitting us," Fox said. "Do they normally use sergeants for a job like this? It seems a little beneath you, if you ask me."

"Actually, it's the opposite," he said. "Inspector Campbell is treating you two like foreign dignitaries. Driving you around is a privilege."

"I don't know if I like being *that* important," Fox said.

Fox and A.C. cleaned themselves up. Fox clicked off her electric toothbrush and spat into the sink. She rinsed the toothbrush, put it into her bag, and met with A.C. and Wilson outside. Wilson led them back to the parking garage, where they all climbed into the SUV for another drive around Calgary.

"Let's grab a late breakfast," Fox said. "We haven't eaten yet. Where do you recommend, Sergeant Wilson? Somewhere that has the Alberta hospitality that Campbell was talking about."

"How about the Stallion Rose Saloon and Dancehall? It's a honky tonk bar. Has all that Alberta hospitality vibe you're looking for. The dancing and live music is only at night, but they've got a great breakfast menu."

"Sounds good. Let's try it."

A.C. sighed.

"What is it?" Fox asked.

"I just feel guilty, I guess. We're going off to some restaurant to have a nice breakfast while Harry is a hostage somewhere. It feels wrong."

Fox knew how she felt. "We can't help him right now. I know it's hard, but we have to be patient and wait for Inspector Campbell to get what we need. Trust me, it's no fun to wait on others. I get it. I've been there. But, as a field agent I learned to compartmentalize my feelings. It's the only way to keep my sanity on a mission. Remember, it was only a day ago we were escaping Los Angeles with our lives, and we've gotten terrible sleep since then. We haven't really recovered from that. As guilty as you might feel, this little break is exactly what we need to make sure we're in top form to rescue Pyne."

A.C. smiled painfully and nodded. She relaxed against her seat. It was the mark of someone who hadn't done much field work. She didn't know if that was a good thing or a bad thing. Had Fox become desensitized to the bleak nature of being a field agent? She'd only done it for a few years, and this was easily her most dangerous assignment to date. She thought back to her dinner with Harry Pyne in Casablanca. Did she change any of her hard opinions that she held back then? It was only six weeks ago, but a lot had happened in those six weeks.

Wilson pulled into the parking lot of the Stallion Rose Saloon and Dancehall. The wild west themed decorations on the front of the building came across as a bit tacky, but they certainly portrayed the vibe the saloon wanted. They entered and were cheerfully greeted by a beautiful woman with blonde hair dressed in jeans, blue button-down shirt with one too many buttons undone at the top of her shirt, and brown boots. She casually flirted with Wilson as she led them to their table. Fox felt sick to her stomach. I can see why the men like this place, she thought.

Between the wooden architecture, the twang and cadence of the music with its unique string instruments, and the many men dressed in jeans, button-downs, and Stetsons, Fox thought for a moment that she was in Texas and not Alberta. There were pictures above every table showcasing highlight moments from the Calgary Stampede. They sat down and Fox saw the picture above their table was of a man bull riding in a stadium full of thousands of spectators.

"The stairs over there at the other end go up to the dance floor," Wilson said. "That's where they have live music at night. It's a fun little place. I've brought my wife here a couple of times, but neither of us are really into the whole cowboy thing. We had a good time, though."

The waitress arrived. She was just as beautiful as the hostess and dressed similarly. She took their drink orders. They all wanted coffee. A.C. made a comment after the waitress walked away.

"The saloon owner certainly has a type, doesn't he?"

Fox laughed. The waitress returned with the cups of coffee. She took their food orders.

"I'll have the breakfast vegetable scramble with wheat toast and a slice of turkey sausage," Fox said.

"Excellent choice," the waitress said. "I think you'll be pleasantly surprised by how tasty the veggie scramble is."

A.C. ordered pancakes and a bowl of fruit. Wilson asked for another cup of coffee. He'd already eaten that morning.

A few people at the restaurant saw Wilson and chatted with him. It was idle gossip about people and places Fox didn't know. Their police escort turned out to be a popular guy.

The food came, and it was just as good as the waitress said it would be. It was a balanced blend of bell peppers, kale, spinach, avocado, and eggs. Fox used the wheat toast to make a quasi-veggie breakfast sandwich. She spread some of the veggies onto the toast and took a bite. She liked it so much that she ate the entire piece of toast that way. She ate one bite of the turkey sausage but no more.

Wilson drove Fox and A.C. to other parts of the city after the meal. He told them the best places to visit were the outdoor spots outside of the city limits. The helicopter ride while looking for Blaze's diamonds would be their best bet to catch Alberta's beauty. Fox enjoyed Calgary, and she was sad the visit was so brief. Duty called, but she made a mental note to visit Calgary again someday, maybe in the summer. Thirty-three degrees in the thin mountain air with the sun shining wasn't too bad, but it was still cold.

Finally, Wilson got a phone call.

"Yep, I'll bring them back. On our way."

Back at the Mountie detachment, Fox and A.C. went into Inspector Campbell's office and sat down at her desk. She smiled widely.

"I've got good news and bad news," she said. "Bad news first. The bad news is that I didn't get permission to use the helicopter. We're stretched thin, and this whole search could be for nothing. Just too many unknowns to commit resources to a wild goose chase. Your time crunch certainly didn't help me make my case."

Fox was deflated. "What's the good news?" she asked.

"The good news is that we're going to use the helicopter anyway."

CHAPTER 38

Inspector Campbell wasted no time in getting everyone out the door for the operation. She'd obviously been thinking of doing the search on her own for a while, but she just needed the right push to do it. Fox and A.C. gave her the push she needed.

Campbell enlisted Wilson for more driving duties, which he was happy to perform. She directed him to drive their group of four to a sportsman's outfitter. She instructed him to park a block away. Campbell turned to Fox and A.C. in the back.

"OK, my contact for the diamond mine is a guy named Levi Stewart," she said. "He works at the sportsman's shop just over there. You'll recognize him right away. You'll find him in either camping or footwear. Check both sections. He's got long curly brown hair, brown eyes, and a perpetual five o'clock shadow. He trims it that way on purpose. The beauty scruff or whatever it is. The hipster beard. I don't know." Fox and A.C. looked at each other and laughed. Campbell couldn't help but laugh, too. Even Wilson giggled as he scratched his own facial hair. "Anyway, do just like what you told me back at the office. Go in and pose as tourists looking for somewhere cool to hike, get him talking, and see if you can get him to mention the diamonds."

"We're on it," Fox said. She and A.C. got out of the car.

Wilson spoke as they exited the car. "For the record, my facial hair is just because I'm lazy when it comes to shaving."

A.C. shut the door.

"Do you want me to do all the talking?" Fox asked.

"Yes, please. Still not sure I'm good at the whole undercover thing."

"No problem. I've got your back."

They walked down the block and came upon the massive outdoor equipment and apparel supercenter. Fox grinned. *Now* she felt like she was back home in Florida, other than the fact that it was fifty degrees colder.

"My grandfather shops at places like this all the time," Fox said. "I bet if I called him right now, he'd be at the shop looking for a new fishing pole."

"Sounds like you miss him," A.C. said.

Fox hadn't thought about it, but she knew A.C. was right. There was something about this mission that made her homesick, and she hadn't talked to her grandfather since before she left for Morocco.

"I do," Fox said. "He's in his eighties now, and he's the only family I have left. I didn't used to think about losing him, but lately I've thought about it more and more." Fox paused and laughed. "Knowing him he'll stick around for another fifteen years and complain about it the entire time."

Suddenly, and without warning, Fox felt guilt swarm over her. Her mind flashed to Theseus Kastellanos and the cliffside duel among the flames of the race car crash. Fox still wondered if there was more she could have done to keep him from dying. Theseus had made it clear that their encounter would only end with one of them dying, but was that a legitimate excuse? Nothing prepared her for the guilt and shame that came with taking another's life, even in a life-or-death situation like the one Fox faced with Theseus. The movies definitely had it wrong. There was a level of remorse she felt at that moment that never came up with the main characters in any action film. She shook off the thought as she and A.C. walked into the outdoors supercenter. She had work to do, and somehow, she had to push away the guilt until later.

Fox and A.C. walked through the superstore to the footwear section. Fox saw a man matching Levi Stewart's description, including the hipster beard. He seemed bored as he offered help to one man. "Can I help you find anything?" he said.

"No," the man said. Fox casually strode into footwear with A.C. on her tail.

They browsed the women's size boots, doing their best to show that they were two customers who needed help. Stewart didn't budge from his spot near the front of the footwear section. Was he shy or lazy? After another few minutes, Fox decided to take a more direct approach with the man. She went up to him and smiled warmly. She knew she had the right guy when she saw "Levi" on his nametag.

"Hello," she said. "Can I get your help real quick? I was wondering if I could get your opinion on a couple of different pairs of boots."

"Uh sure yes no problem." Stewart followed Fox back to where A.C. stood by the hiking boots. Fox held up two different pairs of boots.

"These are about the same price. Can you tell me the difference between the two?" Fox sighed. "Silly me. I remembered to pack everything for our trip except the one thing I needed, boots. Just my luck, right?"

"Sorry to hear that," he said. "So here's the difference between those two brands."

Stewart went into a long explanation about the two sets of boots to which Fox only partially listened. The message Fox got out of the long-winded briefing was that there wasn't much difference at all between the shoes, but Fox respected Stewart's hustle to try and make a sale. He finally made a recommendation on one of the pairs.

"So if I were to do some spelunking after hiking to my destination, which shoe might be the better choice?"

Stewart then dove into another comparison of the two, and this time he insisted that the opposite pair was better for caving than hiking.

"If you're planning to do both, you might want to think about buying both pairs of boots, one for hiking and then changing into the others for spelunking."

It took a lot for Fox to not laugh right there in the store. This guy was trying to squeeze every penny he could out of this potential sale. Fox noticed A.C. holding back the same laughter.

Instead, she said, "It sounds like you really know your stuff. I'm glad we came in here. Do you know any good hiking spots around here?"

Stewart named off the usual places. A.C. was getting impatient. Fox gently squeezed her arm. Just hang on, Fox thought.

"Those are the main spots around Calgary," Stewart said. "Where are you guys from originally?"

"Down south. Tell me, are there any places we can go that aren't necessarily open to the public?" Fox leaned in conspiratorially and lowered her voice. She knew she had to play up the charm here, so she placed a friendly hand on Stewart's shoulder. "Places that might be a little, you know, unsafe? My friend over here, she's the shy one when it comes to talking to people, but she's kind of a daredevil once you get to know her." A.C. looked over Fox's shoulder and offered a mysterious shrug to Stewart. Fox continued, "Do you know about any old coal mines where we might be able to go sneak around? Places like that?"

Stewart hesitated, "Why do you want to know?"

Fox backpedaled. She didn't want to spook him.

"Well, you can't tell anybody what I'm about to tell you, cool?" Fox said.

Stewart seemed unconvinced. Fox figuratively batted her eyelashes as well as she could.

"OK, what's up?"

"Well, my friend and I are treasure hunters." Fox threw her hands up. "No joke. I swear. We like to explore abandoned mines and see if there's anything valuable left behind. We heard Alberta is full of old mines, and so we thought we'd come up here and check them out. But hey, if you don't know about any, don't worry about it. I'm sure we'll find some."

"Treasure hunters?" Stewart asked. "Like Tomb Raider?"

Fox clasped on the shoulders. "Yes! Exactly like Tomb Raider. So do you know any places around here where we can find some valuable loot?"

A.C. spoke for the first time. "We'll even cut you in on a small percentage if you can tell us about some good spots."

"Right!" Fox added. She smiled and raised her eyebrows in surprise at her friend's willingness to join the undercover fun.

Stewart was still hesitant, but he relented his stance. After all, how often do two gorgeous treasure hunters come into this store and show him this much attention? At least that's what Fox assumed he was thinking. It was obvious by the expression on his face, she thought.

"OK check this out," he whispered. "I heard a while back from a buddy that some sketchy looking folks were up by Mount Columbia hauling out truckloads of crates from a cave. He said there were diamonds in those crates and then somebody took a shot at him! He got away, but he said it was crazy. He'd never experienced anything like that before, somebody shooting a gun at him."

"Diamonds!" Fox feigned intense excitement, like her character had hit the mother lode. She looked at A.C. with the same excitement, and A.C. did her best to match it, but it was much more sarcastic than Fox's acting effort. "And you said he saw this cave and these sketchy people up at Mount Columbia?"

"Yeah, totally. There was a cop that used to come in here, and I tried to keep my mouth shut after that. I didn't want to get my buddy in trouble. So please don't say that I told you anything."

"Hey no problem! Your secret's safe with us." Fox pulled out some cash and subtly handed it to Stewart. "You've been a huge help. And there's more where that came from if we find anything valuable up in Mount Columbia."

"Wow! Awesome."

"How far is Mount Columbia from here?"

"A little less than a four-hour drive, maybe? About three-hundred kilometers."

Fox took a pair of boots with her and started heading for the cash registers up front. Once they were out of sight of Stewart, she dropped the boots near a display. She and A.C. then left the store and re-grouped with Campbell and Wilson in the SUV. Fox recapped what Stewart told them.

"Mount Columbia? That's the narrowest search parameter we've had in this case," Campbell said. "You two did an awesome job. I'll get the boys on the horn and get your snowmobile transported up to our waystation in that area. It's about twenty kilometers out from the base of the mountain. I figure by the time we get done searching in the helicopter, they'll be there with your snowmobile. We'll know either way whether there are diamonds up there."

"I don't know what to say," Fox said. "You're putting a lot of faith in us with very little to go on. I'd hate for you to put your job on the line, especially if we don't find anything."

"Don't worry about that. The worst they'll do is demote me, and I might thank them for it."

CHAPTER 39

Fox and A.C. sat in the helicopter's backseat and were treated to some of the most breathtaking scenery in the world. The Canadian Rockies were impressive from afar, but up close they were nearly indescribable. The helicopter soared over the snow-capped peaks with the trails of rivers leading to lakes well below. Fox reminded herself not to get caught up in the scenery because she had to keep her eyes peeled for anything seemingly out of place.

"We're coming up on Mount Columbia," Inspector Campbell's voice came on in their headsets as she sat next to the pilot. "It's the highest peak in Alberta, a little more than twelve-thousand feet, but there are a few trails that make it fairly easy to climb for just about anybody. I can see how your diamond thieves got caught. Crazy that there are diamonds buried there. Who would have thought?"

A search of this scale was tedious. The search area was small by comparison to what RCMP had prior to Fox's intervention, but the team still had a fifty-mile radius through which to fly. It required concentration by Campbell, Fox, and A.C. as all of them watched the surface from behind their respective windows. There wouldn't be a welcome sign with the message, "Villain lair here, please take off your shoes before entering." The hope was that Mickey Blaze made a mistake out of desperation that betrayed her position in the mountains.

Fox watched the ground with a bit of desperation of her own. The first signs that winter was coming to an end showed through the snow as Fox saw glimpses of green from the trees. The glacial coating that enveloped the lakes had broken to give off the dark earthy tint from the bed beneath the water. The higher elevations featured the white dreamworld that Fox had expected out of Canada, and she hoped that the diamond mine was at these heights. With the lower levels thawing out, they provided a natural camouflage into which Blaze could more easily hide, but she'd have to be careful up in the snowy locations.

It was late afternoon by the time the helicopter made its round at Mount Columbia. The majestic composition protruded from the earth high above the surrounding rock formations with a slope on its back that led down a winding path where hikers could make their way up and down from its peak. On its front side, the mountain curved straight down to a valley and a lake. Fox wanted to enjoy the spectacle, but she kept her focus on anything out of the ordinary. The team had only a few hours of sunlight left and even less fuel in the helicopter.

No one saw anything of note on that first pass. The pilot weaved across the valley with everyone remaining silent and watching the scenery. The pilot flew in a northwestern direction along the mountain range before Campbell directed him to turn back and circle the target area.

This continued for about an hour and a half, and still no one saw anything. Fox began to doubt the informant's story. It was a second-hand account, and she felt foolish for buying into the story. She was running out of time to catch Mickey Blaze, and she wondered if this had all been some fool's errand. What if Blaze had sent Harry Pyne in this direction as some sort of distraction? Surely she'd suspected a tracking device even if she couldn't prove that Pyne had one. What if this was all a ruse to allow Blaze to escape to the real diamonds? Maybe somewhere in Africa? Europe? Fox felt sick to her stomach, but it wasn't altitude sickness. It was a whole lot of doubt.

"We have to land soon, Inspector," the pilot said.

"Let's give it another half hour," Campbell said.

Fox couldn't give up yet. She relaxed her shoulders and observed with patience. If there was one thing she learned in her time as an operative, it was that a person who was too tense missed important details. It was the person who went in with a sharp mind and reasonable expectations that prevailed. Fox exhaled slowly and allowed herself to think clearly about clues. Stop looking for a mine, she thought. Instead, look for something that might indicate unusual activity in the area.

Of course, that was easier to do when there wasn't so much *usual* activity in the area. Campbell mentioned that hikers frequented this mountain. Fox made a mental list of things that might look like natural hiking, and that list didn't include a large set of tire tracks that carried from the road through the mud on the low levels and up through the snow and into the direction of Mount Columbia. Fox smiled. Had she accidentally stumbled upon a clue to the mine's whereabouts?

"I think I have something," she said. "Hold this position for a moment."

Fox brought the binoculars to her eyes and came upon the area where she saw the tire tracks. They were heavy and carried mud up the mountain and left a fresh brown trail across the snow. She might have missed them as they got lost through the trees.

"Can we move closer into that spot?" Fox leaned over the pilot and pointed to exactly where she wanted to move the helicopter.

The pilot dropped the helicopter's altitude and moved down to where Fox indicated. Fox was satisfied with the position and tapped the pilot on the shoulder to indicate to stay put. She followed the trail of tire tracks through the snow and around the lake up to the base of the mountain until they came to a hiking trail. The tracks grew deeper into the mud below the snow, and it looked as though whoever drove the vehicle onto this part of the trail did so carefully and slowly. The tire tracks suddenly vanished into a rock formation. Fox took out the binoculars and studied the rock formation. There was something odd about it, but she couldn't quite put her finger on it, but it was almost as if the coloration of a section of the rocks didn't match the rest of the cliffs.

"Inspector Campbell, I insist we turn back now," the pilot said.

"Miss Fox?" Campbell asked.

"It's fine. I think I see a place where I want to take the snowmobile. Here, take a look real quick before we head back."

Fox handed the binoculars to Campbell. The inspector peered down from the helicopter through the lenses.

"Hmm," Campbell said. "I see it. You might have something."

She handed the binoculars back to Fox, who then handed them to A.C. The armory chief leaned over Fox and looked down.

"That's clever," A.C. said. "Trick door."

Campbell told the pilot to head back to the waystation, which was about fifteen miles away. It would be a long ride through the snow back to this spot, Fox thought, and it would be in the dark. She expected another rough night in her attempt to arrest Mickey Blaze.

The pilot landed the helicopter on the helipad at the mountain waystation. The truck hauling Fox's equipment had already arrived. A.C. inspected everything to make sure nothing was damaged. She said it all looked to be in working order as she and Fox suited up for the trip through the snow. Fox placed the holster at her chest for easy access to her Beretta, and she slipped the night-vision goggles over her beanie. She hid the handcuffs and pepper spray inside her coat opposite from the Beretta holster. A.C. retrieved the long-range listening device and what looked to be the airsoft needler that she had worked on building a month earlier. Fox was taken aback when she saw it.

"I didn't think that thing was ready yet," Fox said.

"Remember that cross country trip I took? I told you I had a lot of time to think about my projects, and the needler was one of them. I figured out the jamming problem. She's ready now."

The sun had retreated behind the British Columbia Rockies west of the Alberta border. The orange glow of evening had been replaced by the blue glow of twilight. The temperature dropped at least ten degrees in that short time. Fox felt a sense of urgency running through her. She suspected that if Blaze and her team were still in the mountains, they were waiting until nightfall to escape with the diamonds. Fox and A.C. had to get on the snowmobile as soon as possible.

Campbell approached them. She took a long look at the snowmobile and nodded her approval.

"This thing really has weapons?" Campbell asked.

"It sure does!" A.C. sounded like a proud parent.

Campbell nodded again. She turned to the two women.

"It's late in the season, so the snow is going to feel like gravel. It'll be an uncomfortable ride. I wish I could offer you more tactical support. I hate sending you out there by yourselves."

"You've done more than enough," Fox said. "Besides, I'm sure you have phone calls to return that you've been avoiding all day."

"You're right. I have some hell to pay for taking the helicopter without permission." Campbell paused and exhaled a large cloud from her mouth. "Go catch these guys, and that'll soften the blow, OK?"

"We'll round them up, but stay close to your radio," Fox said. "We might need your help transporting them to jail."

Campbell laughed. "I can help with that."

Fox climbed onto the driver's seat, and A.C. boarded behind her. A.C. glanced to the rear of the snowmobile where she had constructed the missile launcher.

"I wonder if I built it too close to the passenger seat," she said.

"Just scoot up when I'm ready to blow something up," Fox said.

Fox ignited the engine and pressed forward on the accelerator. Her broken thumb ached as she pressed the gas, and it was an instant reminder that she was attempting to complete this mission while injured. It had been a bizarre sixty hours, starting with the Open Circuit Challenge in California and leading to a snowmobile ride in the Rocky Mountains. Fox's body had taken a heavy toll in that time, including the unprotected body blows by Blaze. Pushing through pain was great in theory, but so much more difficult in practice.

The conveyor belt wheels gobbled the snow as the armory chief's new war machine glided along the hiking trail aimed at Mount Columbia. The cobalt sky turned darker as the vehicle cut through the frozen landscape, and Fox opted to keep the headlights off. Instead, she lowered the night-vision goggles over her eyes and let the green and black screen show her the way. Of course, this made A.C. nervous.

"I hate this. Are you sure you don't want to use the headlights?"

"They may hear us coming," Fox said, "but I won't let them see us coming."

"OK, but can you even see?"

"Totally! The night-vision goggles are working great."

The commute took about a half hour. There were a few spots on the trail where Fox was able to open up the speed on the snowmobile. However, Fox had to slow down to a comfortable speed several times for her friend. It didn't matter that A.C. designed the snowmobile; she was scared to death of it. It also didn't help that the snow was as icy and solid as Campbell predicted. It really felt like the snowmobile grinded chunks of rock as it trudged across the frozen tundra.

They reached the valley under the mountain. Fox recognized the landscape and where they flew the helicopter a short time earlier. There was some tree growth near the lake, and Fox drove near that spot. The tire tracks she saw from the sky earlier were still present. The vehicle that left them was heavy and sank into the mud.

"Looks like a semi-truck," Fox said.

"Very dangerous to drive that through here," A.C. added.

"They're in a hurry. No time for safety."

Fox followed the tracks. They weaved back up onto the hiking trail and up onto the mountain until they came upon the anomaly they saw from the helicopter. Fox looked down the hill from this position. They were sitting ducks in the event of a trap. There was too much open space and positions from which to fire long-range weapons. She didn't like this at all. If this was a mine, it was a classic case of hiding the entrance in plain sight. It also gave the *real* masterminds a perfect view of the operation.

Fox shut off the snowmobile and stood up from the seat. She removed the night-vision goggles and allowed herself a moment for her eyes to adjust to the natural light from the moon. She watched the clouds of breath leaving her mouth in the moonlight. She and A.C. walked over to the rock wall, snow crunching under their feet. A.C. tapped it gently. There was a curious echo that came off it.

"Metal?" Fox asked. She slid her hand across the surface. It certainly didn't feel like rock. She moved horizontally, trying to find the edge. She eventually swiped past it onto solid rock. She peered closer and dug in where the rock met the metal. Sure enough, there was a subtle crack in the mountain face.

A.C. had done the same as Fox on the other side. They looked at each other, pleased that they seemingly discovered a door into the mountain.

"How do we get it open?" Fox was sincere with her question. She needed A.C. the engineer to take over in this spot.

"It doesn't look electronically held in place," A.C. said. "It'll take me a minute to figure it out. Hang tight."

Fox went back to the snowmobile and spotted the long-range listening device. She decided to do some reconnaissance while A.C. figured out the door. Fox brought the listening device with her and knelt down. She turned it on and directed it at the door. There was commotion right away. All sorts of activity was going on inside, and she waited for her ears to adjust while listening for anything specific. There were voices inside, as if the door weren't proof enough that they were in the right place. The voices were muffled. It was hard to hear exactly what they said. She picked out a few words, but it was difficult to make out complete sentences behind the barrier. There were more than a few voices. Some of them were high pitched. There was even some indistinguishable noise that sounded similar to crying. Odd, Fox thought.

"Got it," A.C. said. "There's a tab over on this side. Check the other side. Should be another one."

Fox did as A.C. instructed. She searched around near the ground where A.C. found the tab on her side. Fox felt a notch and jiggled it. It came undone, and there was a slight nudge from the frame.

"OK, help me lift it," A.C. said.

She and Fox dug their fingers under a slight crevice and hoisted upward. As expected, the door was heavy, like an auto shop garage door but without any of the contraptions that made it easy to open. It opened outward as Fox and A.C. took steps back with each lift. But, just like a garage door, once Fox and A.C. lifted past a certain point, the hydraulic arms on the inside took over and the door whipped up on its own to reveal the tunnel down into the mountain. A rope dangled from the door in front of them. This was clearly used to close the door from inside the mountain.

Fox felt melodramatic as she watched the cave turn downwards into the hellish underworld.

"Down we go into the dragon's lair."

CHAPTER 40

Fox readied her Beretta and led the way into the cave with A.C. at the rear holding her airsoft needler rifle, a dangerous weapon in its own right. The cave was exceptional, and Fox couldn't believe that Mickey Blaze's criminal syndicate managed to keep it a secret for as long as they had. How did they blast through the mountain? How did they extract the diamonds? How did they do these things without getting caught? It further proved that Fox was in over her head when dealing with these people. Blaze was the tip of the iceberg, and getting her out of here in handcuffs and *not* in a body bag was the most important goal to accomplish right now. The world was at risk and needed more information about this group.

The voices down the end of the tunnel grew louder, and Fox saw faint light at the end where the people attached to those voices convened. Just like outside the mountain, there wasn't much cover into which Fox and A.C. could hide, and this confrontation was likely to get started quickly as soon as anyone turned around to see them walking through the cave. Fox motioned for A.C. to step carefully as they tried to muffle their movements.

She registered the voices now. One of them was definitely Blaze. Then, Fox's heart stopped as she heard the sound of crying just as she did when using the listening device. It wasn't the sound of an adult crying. It was the sound of a child. It was followed by a distinct "Shut up" coming from a man. The crying stopped. Fox and A.C. glanced at each other. They both had the same concerned expression. Did Blaze have a child inside the cave?

Fox crept forward, and the room came into view. The lighting was dim, just a few mobile towers powered by small generators. Fox and A.C. would be able to hide as long as they didn't draw attention to themselves. However, the situation was even worse than Fox expected. It wasn't just one child in the cave. Fox spotted five children huddled together in a group monitored by a guard holding a gun. The children were four boys and one girl. There were three other guards in the room. Fox recognized all of them as the guards from Blaze's mansion. They moved around the cave, carried large boxes, and placed them into the semi-trailer truck. They struggled to lift and move the largest crates. The lid was open on one of the crates, and it was filled to the brim with raw diamonds that had been hacked away from the cave walls. Fox turned her attention to Blaze, who barked orders to the guards and also held a gun.

Fox and A.C. knelt onto the rocky tunnel surface. Fox studied the children. They were dirty and bruised. It was clear to Fox why they were here. They were used as slave labor to mine the raw diamonds. Fox's stomach dropped and her heart hurt. All five children looked to be between the ages of ten and twelve years old. Why did that seem so familiar to Fox? Her mind raced, and the answer hit her a few seconds later as her eyes went wide. These children were the ones mentioned in the analyst report she encountered last month. They were the children that went missing from foster homes all across the United States. The FBI was looking for these missing children.

Mickey Blaze was responsible for all of it! The unconfirmed report of the diamond mine in Canada. The missing children. Blaze was the criminal behind both reports. Smuggling, kidnapping, and murder, a trifecta of villainy. Fox's blood boiled. She'd experienced a wide range of emotions during this investigation, but she'd always kept her composure or at least bounced back in a positive way. However, this crossed the line. They were no longer playing a lady's game. Blaze was not a rival playing on the wrong side of the law. She was a twisted villain, and Fox expended her last ounce of patience to not pull the trigger on her Beretta.

We need her alive, Fox thought. She glanced at A.C., and her friend showed the same anger. Fox had more experience than A.C. at repressing impulses. It's why Fox immediately forgave her friend for what she did next. The armory chief lifted her airsoft needler and aimed it directly at the guard standing above the children. She pulled the trigger, and the low hum of the dart exploding from the chamber with the push of the CO_2 echoed through the cave. The dart zipped toward the guard in a flash and impaled the back of his shoulder. The guard wailed in pain, and the children shrieked.

Everyone whirled in the tunnel's direction, and their faces widened in recognition. They pulled their weapons up as A.C. fired two more darts, knocking down two guards with shots at their legs. Fox scrambled for Blaze, who raised her gun to shoot at A.C. Fox fired the Beretta first, a non-lethal direct hit at Blaze's hand. Shrapnel and blood exploded from Blaze's hand as she crumpled in agony.

Machine gun fire sprayed around the tunnel entrance from the two unharmed guards. Fox barreled forward toward Blaze, who heaved the pieces of her broken gun at Fox, despite the injury. The distraction was just enough to catch Fox off guard. Blaze lurched forward and tackled Fox into the opened crate of raw diamonds. The box spilled the minerals onto the ground, as Fox and Blaze followed end over end. Two more low thuds blasted from A.C.'s direction, which were followed by two more wails of pain from the guards.

Fox pushed Blaze away and turned to A.C. The guards were disabled by her darts, but one of them garnered enough strength to pull his weapon into position and aim it at A.C. Her attention was on the children as she rushed over to them. Fox fired the Beretta at the staggered guard and hit him square in the chest. Her heart ached from the kill, as this officially became her bloodiest job to date.

Blaze gave her no quarter. The lunatic race car driver struck Fox with something heavy. Fox turned with just enough time to block the blunt blow from being fatal, but it was a disastrous hit that left Fox staggered and prone to another attack.

"How!?" Blaze shrieked. "How did you find us!?"

Fox noticed the weapon now. It was a hulking clunk of raw diamond. Blaze swung it down. Fox blocked weakly. It was enough to keep from taking another strike to the head, but Blaze stayed atop her.

Fox heard A.C. comforting the children. The girl cried and embraced A.C. when A.C. told her that she and Fox were with the police and came to rescue them. Fox directed her attention back to Blaze just in time to block another flurry of strikes. Fox found an opening in Blaze's ferocity and retaliated with the pepper spray in her coat. Blaze yelped, and her hands went up to her eyes. Fox pushed Blaze off and retrieved her gun. She aimed it at Blaze.

"I can't believe I felt pity for you," Fox said. "Here I thought you were a victim of circumstance. I could reason with you. But no. You're just as bad as whoever's pulling the strings. Kidnapping children. Pitiful." Fox pulled out the handcuffs from her coat and tossed them onto the ground in front of Blaze. "Put those on."

The three guards that were still alive surrendered their weapons while grasping their wounds. Fox tossed another pair of handcuffs to A.C., and A.C. pulled out two pairs of her own to restrain the guards.

"Can we go home now?" one of the boys asked A.C. in a soft voice. It was the same question that A.C. asked Fox in Blaze's dungeon. This time, A.C. was the one who got to be the hero and answer the question.

"Yes, we're getting you out of here."

Tears streaked down Blaze's face from the pepper spray as she snapped the cuffs onto her own wrists behind her back. She stared at Fox with red eyes and mouth in a scowl. Before the children were involved, Fox might have come up with some snide remark, but she didn't feel it right now. All she felt was disdain for Mickey Blaze kidnapping these children and forcing them into slavery for her criminal syndicate. However, she was also upset with herself. How much time had she wasted preparing to race in the Open Circuit Challenge when she could have been searching for the missing children? She intercepted the report a month ago. These children had been away from home for a long time, and Fox felt responsible that she didn't drop what she was doing to help them.

She shook it off. She was in the middle of a mission, and all that mattered was getting everyone out alive.

"Where's Pyne?" Fox asked.

Blaze remained silent for a moment before she gave in. "He's in the truck. Sleeping off the surgery."

A.C. rushed to the truck. He wasn't inside. She moved to the trailer and climbed inside. She gasped and moved out of Fox's line of sight. After a moment, she came back out. Fox saw the relief on her friend's face before she spoke.

"He's OK," A.C. said. "He really needs a hospital, but he's OK. Fast asleep. These monsters are keeping him in there like he's another storage item."

Fox spoke into her two-way radio. "Campbell, it's Fox."

"Go ahead, Fox."

"Diamond mine confirmed. Suspects apprehended. Suspects had hostages. Hostages are alive. All of them are children. We need your help getting them out of here."

"Copy that, Fox. We're sending a team. Wait. What the hell? What's that? Go check that out. Hang on, Fox. Something's going on out here."

Fox turned to Blaze, who looked even more terrified than Campbell sounded, almost as if she knew what was happening. It wasn't the look of someone who was about to be rescued.

Campbell continued, "It's a helicopter. Dammit, I didn't think they'd send someone to relieve me of my duties so quickly. How the hell did they get here so fast?"

Fox's heart rate picked up. "Blaze, what is it? What's happening out there?"

"It's them."

"Who's them?"

Blaze's skin had turned pale white out of fear. "The people pulling the strings, as you so *eloquently* put it."

"Campbell!" Fox shouted into the radio. "Campbell, wait!"

Fox heard the distinct clatter of machine gun fire and the shattering of glass, and then the two-way radio went silent on Campbell's end.

"Campbell! Campbell! Are you alive? Campbell!"

"It's too late," Blaze said. "Your friend is dead."

"What's going on? Tell me!"

"The order's been given. The Board of Directors is cleaning up my mess."

"What does that mean?"

"They're coming here," Blaze said, "and they're going to kill all of us, including me."

Genuine panic crept into Fox. She should have expected something like this. She *did* expect something like this. Yet, as she stood in front of her adversary holding the Beretta, she still wasn't prepared for it to happen. Fox had done her job *too* well. She humiliated Blaze on national television, and the syndicate that had bailed her out in the past had given up on her. They turned against Mickey Blaze, and it meant death for everyone involved with her.

CHAPTER 41

Jett Fox slowed her breathing. She took a moment to relax and think about the situation. The first thing she needed to do was reassure the children. She put the Beretta back into her winter coat and joined A.C. by the children. They looked up at the two of them with sheer terror in their eyes. Fox bent down so she could look them in the eyes.

"We're going to get you out of here," Fox said, "but it might take a little longer than we thought. How about you kids go get in that truck and sit in the backseat. Keep each other warm, OK?"

The children hesitated, but one by one they nodded and walked to the truck. A.C. helped them all inside and made sure they were comfortable. She closed the door gently.

"What's the plan?" A.C. asked.

"I have no idea." Fox glanced at the tunnel and remembered that they left the door open. "We need to close the cave door. Buy as much time as possible to come up with an escape plan."

They walked over to the three injured guards. Fox sighed as she saw the one she killed slumped near his three buddies. "You three understand that all of us are marked for death, right?"

They all nodded. Fox moved around them and unlocked their handcuffs.

"What are you doing?" A.C. protested.

Fox ignored her and addressed the guards. "I don't care how bad you're hurt. I need you to get all the diamonds out of the trailer. You three are riding back there. If we come back and you've laid even one hand on those kids, I'll kill you. Do you understand? You want to survive this, you'll do everything I say." She turned to A.C. "Come on."

Fox moved to Blaze, who remained still in her handcuffs. Her expression toward Fox hadn't changed. She had mostly recovered from getting pepper sprayed. The tear streaks had dried, and the red eyes burned with amazing fury. Her expression then turned smug.

"Looks like you're getting your wish," Blaze said. "Get me out of this, Jett, and I'll tell you everything you want to know about the organization."

"How many of them will they bring? I already know they have a helicopter, but what else are they bringing?"

"Large squad, about twelve or thirteen soldiers. Given the terrain, most of them will be on snowmobiles. You'll have a few on foot to stay back in case of any diversions."

"And they want you dead first and foremost?"

"Yes."

Fox sensed a plan coming to fruition. However, she wanted to kill Blaze. The desire burned within her. She hadn't allowed herself to cool off after discovering the kidnapped children, and she knew she needed to keep her distance from the automotive mogul. Fox turned on her heel and refused to engage with Blaze any further.

Fox hated herself like this. She didn't have control over the situation or her emotions, and she desperately needed both if everyone in the cave was going to get out of this alive.

She and A.C. made their way back up the tunnel and outside. Fox dragged the snowmobile into the cave, and then the two of them pulled down the massive garage door to hide the cave once again.

"It won't buy us a lot of time," Fox said, "but at least it's one more barrier to give us a chance."

"Mind letting me into that head of yours?" A.C. said. "I think you have a plan, but I don't think I like it."

"I have an idea, but it's a little crazy, and I need to talk to Pyne before we do it," Fox said. "Let's go wake him up."

The guards had moved a few of the crates by the time Fox and A.C. returned. They were in pain and moving slowly after getting shot by the armory chief's dart thrower. Fox and A.C. climbed into the truck and knelt beside Pyne's makeshift bed. They gently woke him up. His eyes opened, and he smiled when he recognized his friends.

"I never had a doubt," Pyne said. His eyes went wide. "The children! Are the children all right?"

"They're OK," A.C. said. "They're in the truck."

Pyne relaxed. "I wanted to help them, but there was nothing I could do. I just had to wait for you to find us. But we're safe now."

"Unfortunately, we're not out of this yet," Fox said.

"What do you mean?"

Fox reiterated everything to Pyne about Blaze's organization tying up the loose ends.

"Then give me a gun and let me help," Pyne said.

"Pyne, you just had major surgery."

"I don't care. Whether we live or die, this is my last mission." He motioned toward his legs. "This is the end of the road for me. I want to make it count. Put me in the truck and let me kill anyone who comes near those children."

Fox considered. In truth, her plan required an extra pair of hands to protect the children and the truck driver as they escaped the cave. The original plan formulating in her head would have forced A.C. to do both on her own.

"Guard them with your life, Pyne," Fox said. "Let's get you into the truck."

Fox and A.C. carefully moved Pyne from the trailer and helped him into the front seat of the truck. The children were awake and silent. All of them were on edge. Fox reassured them that they were going to be leaving soon.

"This is Harry," Fox said. "He's going to protect you."

"I saw them hurt you," one of the boys said to Pyne.

Pyne turned around to see the children in the backseat. He said, "Just a few scratches. Nothing I can't handle."

"Are you guys like secret agents?" another of the boys asked.

"Yes," Fox said, "and Harry is the best one. You're safe with him."

Pyne turned back to Fox. "So what's the plan?"

"Classic misdirection. We'll set up explosives at the entrance, a controlled blast that won't bring the mountain down on us. Just enough to grab everyone's attention and maybe take out a couple of their foot soldiers. That's when I'll ride out on the snowmobile with Mickey Blaze hogtied to the back of it. She's the bait to get the enemy to follow me. I'll get as many of them chasing me as I can, and that's when A.C. drives the truck out of the cave and escapes with the children to safety. And Pyne, you'll shoot any stragglers. Simple enough, right?"

"I was right," A.C. said. "I don't like the plan, Jett. You're going to get yourself killed!"

"I don't see another way, A.C." Fox felt the fear coming over her, and she did her best to ignore it. "No matter what, we have to get the children out of here safely. This is the safest plan for them. We can't worry about me."

Fox returned to the injured guards, who had finished removing the diamond crates from the trailer. They looked awful, and Fox was disgusted with herself that she was pleased with their pain.

"Where are your explosives?"

One of the guards motioned to a pile of crates. Fox moved to the boxes and opened one. There were bars of C-4 inside. She motioned for A.C. to join her.

"Any chance you can cut one of these down to a distraction-level explosion?"

"On it," A.C. said.

Fox returned to her nemesis. Blaze was stoic. She sat on the cavern floor in silence with her wrists restrained by the cuffs. She watched Fox closely, and Fox approached her slowly, expecting a surprise attack.

"We have a plan. I'm taking you out on the snowmobile to give the others a chance to escape." Fox kept her distance from Blaze as she spoke her next words. "Any attempt to betray me, and I'll leave you in the mountains to die. Do we understand each other?"

"Yes."

"Good. Get up."

Fox lifted Blaze by the arm and pulled her to the snowmobile. She picked out rope from her miscellaneous items. She motioned for Blaze to sit down.

"You don't really expect me to sit tied down, do you?"

"I'm not letting you out of your handcuffs, and I can't have you bouncing off the snowmobile because you aren't able to balance yourself."

Blaze grimaced, but she gave in and sat in the passenger seat. Then, in the spirit of Cowtown, Fox looped the rope through the snowmobile and around Blaze like she was competing in the Calgary Stampede. She secured the roping with a tight knot. She nudged Blaze a few times until she was satisfied that Blaze couldn't move.

A.C. passed them on her way to plant the explosive. She took a long look at Blaze and the rope job. She grinned sardonically.

"Still not sure I like the idea of you being alone with her, even if she *is* tied up," A.C. said.

"It's OK." Fox looked Blaze right in the eyes. "She knows I can kick her ass if she tries anything."

Blaze glowered at Fox. She ignored the mogul and grabbed the listening device. She joined A.C. at the tunnel entrance. A.C. placed the miniaturized explosive onto the door and applied adhesive to keep it in position.

Fox put on the headphone and pointed the listening device at the door. She heard motorized vehicles outside. Those must be the snowmobiles, she thought. There were a few incoherent voices, although she heard the phrase "kill everyone inside." It was likely that they were getting into position. She was more interested in what she didn't hear. The repetitive choppy pounding of propeller blades didn't register on the listening device.

Either the helicopter wasn't near them yet, or it had landed somewhere in the valley. Blaze's organization expected a long night and didn't want to expend fuel, Fox thought.

"Bomb is ready," A.C. said.

"They're setting up out there," Fox said. "Whoever opens the door first is going to be at a disadvantage. They're willing to wait as long as *we* are willing to wait."

There was an advantage and disadvantage to using old technology like the manual garage door standing in front of the tunnel entrance, and they were the same pro and con for both sides. The advantage was that the shooting wouldn't start until both sides were absolutely ready for the fire fight. The disadvantage was that neither side gained a true leg up on the competition without sacrificing manpower just to open the door.

The one advantage Fox had over Blaze's former employer was that time was on her side. The longer this went on, the less time the enemy had to complete its mission and escape the wrath of the Royal Canadian Mounted Police. Fox was confident the enemy would blink first. She just had to keep the morale high inside the cave. That was easier said than done while they were trapped with murderers and kidnappers.

Fox and A.C. returned to Blaze.

"Where's your food? Or did you forget to bring any?"

"I thought we'd be out of here by now," Blaze admitted.

"So nothing?"

"There might be something down the tunnel a little way. We built a small break area close to where we mine the diamonds. There's a cupboard, but we didn't stock it. If there's anything in there, it's from the last dig. Might be stale."

They left Blaze and moved to the guards by the truck. As angry as Fox was at Blaze, she wasn't nearly as mad at these men. They weren't saints, and they were looking at serious prison time, but they weren't the masterminds. Everyone has to put food on the table, Fox thought. It was no excuse, but she understood that sometimes there were extenuating circumstances.

"Time to get in the trailer," Fox said.

The guards wearily stood and marched to the back. They climbed in.

"It's going to be a long night," Fox said. "Do your best to get comfortable."

Fox pulled down the trailer door and locked it into place.

"I'll check on Harry and the kids," A.C. said.

"I'll see if there's any food for them."

Fox moved carefully through the mine, wary of any last-second traps set by Blaze. She reached the cupboard and opened it. There wasn't much inside, a few oat and honey granola bars and an unopened sports drink. Fox returned with the snacks. The children were all still awake as Pyne was in the middle of reciting a story.

"So, there I was at the pyramids several miles outside Cairo. Agent Konnikova and I were attacked by a man the size of The Incredible Hulk. I can't remember his name. Let's call him Bonecrusher. He lifted a large stone over his head, and just as he was about to throw the stone onto Agent Konnikova, I grabbed him by the leg. He lost his balance and dropped the stone onto himself!"

The children gasped.

"But it didn't hurt him! The man was inhuman!"

"You're kidding me!" one of the boys exclaimed.

"Agent Konnikova and I escaped, but we had to hike through the desert all the way back to Cairo, and that was not the last time we'd encounter Bonecrusher."

Fox whispered to A.C. "This sounds a lot like *The Spy Who Loved Me*."

"I think it is," A.C. whispered back. "Agent Konnikova is Anya Amasova, and Bonecrusher is obviously Jaws."

"And Pyne is James Bond. Got it."

Fox divvied out the snacks to the children. She tested the sports drink to make sure there was nothing wrong with it before letting the children drink from the bottle. The girl had settled down significantly from when they first saw her. She was enamored of Harry Pyne and only took her eyes off him to eat her snack and sip from the sports drink. One by one, the children fell asleep. A.C. and Pyne also fell asleep. Fox noticed her own fatigue and was tempted to give into her drowsiness. She shook herself out of the daze and kept her eyes open. She got out of the truck to walk around the cave.

A long time passed, although Fox wasn't exactly sure how long had passed. Then among the quietness inside the mountain, Fox finally heard the thunderous mechanical rattle she had expected to hear. The helicopter woke up.

Fox ran to the truck and nudged A.C. and Pyne. They came to their senses quickly.

"It's time. They're getting ready to breach."

Fox's heart pounded hard just like it did before the race in Los Angeles. She allowed herself a second to calm down and then turned to her friends. Pyne must have recognized the look on her face. He spoke first.

"Ride fast and hard. Drinks are on me when we get out of this." He paused. "Fox, I trust very few people in this world, but you're one of them. I know you'll get us out of here."

Fox felt a smile form on her face. When Harry Pyne wanted to be kind, he was extraordinary at it.

"Could you say something elitist and condescending? You're making me uncomfortable with kindness."

Pyne smiled. "Very well. We both know that I'd ride that snowmobile much more effectively if my legs weren't shot to hell."

"That's more like it."

She turned to A.C., who was on the verge of tears. She performed admirably in her first field assignment, but the toll was high.

"No time to cry, A.C. We have work to do. Keep these kids safe."

"Buffalo chicken salads on you when we get back to New York?"

"Deal."

Fox gave her friends one last look and took in their faces, as if she might never see them again. Operatives were trained to avoid those thoughts and feelings, but Fox disagreed with that technique. It was only natural to think about death and how one might avoid it. This was the most scared Fox had ever felt, and she had a lot to lose if the mission failed. So she chose to embrace the possibility. She thought about death, but she also thought about the skill she needed to employ over the next half hour or so to avoid that fate. After all, survival for the children, Pyne, and A.C. relied on Fox staying alive long enough to provide a quality distraction.

Fox reached the snowmobile and shoved Blaze. She was already awake.

"I heard the helicopter," Blaze said.

"It's about to get a lot louder."

CHAPTER 42

No listening device was necessary. Jett Fox heard the squad outside mobilizing into position. The helicopter hovered in place a short way off from the mountain. The fireworks would ignite in a matter of seconds.

Fox spoke into the two-way radio. "Big Sister to Little Sister. Come in, Little Sister."

"I read you, Big Sister. Over."

"Standby to detonate the tunnel on my mark."

"Copy that."

One final calm before the storm settled over the impending battlefield. Fox felt a chill run down her spine, and she wasn't sure if that was the thrill of war or Blaze's ghastly exhalation making the hairs on her neck stand up straight.

"Jett, I have to tell you something," Blaze said.

"We're past it, Blaze."

"Please, just in case we die, I have to get this off my chest."

Fox sighed. "Go ahead."

"I feel bad about all of this. I know you think I'm a monster, and maybe I am, but you just don't understand this organization, Jett. If they want you, they'll get you.

I had no choice in joining them." Blaze sighed. "Or maybe I did, but they enticed me so well that I was already in before I realized it was too late to get out."

Fox wanted to believe Blaze was telling the truth, but there were five reasons to not believe Blaze sitting in the truck with A.C. and Pyne. There was also the woman for whom Fox dedicated this entire investigation, Sharon Graham.

"I get smuggling to try and make an extra buck, but why murder and kidnapping? Sharon Graham didn't need to die, and those kids didn't need to be stolen from their homes."

"That's why I targeted orphans! I..."

Fox cut Blaze off. "I don't want to hear it! There is no excuse to make me believe you were justified in kidnapping children!"

There was scratching and clicking at the entrance. The enemy soldiers had unlatched the door. A creak followed as the door lifted from the ground outward.

Fox spoke into the radio, "Get ready, A.C."

Sunlight shone through the tunnel opening. They had been inside of the cave all night as the morning glow came in around the feet of the opposing henchman. Fox waited for the precise moment. Just as the hydraulic arms began to take over the rest of the work for the henchman to open the garage door, Fox shouted to her friend.

"Now!"

Flames erupted and engulfed the two men who opened the door. They were the poor saps chosen for the suicide mission, and they had no chance once A.C. pressed the detonator. The explosion rocked the cave with a boisterous boom, which made Fox nervous that the mountain would fall onto them. The echo through the tunnel was nearly unbearable, like standing next to a rocket inside a silo as it launched toward the sky.

Fox pressed down on the accelerator, and the snowmobile lurched forward through the tunnel and into the smoke. Gunfire was upon her in an instant. The snowmobile barreled ahead of the smoke and out into the open air. Fox got her first look at just how seriously Blaze's organization took this assassination attempt. There were just as many troops as Blaze had predicted, a large squad of fourteen men both on foot and machine. The helicopter hovered above them like a dragon waiting to incinerate its prey. Fox kept her aching thumb on the throttle and turned the vehicle west, the opposite direction of where A.C. was to drive the truck. Please see that the woman on the snowmobile is Blaze, Fox thought. Follow me.

The machine kicked up snow as Fox raced westward deeper into the mountains toward the Alberta and British Columbia provincial border. The morning sunrise was at her back to show her the way. Fox heard the heavy sound of vehicles trailing behind her. She glanced quickly and smiled. Every machine chased after her, including the helicopter. The only ones who stayed behind were the foot soldiers, and Fox was confident A.C. and Pyne could handle them. The diversion worked. These people *really* wanted to kill Mickey Blaze.

Gunfire came from all directions. Fox swerved the snowmobile to make the target more difficult for them to hit. She accelerated to dangerous speeds, and one wrong move would mean death from a crash rather than bullets. Fox reached a switchback that would take them down the mountain toward the valley. She used it. She checked to see that her pursuers followed. The helicopter zipped across to try and cut Fox off. The gunner on the chopper fired the heavy gun, and snow and mud exploded all around Fox as she maneuvered. Blaze shouted all sorts of obscenities from the passenger seat.

Now was the time for Fox to lose some of her pursuers. She spotted an open field and turned toward it. She decreased her speed just enough to lure in her enemies. They picked up their speed in turn. Fox went through her mind back to the day A.C. introduced her to the super snowmobile and all of its features. A.C.'s voice chimed in her head about "a spike drop on the underside to ward off any unwanted followers with unfriendly debris."

Fox cycled through the features and came to the spike drop. She cranked the wheel on a dime and threw ice into the air. She pressed the button for the spike drop. A trail of metal jagged burs littered across the tracks that

Fox left in her wake. The three pursuers closest to Fox matched her turn and veered right onto her track. There was a snap, crackle, and pop of their snowmobiles sucking in the metal debris, and then all three engines coughed and sent the riders crashing into the snow.

The remaining snowmobile riders drove around the trail to avoid the spikes. Fox had turned and faced their direction. They opened fire on her as she whirled the snowmobile around to chase the stragglers. She cycled on the touchpad up to the machine guns. The double barrels opened from the headlights. Fox held her off-hand over the trigger and pulled. The snowmobile rollicked at the blasts from the heavy guns as her machine gun fire lit up sparks and snow eruptions around the enemy riders. One man clutched at his leg after getting hit. He crashed his vehicle and then lay in the snow grasping his leg in pain.

Fox moved toward the southwestern direction and accelerated at breakneck speed away from the others. They adjusted and chased her once again. She felt pleased with herself as she had taken out half the snowmobile riders with the spikes and machine guns. However, the super snowmobile only had one trick left, and she wanted to save that one for a last resort.

"Blaze, are you still alive?"

"Yes, damnit!"

The remaining four riders barreled down the hill after Fox, followed closely by the helicopter. The heavy gun erupted from the sky once again. Fox weaved the armory chief's special weapon around mounds and rocks to stay out of fire, but she was running out of space. The maneuvers cost her as the snowmobiles closed the gap.

Fox pulled out the Beretta from her holster. She looked over her left shoulder and saw the driver gain ground. He had aimed his own machine pistol at Blaze. Fox jerked the snowmobile, and the man's shots sailed over their heads. Fox retaliated with three shots from her Beretta. The first connected with the man's shoulder, the second ricocheted off the throttle, and the third pierced the man's hand. He lost control of his vehicle and collided with another driver. The two of them tumbled end over end, snowmobiles crumpling into twisted metal. That left only two more riders!

A thicket of trees sprung out a short way down the mountain. Fox aimed the snowmobile at the trees and picked up speed. The helicopter pilot must have anticipated her movement as the machine whirred ahead. The gunner fired leading shots at the tree line to force Fox to shift away from the target area.

Fox backtracked and saw the carnage she left behind. In front of it were the two remaining riders with their machine pistols drawn and ready to fire. They unleashed a merciless barrage of bullet spray. Fox dropped her head behind the throttle and yelled for Blaze to do the same. Fox felt Blaze's head nestle against her back as they charged toward the two men.

Fox activated the double barrels on her super snowmobile and let out her own fury.

She didn't see it happen, but she must have hit one as the snowmobile to her left skidded away. Fox cranked her handles in that direction. She saw the wounded soldier in the fetal position on the ground with the snowmobile wrecked a short distance from him. The final rider rounded after passing Fox and began pursuit once again. Fox looked at the gauge on her snowmobile guns. She was out of ammunition. She checked with Blaze again to make sure that she was still alive. Blaze confirmed.

The soldiers inside the helicopter had made up their minds about which direction they wanted Fox to drive. The heavy turret fire continued as Fox frantically darted the snow machine in and out of the line of fire. They directed her away from the trees to keep her in the open. They hadn't been able to hit her yet, but how long could she keep this up? Fox decided to make a break for the lake in the valley.

Fox pressed hard on the throttle, ignoring the searing pain shooting through her hand. She knew that snowmobiles could outrun helicopters, but it was incredibly dangerous to try it. She heard the heavy turret fire raining from the sky. Fox's snowmobile gained speed, and the shooting ceased. The gunner must have failed to crank the turret in her direction fast enough, Fox thought. A motor hissed a short distance behind her.

Fox spared a look and saw the final snowmobile picking up speed to catch her.

Icy chunks floated on the lake's surface, but for the most part it had thawed this late in the winter. Fox improvised a plan in her mind as she spotted a log and other various debris along the muddy banks. The snow grew thinner down at this lower elevation, and Fox risked her own snowmobile consuming unwanted scrap. The pursuer fired a continuous spray from the machine pistol. Fox shouted for Blaze to keep her head down again. Fox spun and used the momentum of her own legs to help the snowmobile turn on a dime to face the pursuer. She lifted the Beretta and fired a few rounds. Keeping track of her count, she had only three shots left. The driver ducked to avoid her fire. Fox wrenched her hand over the throttle and burst ahead back toward the mountain, passing the pursuer in the process. Fox glanced backward and saw her plan come to fruition. The final snowmobile toppled over the forest debris and launched the driver forward until he splashed into the lake. The snowmobile coughed and died.

All ground troops eliminated in one form or another! Fox thought. She turned to face the helicopter just as the gunner aimed the turret in her direction. There was no reprieve. The heavy blasts boomed from the gun toward the earth, and Fox slammed the throttle yet again. A spray of ice came down over Fox and Blaze, as Fox narrowly escaped the machine gun's turbulence.

"Little Sister to Big Sister." It was A.C.'s voice coming in over the walkie-talkie. "We're on the move. We can hear your distraction from here. King George has neutralized the enemy foot soldiers. Stay alive. We'll see you in a bit."

Suddenly, the firing ceased from the helicopter gunner. The steel beast in the sky changed direction away from Fox. As the blades sliced through the air, and the chopper sailed westward, Fox's eyes went wide. Whether it was A.C.'s broadcast that they intercepted or a straggler among the foot soldiers who survived and made contact, the message had been relayed, and now the helicopter headed straight for Fox's friends. The diversion worked briefly, but the assassins in the helicopter picked up on the plan. A.C. and Pyne were exposed.

Fox saw her path around the lake. She'd cut it close, but she could make it and save her friends from doom. But just as she wrenched the throttle, a noose went around her neck. Her windpipe tightened, and her body thrust backward. The snowmobile kicked forward and then toppled onto the ground as Fox lay gasping for air with something around her neck choking the life from her body. Panic set in, and Fox knew what had happened. Somehow, Blaze escaped her bonds and gripped tightly to Fox.

CHAPTER 43

Jett Fox had no time to assess the situation. The long and short of it was that Mickey Blaze used the last trick card up her sleeve and had Fox dead to rights. Blaze waited until she had a glimpse of hope for escape. Fox did the dirty work by eliminating the assassins. Blaze needed only to finish off Fox, and she could disappear. How long had Blaze pretended to be restrained on the snowmobile? Did she break out of her bonds in the middle of the night while Fox shared snacks and stories with her friends? Did she do it while they raced across the mountainside avoiding gunfire?

The rope around Fox's neck was the same rope that she used to restrain Blaze. Her adversary had given her a taste of her own medicine. Fox escaped from Blaze's mansion in improbable fashion, and now Blaze had done the same in the Canadian Rockies. Fox might have felt sorry for herself had she not been gasping for air and scrambling to break Blaze's grip. As it stood, Fox thought only to keep from suffocating and looked everywhere for her gun that must have bounced away when Blaze initiated her attack.

Blaze surprised Fox with her strength. She used raw ferocity to keep the spry Fox at bay. Fox reached for Blaze's hands while working on pure instinct. The death grip sank deeper, and Fox saw darkness slipping over her vision. The mountain and lake became blurry. The helicopter flew farther and farther away in the direction of her friends.

"Be a good girl and die, Jett."

The words dripped from Blaze's mouth like venom. Fox felt her strength waning. Her legs kicked involuntarily. She kicked away the layer of snow under feet and splashed in the mud. She jerked against Blaze's body, but that just made the hold around her neck that much worse. Fox was stronger than Blaze, and if she had enough time, she'd break free of Blaze's grasp. However, Fox was sure to suffocate before Blaze's adrenaline-powered stranglehold ceased. She had mere seconds left before she died.

Fox faced the worst possible outcome. The mission report on Solace's desk would read something like this: Fox died, her friends died, the hostage children died, and Blaze escaped. It was a critical failure of humiliating proportions, and there was no one left to pick up the trail. The secret organization that kept Blaze afloat stayed in business. Blaze fled the country and was still at large. No one would ever see her again. Yes, that would be the final report that Solace would lock behind a secure firewall. She would disavow Fox and A.C. and delete the paper trail leading back to Harry Pyne.

That would have been the final report had Fox not seen the handcuffs dangling from Blaze's right wrist. The left cuff remained perfectly intact without an arm to hold in place. So that was it! Blaze had escaped the handcuff using Fox's exact same masochistic tactic. She broke her own thumb to slip her hand through the cuff, and then she used the steel to cut into the ropes. It must have taken her all night, and she waited patiently for the right moment to spring her trap on Fox after the assassins were neutralized. Clever, Mickey Blaze!

With one final gasp before her life ended, Fox thrust her hand over Blaze's left thumb. She applied all the pressure she had left and waited for the pain to overcome Blaze. The banshee's wail nearly ruptured Fox's eardrum. The grip loosened. Fox doubled down on the pressure, cranking the thumb backward. Fox felt the bone snap like a chicken wing, and the rope around her neck slackened completely. Blaze shrieked and rolled in the snow in agony. Fox desperately sucked in the cold mountain air and coughed out the death inside of her.

Fox spotted the tree line on the other side of the lake. The helicopter would be on top of her friends in just a few minutes. She stumbled to her feet and fell back down into the snow. She breathed heavily. Her respiratory system raced to catch up and balance itself. Fox looked around the area and saw her gun near the shore. She stumbled across the snow and into the soft dirt. She picked up the gun and then turned to face the lake.

Something stirred in the water. A man emerged. The icy water poured off his body as he marched at a snail's pace like some sort of sea zombie. It was the assassin from the snowmobile! He had conviction in his eyes. His body trembled from the cold. He raised his arm to reveal the machine pistol. He ignored Fox and aimed the lethal weapon at Blaze. Beleaguered, Fox aimed the Beretta at the man and pulled the trigger. The shot missed, but it drew the assassin's attention away from Blaze. He whirled to aim at Fox. She pulled the trigger a second time. A direct hit at the man's shooting hand! The machine pistol clattered away, and the chilled assassin dropped to the ground and clutched his arm. Fox approached him and whipped her gun across his head to knock him unconscious.

She then trudged up to Blaze. The two women stared at each other without saying anything. Fox then pointed the gun at Blaze's leg and pulled the trigger. Blaze let out another shrieking wail. Fox had aimed carefully for a non-fatal part of the leg, and she was satisfied with the flesh wound after hitting the shot.

"Don't go anywhere."

Fox stashed the empty Beretta back into her jacket and ran to the snowmobile. She lifted it from the ground and climbed onto the driver's seat. She ignited the engine and rammed the throttle. She lost precious time dealing with Blaze and the assassin, and the dark cloud of gloomy doubt hovered over her as she raced against the clock to catch up to the helicopter.

How much time had she wasted wrestling with Blaze in the snow? She saw the helicopter scouring the hiking trails on the opposite side of the lake. It had the distinct advantage of flying over terrain, whereas Fox worked her way around the lake back toward the mountain. She remembered the trees that the helicopter gunner prevented her from entering earlier. She could use those as a shortcut, but she would have to be precise with her driving to avoid wrapping the snowmobile around a tree and killing herself. She then looked to the lakeshore. Might that be a possibility? No, the snow along the shore was far too slushy that she'd suck mud into the snowmobile's engine. The trees were the best option to keep her friends alive, but it required Fox at her best. Even then, Fox knew that A.C. would have to buy her time with defensive driving.

Fox neared speeds of 100 mph as she sped up the mountain toward the trees. She let off the gas and saw the men who were still alive sitting up and figuratively licking their wounds. They watched Fox speed past them, but they made no motion to attack her. She raced inside the forest and adjusted her driving style. Getting through these abbreviated woods wasn't about pulse-pounding RPMs, but rather precision and maneuverability. Fox moved her eyes from side to side and kept the obstacles in her line of sight at all times. However, the sun had fully risen by this point, making it extra difficult for Fox as she drove into the glare. A.C. built a hell of a machine, Fox thought, as the super snowmobile proved every bit as reliable, weaving in and out of trees, outrunning the assassins as it did.

She saw the fuel gauge. It was low, but it wasn't a concern yet. This encounter with the assassin helicopter would be over one way or another before she ran out of fuel. She switched the panel over to the final weapon she had in her arsenal, and the only one that could save her friends. The image of the heat-seeking missile pulled up on the screen. She wondered if she could get to her friends in time to use it, or if she held onto false hope.

Come on! Fox thought. Faster, damn you!

An explosion rocked the mountain. Fox felt the tremors come up from the ground and shake the vehicle. She allowed herself a moment to glance up through branches and saw the orange glow of flames. The helicopter fired one of its rockets. She feared the worst. Was she too late? Had the helicopter already incinerated her friends? Machine gun fire followed from the turret. No, they weren't dead yet, but they were running out of time. Fox dared herself to pick up the pace in the dense wooded traffic. The snowmobile accelerated, and Fox nearly missed seeing a wounded foot soldier. He limped through the woods and saw Fox driving toward him at her deadly pace. He dove out of the way at the same time she tilted the bars to avoid hitting him. She corrected her course and missed hitting a tree by only a few centimeters.

"Jett! The chopper is on us! Are you still alive?"

Fox couldn't afford to answer A.C. without losing her focus on the narrow woods. She left the two-way radio alone and drove at a quickened pace while bouncing her vision left and right between the trees and directing the snowmobile with the perfect precision necessary to keep it from crashing. She saw the clearing up ahead. At last! After a few more maneuvers to keep the super machine upright, Fox barreled ahead through the clearing, breaking a few branches on the way. She soared across a mound of ice and turned the vehicle onto the trail. She fishtailed slightly, but corrected smoothly and carried on ahead.

The semi-trailer truck's tracks were fresh. Fox followed them and saw the helicopter about a half mile ahead of her. Too far! She red-lined the RPMs, and the super snowmobile jerked forward, nearly knocking her backward. This was it, the final gasp. She reached point-of-no-return speed on the machine. Her heart pounded at the same speed against her chest. Finally, the truck came into view. She saw Pyne's head out the window. He fired off a few shots at the helicopter with his gun. They were impossible shots. He made them out of desperation. The helicopter fired another rocket, and A.C. jerked the wheel to narrowly avoid the explosion. Fox had to do the same thing on the snowmobile. She felt the heat from the flames as she whizzed by the spot of the explosion. Pyne leaned out the window again and fired off another shot. He turned and saw Fox catching up to them on the snowmobile. Fox heard him shout to A.C. "It's Fox!"

Fox spoke into the walkie-talkie. "A.C., slam the brakes! I'll take it from here!"

The red taillights illuminated, and Fox gained considerable ground on the semi-trailer truck. She moved to pass around it, as the helicopter zoomed ahead. Fox moved back onto the road ahead of the truck just as the pilot flipped the helicopter around. Fox faced the helicopter dead on, each on a collision sprint. She swiped the snowmobile's missile system. It registered the chopper's heat signature. "Pull the trigger to launch the missile." It indicated the same trigger that Fox used to fire the snowmobile's machine guns. Fox looked up at the helicopter. It looked ready to fire its remaining weapons at her. She held her hand over the trigger and initiated the launch.

The explosion at the snowmobile's rear startled her. She expected it to sound somewhat like a bottle rocket on the Fourth of July, but it was much louder than that. The heat that emanated from it felt like a burn on her back. A.C. was right. She built the mini-silo too close to the passenger seat. The rocket would have left considerable burns on Blaze's body had she still been restrained.

The armory missile torched the sky. The dragon that hauntingly hovered above the syndicate assassins earlier readied a rocket of its own to deliver the death blow to Jett Fox. But that assault never came. Instead, the mechanical beast ruptured into an orange ball as bright as the sun. The blades that propelled it upward into the sky broke away and sliced onto the ground like darts. The flaming carcass dropped like an anvil and crashed into the snow with a destructive boom that echoed through the valley and up across the face of Mount Columbia. Fox steered the snowmobile off the road to narrowly avoid falling debris. She crashed the vehicle and thudded onto the ground as all she heard were the flames that emanated from the assassination chopper and the idle engine of the semi-trailer truck.

"*Nossa Senhora!*" Fox sighed in Portuguese. It was the Portuguese version of "OMG!"

Fox lay for a long moment until she heard engines coming from the southeast. She sat up. She checked the weapons in her coat. She had nothing left. Out of options, she stood and raised her arms up above her head in surrender. We tried, she thought. We're out of moves. She could only hope for mercy now.

She spotted the vehicles through the smoke. They were snowmobiles, but the riders weren't dressed like the assassins. These riders looked more official. In fact, the rider at the front looked familiar. Fox smiled. It was Inspector Campbell! Fox waved like a happy idiot. Campbell did the same.

Campbell and her team survived the attack by assassins. She pulled up the snowmobile next to Fox and shut off the engine.

"Were you the one that blew that thing out of the sky?"

"Sure was."

"It was one hell of a show, Fox! One hell of a show!"

A.C. approached with the five children from the truck. Fox looked to Pyne at the truck and gave him the thumbs-up sign. He returned the gesture. She turned back to Campbell.

"Get a hold of the FBI as soon as you can. They are looking for these children. We have another hostage in the front seat of the truck. He recently had surgery and can't move his legs. Be careful with him. And then we have three prisoners in the trailer."

"What about your suspect? Where is she?"

Fox looked west. "Across the lake. We'll have to go back for her. There are a lot of people to round up. Some of them are armed. Tell your officers to expect a fight."

Campbell smiled. "The Mounties *always* expect a fight."

The Mounties broke into two teams. One team ushered the children to a medical vehicle, and the other rallied to find the remaining assassins.

They returned a short time later with all prisoners in custody. Fox got to look Blaze in the eyes one last time as two individuals escorted her by the arms. Fox and Blaze simply stared at each other. Neither of them said a word, and then they went their separate ways.

CHAPTER 44

Jett Fox sat uncomfortably in the seat across the desk from Chairwoman Solace. She was turned around as they watched the news report on the television mounted on the wall. Again, it wasn't Solace's usual viewing. She had the channel turned to the Sporting Times Network. Fox's new acquaintance, Rhiannon Misrasi, delivered a news report about Mickey Blaze and the arrest in Canada.

"Given the jurisdictional complications, the United States, Canadian, and British governments compromised to have Blaze tried for all counts of smuggling, kidnapping, and murder at the International Criminal Court in the Netherlands..."

"It's not the usual story you'd see on the sports channel, is it?" Fox said.

"I told you not to underestimate the sports channel," Solace said.

They watched more of Rhiannon's television report. "... Blaze named members of the British Parliament and the United States Congress in her testimony, although it may take years to substantiate the accusations. Blaze claimed that all of them, including herself, were part of a secret criminal organization known as I Kingmakers. This group used Blaze's automotive empire as the means for smuggling everything from diamonds to drugs…"

"The Kingmakers," Solace said.

"Have you heard the name before?" Fox asked.

"No. This is new, and that's what scares me. Maybe if I'd heard of them, I could advise you better on how to handle them."

"They're not too scary," Fox said.

"Oh?" Solace looked genuinely confused by Fox's sudden bravado.

"Blaze got on the witness stand. If these Kingmakers were untouchable, she never would have made it this far."

Solace cracked a brief smile before it faded. "An astute observation, Agent Fox." She turned off the television. "I have to say, all things taken into account, this mission was a smashing success. You did excellent work."

"Thank you, ma'am."

"The FBI also sends its thanks for finding the missing children."

Fox became somber. She wasn't so sure it was her hard work that found the children. She lucked into them, and she hated getting credit for it. She was happy that they made it back to their foster homes safely, but she couldn't help but wonder how much worse things might have gotten for them had she not arrived in Calgary when she did. She shook off the thought and accepted the thanks.

"That's very kind of them."

"I think that wraps up this case. Well done, Agent Fox. See you in two weeks."

"I wish you weren't forcing me to take time off."

"Resting to heal your injuries is an important part of the job. The toll your body takes adds up, and it affects future assignments. Don't worry, hopefully Agent Stonecreek and I have more information on the Kingmakers by the time you get back."

Fox sighed. "Understood."

Solace studied her agent for a second. "You should fly home to Miami during your time off. Say hello to your grandfather for me. And while you're down there you might consider talking to a friend of mine. It seems he has a small problem and could use a little bit of help."

Fox and Solace shared a knowing smile. Solace handed a half-sheet of paper to Fox. Now this is more like it, Fox thought.

Fox returned to her desk to pack up her things for the day. She received a phone call from Rhiannon Misrasi.

"Did you see my report?" Rhiannon asked.

"Yes, sorry to force a little twist to your big post-race feature."

"Are you kidding? That turned out even better than I thought it would. I knew at the luncheon you were some kind of cop, but then all the craziness happened at the race and I realized you were insane."

"I appreciate your discretion, by the way. It was basically impossible not to blow my cover while investigating a celebrity."

"Happy to help, but it's not like I know your real name. You're still the ghost Juliana Ferreira."

"Tell you what, if you can correctly guess who I am, I'll confirm it for you."

"Do I get a hint?"

"Now where's the fun in that? You're the reporter. Use your journalistic tenacity."

"I bet I'll know the answer by the end of the day."

Fox changed the subject. "Hey, thanks for that warning you gave a couple days before the race. The one on TV about Blaze's team doing whatever it takes to help her win. It helped me prepare for the ambush on race day."

"I spent a lot of time around Mickey Blaze leading up to the race, and something seemed off about her. I had to get the word out to you. I'm just glad you knew what I was saying."

They wrapped up their phone conversation and Fox left to meet A.C. and Pyne at a bar down the street. She walked in and sat down. A.C. entered shortly thereafter pushing Pyne in a wheelchair.

"I look worse than I am," Pyne said. "I start physical therapy next month."

"I didn't say anything."

"Your face did."

"Are you sure you should be here? Isn't the normal rule to wait two weeks after surgery before you can drink alcohol?"

"Stuff the rules," Pyne said.

"You're fighting a losing battle, Jett." A.C. parked Pyne and sat down.

"I'll order our drinks. Double bourbon for Pyne and red wine for you?"

They both nodded in the affirmative. Fox went up and ordered the drinks. She sat back down just as she received a text message. It was from Rhiannon Misrasi.

"You're Jett Fox. You played volleyball at Yale."

Fox texted back with the thumbs-up emoji. She put her phone away.

"The Service officially removed me from field work," Pyne said. "If I want to go back, it will be a desk job."

"What did you tell them?" Fox asked.

"I tendered my resignation, effective immediately."

There was a short silence at the table. Fox broke it. "Are you happy with that choice?"

Pyne looked at A.C. The two of them smiled at each other.

"Yes, I am."

Fox didn't pry into what was next. The two of them needed space to figure out their relationship outside the context of an espionage adventure.

The waiter arrived with the drinks. The three of them debated whether they should toast to Sharon Graham or the Takahashi 72. They ended up doing the real toast to Sharon Graham and a subsequent less serious toast to Fox's race car.

"Where are you going for your forced vacation, Jett?"

"Miami. See my grandfather, catch a Marlins game, and then maybe catch an actual marlin. Oh, and Solace has a rest and recuperation assignment for me while I'm down there. Her friend needs help with a problem. So, you know, keep the phone line open, A.C. I might need to borrow some tools."

THE END